"There's only one Leigh Brackett and there's only one Eric John Stark—both stand alone in their field!" —Ray Bradbury

"Leigh took science fiction and lifted it above the genre preconceptions. This is fiction as its most exciting, in the hands of master storyteller." —George Lucas

"Brackett is absolutely at the top of her genre." —*Publisher's Weekly*

"Leigh Brackett combines the best of A. Merritt and Edgar Rice Burroughs with much that is uniquely her own!" —Lester Del Rey

"Miss Brackett's . . . books have been sheer romantic space operas (which no one does better)."

—H. H. Holmes, *New York Herald-Tribune*

"I believe that ***Enchantress of Venus*** is one of the best of the Stark stories . . . the scenes in the strange depths of the gaseous Red Sea lead inexorably toward a final struggle—and a final failure. And indeed, this is a favorite and recurring theme of the Leigh Brackett stories—the theme of a strong man's quest for a dream and of his final failure when it turns to smoke and ashes in his hands."

—Edmond Hamilton, *The Best of Leigh Brackett*

"Brackett not only continued the great romantic tradition of Edgar Rice Burroughs (though with infinitely more sophistication), but she managed to sneak into the Puritan pulps . . . a sensuousness which the male writers of the period couldn't seem to achieve, both in descriptive ability and hints that the hero and heroine wanted more than for the former to save the latter from a bug-eyed monster . . . Brackett's works are adventurous world-creating at its best."

—*A Reader's Guide to Science Fiction*

"She approached all she wrote with economy and vigor: everything about her early stories—their color, their narrative speed, the brooding forthrightness of their protagonists—made them an ideal and fertile blend of traditional space opera and sword and sorcery." —*The Encyclopedia of Science Fiction*

N'Chaka
had
a grip
at last
on
the demon
with
yellow eyes
that
hungered
for
his life,
and
he
would
not
let
go.

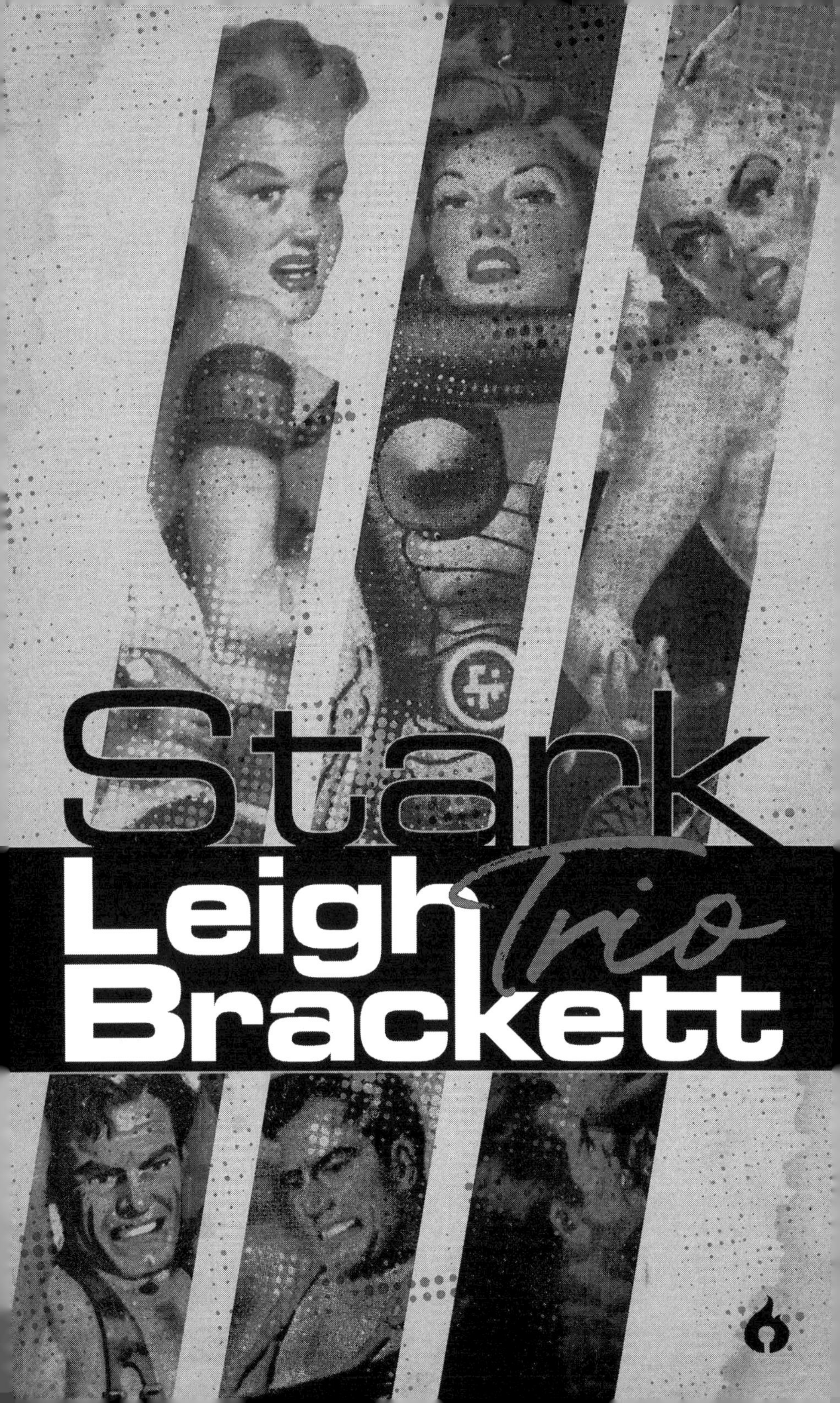
Stark
Trio
Leigh
Brackett

HEATHEN EDITIONS
THEIR BOOKS. OUR WAY.

Published in the good ole United States of America
by Heathen Editions, an imprint of
Heathen Creative
P.O. Box 588
Point Pleasant, WV 25550-0588

Heathen Editions are available at quantity discounts.
Bear witness to the yackety-yak and tomfoolery at:

heatheneditions.com

Social? Tag us! @heatheneditions
Photo? Tag it! #heathenedition

Caution: This book may alter your mind.

Queen of the Martian Catacombs first published in ***Planet Stories*** Summer 1949
Black Amazon of Mars first published in ***Planet Stories*** March 1951
Enchantress of Venus first published in ***Planet Stories*** Fall 1949
Heathen Edition published August 8, 2024

Paperback ISBN: 978-1-948316-30-9
Hardcover ISBN: 978-1-963228-30-4

Book and cover design by Sheridan Cleland
Set in 11.5pt Garamond Premier Pro
Titles in Eurostile, Parts in Quentin

FIRST HEATHEN EDITION

Contents

Heathenry

Thoughts on the Text

I've wanted to do a Leigh (pronounced Lee) Brackett Heathen Edition for a while now because I absolutely love her writing—it's lean and mean, and her dialogue sizzles and pops like a string of lit firecrackers.

While proofing this trio of stories, I found myself more than once rereading her sentences, reverse engineering their structure, and marveling at how she could so consistently *bing–bang–boom!*

It's no wonder Hollywood came knocking soon after her stories started getting published; director Howard Hawks being one of the first, recruiting her for co-screenwriting duty with legendary author William Faulkner, adapting the 1939 novel *The Big Sleep* by yet another legendary author, Raymond Chandler, which makes perfect sense because, as a *Los Angeles Times* article noted, quoting Brackett herself:

" . . . how did she master laconic male dialogue? 'I put myself through an intensive course of studying Steinbeck, Hemingway, Kipling, Chandler, and Dashiell Hammett because they got so much into so little.'"[1]

[1] Hopper, H. (1965, December 28). They Call Her for Salty Dialogue. *The Los Angeles Times*, p. E10.

"It began," says the article, when "Hawks read a hard-boiled detective novel called *No Good From a Corpse* [1944] . . . and decided it had just the kind of rough, tough dialogue he wanted in the Humphrey Bogart movie he was about to make. He phoned the author's agent and said, 'I'd like to see Mr. Brackett.'"

"'Not Mr. Brackett,' the agent told him. '*Miss* Brackett.'"

And "rough, tough" is exactly right as it seems reflective of the gal who said she had a "fiendish temper" and described one of her pastimes as "volleyball, the sandlot kind with only two on a side, and the way we do it you can get your head torn off."[2]

In a 1975 interview, when questioned about the early years of her career as a woman in what was, at the time, predominantly male-driven spheres of writing, she said, "I guess I was liberated on the day I was born, because my mother was a feminine, helpless little person and all of the women in my family were professional ladies with a capital 'L.' A lady never did anything for herself; somebody always did it for her. They looked down on me a great deal because I was big and husky and active, running up and down the beach, playing with the boys and doing things. Oh, goodness, I got so many lectures. I think I was just the opposite type, that's all, and possibly became even more opposite because I so despised their attitude. I thought it was so ridiculous. I didn't believe that you were supposed to sit around waiting for a man to come along and want you and provide you with this, that, and the other. I don't need anybody to provide for me. I'll provide for myself. My father and mother dearly loved each other and they were wonderful people and they got married and he died. So where was she? I always prefer to have a little something in my own hands that I have control of."[3]

Excuse me while I cue up The Spinners' "Could It Be I'm Falling in Love" . . .

---

[2] Leigh Brackett Steps Up and Tells Us About Herself. (1944, Fall). *Startling Stories* (11)2, p. 112.

[3] Roderick, J. & Earnhart, H.G. (1975, October 7). Science Fiction Writing: Experiences as a Writer (Youngstown State University Oral History Program).

Later, in that same interview, Brackett is questioned about the balance she found in her youth between being with friends versus being alone, the interviewer underscoring the question with: "It isn't necessarily the loner that spins daydreams to become a writer."

To which Brackett replied, "I remember that one of the happiest things I used to do as a child was to walk out to the empty jetty and sit on the stringer with my feet in the ocean and just listen to the breathing of the sea and look out at the horizon and just feel and think. I loved being alone . . . I think there is something in being a loner. I think you have to be enough of an individual yourself, or otherwise nothing that is individual is going to come out of you."

singing *Could it be I'm falling in love–with you, baby!*

. . . before I get too carried away, let's pivot and talk Stark.

Brackett has been called "the Queen of Space Opera"[4] and, as per that earlier interview, it seemed preordained, "At the age of eight I was a great reader . . . I got hold of a copy of Edgar Rice Burroughs' *The Gods of Mars* [1913] and I was never the same after that. Suddenly, I became aware of other worlds out there and then, from that time on, I was destined to be a science fiction writer."

Finding inspiration in Burroughs' Mars adventures, Brackett introduced her own planet-hopping "man without a tribe" Eric John Stark in the Summer 1949 edition of sci-fi pulp *Planet Stories* with the razor-sharp "Queen of the Martian Catacombs."

His next appearance occurred in the very next issue, for Fall 1949, with "Enchantress of Venus," which we Heathens believe is certainly the greatest bare-knuckled romp of the trilogy.

Two years later, after *Planet Stories* had evolved from quarterly to monthly, his third appearance was in "Black Amazon of Mars" for the March 1951 issue. And while that story arrived last in publishing order, it is actually second in chronological order, which is how we have presented it here, in our Edition.

Brackett later expanded two of those stories into short novels:

[4] Liptak, A. (2015, July 15). Happy 100th Birthday to Leigh Brackett, the Queen of Space Opera! gizmodo.com

ends next p.

"Queen of the Martian Catacombs" as *The Secret of Sinharat* and "Black Amazon of Mars" as *People of the Talisman*, both first published in a 1964 Ace Double paperback, then again in 1982 as *Eric John Stark: Outlaw of Mars*.

However, those expanded novels have inconsistencies when compared with the originals as first published in *Planet Stories*, which is why we have collected and presented the originals here.

As for the text, little ~~editing~~ Heathening has been required on our part as we've mostly, only jettisoned Brackett's use of British spellings in favor of their American counterparts.

The bulk of our work lies in the over 100 footnotes we've added to provide clarity, context, and commentary as necessary, especially of the literary and archaic words Brackett peppered throughout the stories.

Finally, if this is your first foray into reading the words of Leigh Brackett, then prepare to fall in love . . .

singing *with youuuu, with yoooooouuuuuu!*

Sheridan Cleland
Co-Heathen
August 2024

P.S. If you're a *Star Wars* fan, then you're probably aware of Leigh's connection to the franchise as the first writer of *The Empire Strikes Back* (which will *always and forever* be the best movie of the entire series), but did you know there's a theory that she also ghostwrote the first *Star Wars* movie?!

As a lifelong fan of the original trilogy, I thought the idea was, at first, preposterous, but YouTube channel The Starkiller has a feature-length video[5] on the matter and their presentation of evidence is wildly overwhelming if not wholly convincing!

[5] youtu.be/fhR2qD7D8QY

Introducing the Author

Leigh Brackett

In quite undramatic fashion, I began by being born. Place, Los Angeles, California. Date, December 7, so few years ago that darned little has had time to happen. Ancestry, Scots-English. I weighed ten pounds, had black hair, and a strident personality, especially during the wee sma' hours.

The next few years are somewhat hazy, except that I was very naughty and had an uncanny faculty for imitating dialect. The family was never quite sure whether it had hatched out a Chinese cook or an Italian fruit man.

At an early age I discovered books. It was a sad day for the family. It's a mournful tradition with us that if you want to get me out of a book, you've got to use a good-sized percussion cap.

Presently I was put into a small school in Santa Monica. I may say, with a pardonable blush, that I was the second worst brat on the campus. The worst one had a head start—she was a year older.

This I call my beach-combing period. I lived at the shore, acquired an indelible tan and a mop of straw-colored hair—the black fuzz I started out with having apparently made a mistake. I didn't grow scales and gills, but the fish all called me by my first name.

By this time several alarming characteristics had appeared in me. I was crazy over dogs. I'd have had a dozen or so, if the family hadn't sternly refused to cooperate. I had a nice taste in Elizabethan oaths, garnered from pirate stories. I wavered between four desperate alternatives: whether to be a smuggler like Jim Davis,[1] a pirate like Blackbeard, an all-round daredevil like Douglas Fairbanks,[2] who was my idol, or just to settle for Cowboys 'n' Indians.

And I discovered "imaginative fiction."

There was apprehensive shaking of heads among the female relations. Attempts were made to save me. But it was too late. I devoured Burroughs,[3] Haggard,[4] Balmer and Wylie,[5] Doyle's unforgettable "Maracot Deep,"[6] Jules Verne.[7] Yes, boys and girls, I was hooked. Completely and utterly.

In the meantime, I flunked Latin and algebra, acted in some school plays, fought the neighbor's boy, and made several unsuccessful attempts to go to Mars à la John Carter.

Then we went East, and the Fateful Day arrived.

---

[1] *Jim Davis* (aka *The Captain of the Smugglers*) is a 1911 book by English poet and author John Masefield (1878–1967) about a twelve-year-old boy whose life gets flipped turned upside down when he stumbles upon a band of savage pirates.

[2] Douglas Fairbanks Sr. (1883–1939) was an American actor and filmmaker best known for his swashbuckling roles in silent films like *The Mark of Zorro* (1920) and *Robin Hood* (1922).

[3] Edgar Rice Burroughs (1875–1950) was a legendarily prolific American author, writing over eighty books in thirty-six years, and best known as the creator of *Tarzan of the Apes* and *John Carter of Mars.*

[4] Sir Henry Rider Haggard (1856–1925) was an English writer of adventure fiction romances set in exotic locations, predominantly Africa, and a pioneer of the lost world literary genre.

[5] Science fiction and mystery writers Edwin Balmer (1883–1959) and Philip Wylie (1902–1971) teamed up for the catastrophe sci-fi novel pair *When Worlds Collide* (1933) and *After Worlds Collide* (1934).

[6] *The Maracot Deep* is a short 1929 novel by English writer Sir Arthur Conan Doyle (1859–1930) about the discovery of a sunken city of Atlantis by a team of explorers led by Professor Maracot.

[7] Jules Verne (1828–1905) was a French novelist, poet, and playwright best known for his adventure novels including *Journey to the Center of the Earth* (1864) and *Twenty Thousand Leagues Under the Seas* (1870).

It dawned quite simply. The sun shone, the little birds were doing their stuff, all was quiet and serene. I got out of bed . . .

There was a muffled thunder of psychic drums. Boston quaked to its foundations. And I said to myself:

"Brackett, you're thirteen. Time you thought about things. The days of piracy are over, smuggling has degenerated into bootlegging, and cowboying seems to have lost its siren charm. What's it to be, the Life Work?"

Brackett struggled with this for a long time—five minutes at least. And then,

"I have it! You get good marks in Eng. Lit. You read incessantly. Composition is a snap. Writing is easy. In fact, it's so easy it'll be almost a pity to take money for it.

"Brackett, your future is assured. You will be a writer."

Uh huh. Gruesome, isn't it? My only excuse is that I was young, and no one had ever kicked me very hard.

I wrote a novel, an intensely dramatic problem piece. I wrote short stories. Then two more novels.

They made a horrible stench, burning. My one consolation is that I wrote them in longhand, which in my case is practically illegible, and I think the editors simply stuck rejection slips on them, of necessity, without reading.

We came West again. I entered school, and took a course in writing on the side. It did some good, but not much. Besides, I was bitten by the acting bug about this time and spent most of my waking hours in the school auditorium.

This eventually resulted in my placing second for dramatic reading in the Festival of Arts and Sciences, and teaching speech and dramatics for a year at an up-coast school.

I taught swimming as well during the summers, and had an idea I might be a physical instructor. But writing had become chronic. I couldn't shake it. I turned out incredibly bad stories in every spare moment.

Now we come to the tragic, soul-searing period inevitable in the life of every struggling artist, the time when he's sure his Muse

ends next p.

has deserted him for good. If, indeed, the gal was ever around. In nine years I hadn't sold a word. I was beating my head against a wall, with no way over or around. Writing was easy. *Ha!*

Then, just as I was poised on the edge of a cliff, with a rope around my neck, a bottle of poison in one hand and a gun in the other, Fate stepped in. I found a teacher, heaven bless him. I found a writer willing to help. I found an agent, ditto. I decided life wasn't so bad after all.

Behold me now, laboring in my garret,[8] which overlooks the city of Los Angeles. I've sold a dozen stories. Not much, but a beginning. And some day, maybe . . .

That just about finishes this uneventful chronicle. If physical statistics are of interest, I'm tallish, fairish, and mildly insane on the subject of beach volleyball. I still read. I like eating and sleeping, dislike hats and cats,[9] and dream of globe-trotting.

There's just one more thing—a very important thing. I hope you enjoy—

[8] A small, cramped attic or top-floor room.

[9] We Heathens won't hold her dislike of cats against her.

Queen of the Martian Catacombs

A Stark Tale

Gaunt giant and passionate beauty, they dragged their thirst-crazed way across the endless crimson sands in a terrible test of endurance. For one of them knew where cool life-giving water lapped old stones smooth—a place of secret horror that it was death to reveal!

Queen of the Martian Catacombs

Part 1

For hours the hard-pressed beast had fled across the Martian desert with its dark rider. Now it was spent. It faltered and broke stride, and when the rider cursed and dug his heels into the scaly sides, the brute only turned its head and hissed at him. It stumbled on a few more paces into the lee[1] of a sandhill, and there it stopped, crouching down in the dust.

The man dismounted. The creature's eyes burned like green lamps in the light of the little moons, and he knew that it was no use trying to urge it on. He looked back, the way he had come.

In the distance there were four black shadows grouped together in the barren emptiness. They were running fast. In a few minutes they would be upon him.

He stood still, thinking what he should do next. Ahead, far ahead, was a low ridge, and beyond the ridge lay Valkis and safety, but he could never make it now. Off to his right, a lonely tor[2] stood up out of the blowing sand. There were tumbled rocks at its foot.

---

[1] An area sheltered from the wind.

[2] Hill or rocky peak.

"They tried to run me down in the open," he thought. "But here, by the Nine Hells, they'll have to work for it!"

He moved then, running toward the tor with a lightness and speed incredible in anything but an animal or a savage. He was of Earth stock, built tall, and more massive than he looked by reason of his leanness. The desert wind was bitter cold, but he did not seem to notice it, though he wore only a ragged shirt of Venusian spider silk, open to the waist. His skin was almost as dark as his black hair, burned indelibly by years of exposure to some terrible sun. His eyes were startlingly light in color, reflecting back the pale glow of the moons.

With the practiced ease of a lizard he slid in among the loose and treacherous rocks. Finding a vantage point, where his back was protected by the tor itself, he crouched down.

After that he did not move, except to draw his gun. There was something eerie about his utter stillness, a quality of patience as unhuman as the patience of the rock that sheltered him.

The four black shadows came closer, resolved themselves into mounted men.

They found the beast, where it lay panting, and stopped. The line of the man's footprints, already blurred by the wind but still plain enough, showed where he had gone.

The leader motioned. The others dismounted. Working with the swift precision of soldiers, they removed equipment from their saddle-packs and began to assemble it.

The man crouching under the tor saw the thing that took shape. It was a Banning shocker, and he knew that he was not going to fight his way out of this trap. His pursuers were out of range of his own weapon. They would remain so. The Banning, with its powerful electric beam, would take him—dead or senseless, as they wished.

He thrust the useless gun back into his belt. He knew who these men were, and what they wanted with him. They were officers of the Earth Police Control, bringing him a gift—twenty years in the Luna cellblocks.

Twenty years in the gray catacombs, buried in the silence and the eternal dark.

He recognized the inevitable. He was used to inevitables—hunger, pain, loneliness, the emptiness of dreams. He had accepted a lot of them in his time. Yet he made no move to surrender. He looked out at the desert and the night sky, and his eyes blazed, the desperate, strangely beautiful eyes of a creature very close to the roots of life, something less and more than man. His hands found a shard of rock and broke it.

The leader of the four men rode slowly toward the tor, his right arm raised.

His voice carried clearly on the wind. "Eric John Stark!" he called, and the dark man tensed in the shadows.

The rider stopped. He spoke again, but this time in a different tongue. It was no dialect of Earth, Mars, or Venus, but a strange speech, as harsh and vital as the blazing Mercurian valleys that bred it.

"*Oh N'Chaka, oh Man-without-a-tribe, I call you!*"

There was a long silence. The rider and his mount were motionless under the low moons, waiting.

Eric John Stark stepped slowly out from the pool of blackness under the tor.

"Who calls me N'Chaka?"

The rider relaxed somewhat. He answered in English, "You know perfectly well who I am, Eric. May we meet in peace?"

Stark shrugged. "Of course."

*

He walked on to meet the rider, who had dismounted, leaving his beast behind. He was a slight, wiry man, this EPC officer, with the rawhide look of the frontiers still on him. His hair was grizzled and his sun-blackened skin was deeply lined, but there

pt. ends p. 7

was nothing in the least aged about his hard good-humored face nor his remarkably keen dark eyes.

"It's been a long time, Eric," he said.

Stark nodded. "Sixteen years." The two men studied each other for a moment, and then Stark said, "I thought you were still on Mercury, Ashton."

"They've called all us experienced hands in to Mars." He held out cigarettes. "Smoke?"

Stark took one. They bent over Ashton's lighter, and then stood there smoking while the wind blew red dust over their feet and the three men of the patrol waited quietly beside the Banning. Ashton was taking no chances. The electro-beam could stun without injury.

Presently Ashton said, "I'm going to be crude, Eric. I'm going to remind you of some things."

"Save it," Stark retorted. "You've got me. There's no need to talk about it."

"Yes," said Ashton, "I've got you, and a damned hard time I've had doing it. That's why I'm going to talk about it."

His dark eyes met Stark's cold stare and held it.

"Remember who I am—Simon Ashton. Remember who came along when the miners in that valley on Mercury had a wild boy in a cage, and were going to finish him off like they had the tribe that raised him. Remember all the years after that, when I brought that boy up to be a civilized human being."

Stark laughed, not without a certain humor. "You should have left me in the cage. I was caught a little old for civilizing."

"Maybe. I don't think so. Anyway, I'm reminding you," Ashton said.

Stark said, with no particular bitterness, "You don't have to get sentimental. I know it's your job to take me in."

Ashton said deliberately, "I won't take you in, Eric, unless you make me." He went on then, rapidly, before Stark could answer. "You've got a twenty-year sentence hanging over you, for running guns to the Middle-Swamp tribes when they revolted against Terro-Venusian Metals, and a couple of similar jobs.

"All right. So I know why you did it, and I won't say I don't agree with you. But you put yourself outside the law, and that's that. Now you're on your way to Valkis. You're headed into a mess that'll put you on Luna for life, the next time you're caught."

"And this time you don't agree with me."

"No. Why do you think I broke my neck to catch you before you got there?" Ashton bent closer, his face very intent. "Have you made any deal with Delgaun of Valkis? Did he send for you?"

"He sent for me, but there's no deal yet. I'm on the beach. Broke. I got a message from this Delgaun, whoever he is, that there was going to be a private war back in the Drylands, and he'd pay me to help fight it. After all, that's my business."

Ashton shook his head.

"This isn't a private war, Eric. It's something a lot bigger and nastier than that. The Martian Council of City-States and the Earth Commission are both in a cold sweat, and no one can find out exactly what's going on. You know what the Low-Canal towns are—Valkis, Jekkara, Barrakesh. No law-abiding Martian, let alone an Earthman, can last five minutes in them. And the back-blocks are absolutely *verboten*.[3] So all we get is rumors.

"Fantastic rumors about a barbarian chief named Kynon, who seems to be promising heaven and earth to the tribes of Kesh and Shun—some wild stuff about the ancient cult of the Ramas that everybody thought was dead a thousand years ago. We know that Kynon is tied up somehow with Delgaun, who is a most efficient bandit, and we know that some of the top criminals of the whole System are filtering in to join up. Knighton and Walsh of Terra, Themis of Mercury, Arrod of Callisto Colony—and, I believe, your old comrade in arms, Luhar the Venusian."

Stark gave a slight start, and Ashton smiled briefly.

"Oh, yes," he said. "I heard about that." Then he sobered. "You

[3] A German word meaning forbidden.

pt. ends next p.

can figure that setup for yourself, Eric. The barbarians are going to go out and fight some kind of a holy war, to suit the entirely unholy purposes of men like Delgaun and the others.

"Half a world is going to be raped, blood is going to run deep in the Drylands—and it will all be barbarian blood spilled for a lying promise, and the carrion crows of Valkis will get fat on it. Unless, somehow, we can stop it."

*

He paused, then said flatly, "I want you to go on to Valkis, Eric—but as my agent. I won't put it on the grounds that you'd be doing civilization a service. You don't owe anything to civilization, Lord knows. But you might save a lot of your own kind of people from getting slaughtered, to say nothing of the border-state Martians who'll be the first to get Kynon's axe.

"Also, you could wipe that twenty-year hitch on Luna off the slate, maybe even work up a desire to make a man of yourself, instead of a sort of tiger wandering from one kill to the next." He added, "If you live."

Stark said slowly, "You're clever Ashton. You know I've got a feeling for all planetary primitives like those who raised me, and you appeal to that."

"Yes," said Ashton, "I'm clever. But I'm not a liar. What I've told you is true."

Stark carefully ground out the cigarette beneath his heel. Then he looked up. "Suppose I agree to become your agent in this, and go off to Valkis. What's to prevent me from forgetting all about you, then?"

Ashton said softly, "Your word, Eric. You get to know a man pretty well when you know him from boyhood on up. Your word is enough."

There was a silence, and then Stark held out his hand. "All right, Simon—but only for this one deal. After that, no promises."

"Fair enough." They shook hands.

"I can't give you any suggestions," Ashton said. "You're on your own, completely. You can get in touch with me through the Earth Commission office in Tarak. You know where that is?"

Stark nodded. "On the Dryland Border."

"Good luck to you, Eric."

He turned, and they walked back together to where the three men waited. Ashton nodded, and they began to dismantle the Banning. Neither they nor Ashton looked back, as they rode away.

Stark watched them go. He filled his lungs with the cold air, and stretched. Then he roused the beast out of the sand. It had rested, and was willing to carry him again as long as he did not press it. He set off again, across the desert.

The ridge grew as he approached it, looming into a low mountain chain much worn by the ages. A pass opened before him, twisting between the hills of barren rock.

He traversed it, coming out at the farther end above the basin of a dead sea. The lifeless land stretched away into darkness, a vast waste of desolation more lonely even than the desert. And between the sea bottom and the foothills, Stark saw the lights of Valkis.

Part 2

There were many lights, far below. Tiny pinpricks of flame where torches burned in the streets beside the Low-Canal—the thread of black water that was all that remained of a forgotten ocean.

Stark had never been here before. Now he looked at the city that sprawled down the slope under the low moons, and shivered, the primitive twitching of the nerves that an animal feels in the presence of death.

For the streets where the torches flared were only a tiny part of Valkis. The life of the city had flowed downward from the cliff-tops, following the dropping level of the sea. Five cities, the oldest scarcely recognizable as a place of human habitation. Five harbors, the docks and quays[1] still standing, half buried in the dust.

Five ages of Martian history, crowned on the topmost level with the ruined palace of the old pirate kings of Valkis. The towers still stood, broken but indomitable, and in the moonlight they had a sleeping look, as though they dreamed of blue water and the sound of waves, and of tall ships coming in heavy with treasure.

Stark picked his way slowly down the steep descent. There was

---

[1] Wharfs; stone, concrete, or metal platforms alongside or projecting into water for loading and unloading boats or ships.

something fascinating to him in the stone houses, roofless and silent in the night. The paving blocks still showed the rutting of wheels where carters had driven to the marketplace, and princes had gone by in gilded chariots. The quays were scarred where ships had lain against them, rising and falling with the tides.

Stark's senses had developed in a strange school, and the thin veneer of civilization he affected had not dulled them. Now it seemed to him that the wind had the echoes of voices in it, and the smell of spices and fresh-spilled blood.

He was not surprised when, in the last level above the living town, armed men came out of the shadows and stopped him.

They were lean, dark men, very wiry and light of foot, and their faces were the faces of wolves—not primitive wolves at all, but beasts of prey that had been civilized for so many thousands of years that they could afford to forget it.

They were most courteous, and Stark would not have cared to disobey their request.

He gave his name. "Delgaun sent for me."

The leader of the Valkisians nodded his narrow head. "You're expected." His sharp eyes had taken in every feature of the Earthman, and Stark knew that his description had been memorized down to the last detail. Valkis guarded its doors with care.

"Ask in the city," said the sentry. "Anyone can direct you to the palace."

Stark nodded and went on, down through the long-dead streets in the moonlight and the silence.

With shocking suddenness, he was plunged into the streets of the living.

It was very late now, but Valkis was awake and stirring. Seething, rather. The narrow twisting ways were crowded. The laughter of women came down from the flat roofs. Torchlight flared, gold and scarlet, lighting the wineshops, making blacker the shadows of the alley-mouths.

pt. ends p. 14

Stark left his beast at a *serai*[2] on the edge of the canal. The paddocks were already jammed. Stark recognized the long-legged brutes of the Dryland breed, and as he left a caravan passed him, coming in, with a jangling of bronze bangles and a great hissing and stamping in the dust.

The riders were tall barbarians—Keshi, Stark thought, from the way they braided their tawny hair. They wore plain leather, and their blue-eyed women rode like queens.

Valkis was full of them. For days, it seemed, they must have poured in across the dead sea bottom, from the distant oases[3] and the barren deserts of the back-blocks. Brawny warriors of Kesh and Shun, making holiday beside the Low-Canal, where there was more water than any of them had seen in their lives.

They were in Valkis, these barbarians, but they were not part of it. Shouldering his way through the streets, Stark got the peculiar flavor of the town, that he guessed could never be touched or changed by anything.

In a square, a girl danced to the music of harp and drum. The air was heavy with the smell of wine and burning pitch and incense. A lithe, swart Valkisian in his bright kilt and jeweled girdle leaped out and danced with the girl, his teeth flashing as he whirled and postured. In the end he bore her off, laughing, her black hair hanging down his back.

Women looked at Stark. Women graceful as cats, bare to the waist, their skirts slit at the sides above the thigh, wearing no ornaments but the tiny golden bells that are the particular property of the Low-Canal towns, so that the air is always filled with their delicate, wanton chiming.

Valkis had a laughing, wicked soul. Stark had been in many places in his life, but never one before that beat with such a pulse of evil, incredibly ancient, but strong and gay.

He found the palace at last—a great rambling structure of

---

[2] A caravansary; an inn or hostel built around a large courtyard for the overnight accommodation of caravans along desert trade routes.

[3] Plural of oasis.

quarried stone, with doors and shutters of beaten bronze closed against the dust and the incessant wind. He gave his name to the guard and was taken inside, through halls hung with antique tapestries, the flagged floors worn hollow by countless generations of sandaled feet.

*

Again, Stark's half-wild senses told him that life within these walls had not been placid. The very stones whispered of age-old violence, the shadows were heavy with the lingering ghosts of passion.

He was brought before Delgaun, the lord of Valkis, in the big central room that served as his headquarters.

Delgaun was lean and catlike, after the fashion of his race. His black hair showed a stippling of silver, and the hard beauty of his face was strongly marked, the lines drawn deep and all the softness of youth long gone away. He wore a magnificent harness, and his eyes, under fine dark brows, were like drops of hot gold.

He looked up as the Earthman came in, one swift penetrating glance. Then he said, "You're Stark."

There was something odd about those yellow eyes, bright and keen as a killer hawk's yet somehow secret, as though the true thoughts behind them would never show through. Instinctively, Stark disliked the man.

But he nodded and came up to the council table, turning his attention to the others in the room. A handful of Martians—Low-Canallers, chiefs and fighting men from their ornaments and their proud looks—and several outlanders, their conventional garments incongruous in this place.

Stark knew them all. Knighton and Walsh of Terra, Themis of Mercury, Arrod of Callisto Colony—and Luhar of Venus. Pirates, thieves, renegades, and each one an expert in his line.

pt. ends p. 14

Ashton was right. There was something big, something very big and very ugly, shaping between Valkis and the Drylands.

But that was only a quick, passing thought in Stark's mind. It was on Luhar that his attention centered. Bitter memory and hatred had come to savage life within him as soon as he saw the Venusian.

The man was handsome. A cashiered[4] officer of the crack Venusian Guards, very slim, very elegant, his pale hair cropped short and curling, his dark tunic fitting him like a second skin.

He said, "The aborigine! I thought we had enough barbarians here without sending for more."

Stark said nothing. He began to walk toward Luhar.

Luhar said sharply, "There's no use in getting nasty, Stark. Past scores are past. We're on the same side now."

The Earthman spoke, then, with a peculiar gentleness.

"We were on the same side once before. Against Terro-Venus Metals. Remember?"

"I remember very well!" Luhar was speaking now not to Stark alone, but to everyone in the room. "I remember that your innocent barbarian friends had me tied to the block there in the swamps, and that you were watching the whole thing with honest pleasure. If the Company men hadn't come along, I'd be screaming there yet."

"You sold us out," Stark said. "You had it coming."

He continued to walk toward Luhar.

Delgaun spoke. He did not raise his voice, yet Stark felt the impact of his command.

"There will be no fighting here," Delgaun said. "You are both hired mercenaries, and while you take my pay you will forget your private quarrels. Do you understand?"

Luhar nodded and sat down, smiling out of the corner of his mouth at Stark, who stood looking with narrowed eyes at Delgaun.

He was still half blind with his anger against Luhar. His

[4] Dismissed or suspended from office or position.

hands ached for the kill. But even so, he recognized the power in Delgaun.

A sound shockingly akin to the growl of a beast echoed in his throat. Then, gradually, he relaxed. The man Delgaun he would have challenged. But to do so would wreck the mission that he had promised to carry out here for Ashton.

He shrugged, and joined the others at the table.

Walsh of Terra rose abruptly and began to prowl back and forth. "How much longer do we have to wait?" he demanded.

Delgaun poured wine into a bronze goblet. "Don't expect me to know," he snapped. He shoved the flagon[5] along the table toward Stark.

Stark helped himself. The wine was warm and sweet on his tongue. He drank slowly, sitting relaxed and patient while the others smoked nervously or rose to pace up and down.

Stark wondered what, or who, they were waiting for. But he did not ask.

Time went by.

Stark raised his head, listening. "What's that?"

Their duller ears had heard nothing, but Delgaun rose and flung open the shutters of the window near him.

The Martian dawn, brilliant and clear, flooded the dead sea bottom with harsh light. Beyond the black line of the canal a caravan was coming toward Valkis through the blowing dust.

It was no ordinary caravan. Warriors rode before and behind, their spearheads blazing in the sunrise. Jeweled trappings on the beasts, a litter[6] with curtains of crimson silk, barbaric splendor. Clear and thin on the air came the wild music of pipes and the deep-throated throbbing of drums.

Stark guessed without being told who it was that rode out of the desert like a king.

---

[5] A large bottle or vessel in which liquor is held, typically with a handle, spout, and often a lid, holding about 2 pints.

[6] An enclosed or curtained bed or seat held between parallel poles used to carry a single passenger.

pt. ends next p.

Delgaun made a harsh sound in his throat. "It's Kynon, at last!" he said, and swung around from the window. His eyes sparkled with some private amusement. "Let us go and welcome the Giver of Life!"

Stark went with them, out into the crowded streets. A silence had fallen on the town. Valkisian and barbarian alike were caught now in a breathless excitement, pressing through the narrow ways, flowing toward the canal.

Stark found himself beside Delgaun in the great square of the slave market, standing on the auction block, above the heads of the throng. The stillness, the expectancy of the crowd were uncanny...

To the measured thunder of drums and the wild skirling[7] of desert pipes, Kynon of Shun came into Valkis.

[7] A high, shrill, wailing sound, especially of bagpipes.

Part 3

Straight into the square of the slave market the caravan came, and the people pressed back against the walls to make way for them. Stamping of padded hoofs on the stones, ring and clash of harness, brave glitter of spears and the great two-handed broadswords of the Drylands, with drumbeats to shake the heart and the savage cry of the pipes to set the blood leaping. Stark could not restrain an appreciative thrill in himself.

The advance guard reached the slave block. Then, with deafening abruptness, the drummers crossed their sticks and the pipers ceased, and there was utter silence in the square.

It lasted for almost a minute, and then from every barbarian throat the name of Kynon roared out until the stones of the city echoed with it.

A man leaped from the back of his mount to the block, standing at its outer edge where all could see, his hands flung up.

"I greet you, my brothers!"

And the cheering went on.

Stark studied Kynon, surprised that he was so young. He had expected a gray-bearded prophet, and instead, here was a brawny-shouldered man of war standing as tall as himself.

Kynon's eyes were a bright, compelling blue, and his face was the face of a young eagle. His voice had deep music in it—the kind of voice that can sway crowds to madness.

Stark looked from him to the rapt faces of the people—even the Valkisians had caught the mood—and thought that Kynon was the most dangerous man he had ever seen. This tawny-haired barbarian in his kilt of bronze-bossed leather was already half a god.

Kynon shouted to the captain of his warriors, "Bring the captive and the old man!" Then he turned again to the crowd, urging them to silence. When at last the square was still, his voice rang challengingly across it.

"There are still those who doubt me. Therefore I have come to Valkis, and this day—now!—I will show proof that I have not lied!"

A roar and a mutter from the crowd. Kynon's men were lifting to the block a tottering ancient so bowed with years that he could barely stand, and a youth of Terran stock. The boy was in chains. The old man's eyes burned, and he looked at the boy beside him with a terrible joy.

Stark settled down to watch. The litter with the curtains of crimson silk was now beside the block. A girl, a Valkisian, stood beside it, looking up. It seemed to Stark that her green eyes rested on Kynon with a smoldering anger.

He glanced away from the serving girl, and saw that the curtains were partly open. A woman lay on the cushions within. He could not see much of her, except that her hair was like dark flame and she was smiling, looking at the old man and the naked boy. Then her glance, very dark in the shadows of the litter, shifted away and Stark followed it and saw Delgaun. Every muscle of Delgaun's body was drawn taut, and he seemed unable to look away from the woman in the litter.

Stark smiled, very slightly. The outlanders were cynically absorbed in what was going on. The crowd had settled again to that silent, breathless tension. The sun blazed down out of the empty sky. The dust blew, and the wind was sharp with the smell of living flesh.

The old man reached out and touched the boy's smooth shoulder, and his gums showed bluish as he laughed.

Kynon was speaking again.

"There are still those who doubt me, I say! Those who scoffed when I said that I possessed the ancient secret of the Ramas of long ago—the secret by which one man's mind may be transferred into another's body. But none of you after today will doubt that I hold that secret!

"I, myself, am not a Rama." He glanced down along his powerful frame, half-consciously flexing his muscles, and laughed. "Why should I be a Rama? I have no need, as yet, for the Sending-on of Minds!"

Answering laughter, half ribald,[1] from the crowd.

"No," said Kynon, "I am not a Rama. I am a man like you. Like you, I have no wish to grow old, and in the end, to die."

He swung abruptly to the old man.

"You, Grandfather! Would you not wish to be young again—to ride out to battle, to take the woman of your choice?"

The old man wailed, "Yes! Yes!" and his gaze dwelt hungrily upon the boy.

"And you shall be!" The strength of a god rang in Kynon's voice. He turned again to the crowd and cried out,

"For years I suffered in the desert alone, searching for the lost secret of the Ramas. And I found it, my brothers! I hold their ancient power. I alone—in these two hands I hold it, and with it I shall begin a new era for our Dryland races!

"There will be fighting, yes. There will be bloodshed. But when that is over and the men of Kesh and Shun are free from their ancient bondage of thirst and the men of the Low-Canals have regained their own—then I shall give new life, unending life, to all who have followed me. The aged and lamed and wounded can

[1] Vulgar or lewd humor.

pt. ends p. 20

choose new bodies from among the captives. There will be no more age, no more sickness, no more death!"

A rippling, shivering sigh from the crowd. Eyeballs gleaming in the bitter light, mouths open on the hunger that is nearest to the human soul.

"Lest anyone still doubt my promise," said Kynon, "watch. Watch—and I will show you!"

They watched. Not stirring, hardly breathing, they watched.

*

The drums struck up a slow and solemn beat. The captain of the warriors, with an escort of six men, marched to the litter and took from the woman's hands a bundle wrapped in silks. Bearing it as though it were precious beyond belief, he came to the block and lifted it up, and Kynon took it from him.

The silken wrappings fluttered loose, fell away. And in Kynon's hands gleamed two crystal crowns and a shining rod.

He held them high, the sunlight glancing in cold fire from the crystal.

"Behold!" he said. "The Crowns of the Ramas!"

The crowd drew breath then, one long rasping *Ah!*

The solemn drumbeat never faltered. It was as though the pulse of the whole world throbbed within it. Kynon turned. The old man began to tremble. Kynon placed one crown on his wrinkled scalp, and the tottering creature winced as though in pain, but his face was ecstatic.

Relentlessly, Kynon crowned with the second circlet the head of the frightened boy.

"Kneel," he said.

They knelt. Standing tall above them, Kynon held the rod in his two hands, between the crystal crowns.

Light was born in the rod. It was no reflection of the sun. Blue and brilliant, it flashed along the rod and leaped from it to wake an answering brilliance in the crowns, so that the old man and the youth were haloed with a chill, supernal[2] fire.

The drumbeat ceased. The old man cried out. His hands plucked feebly at his head, then went to his breast and clenched there. Quite suddenly he fell forward over his knees. A convulsive tremor shook him. Then he lay still.

The boy swayed and then fell forward also, with a clashing of chains.

The light died out of the crowns. Kynon stood a moment longer, rigid as a statue, holding the rod which still flickered with blue lightning. Then that also died.

Kynon lowered the rod. In a ringing voice he cried, "Arise, Grandfather!"

The boy stirred. Slowly, very slowly, he rose to his feet. Holding out his hands, he stared at them, and then touched his thighs, and his flat belly, and the deep curve of his chest.

Up the firm young throat the wondering fingers went, to the smooth cheeks, to the thick fair hair above the crown. A cry broke from him.

With the perfect accent of the Drylands, the Earth boy cried in Martian, "I am in the youth's body! I am young again!"

A scream, a wail of ecstasy, burst from the crowd. It swayed like a great beast, white faces turned upward. The boy fell down and embraced Kynon's knees.

Eric John Stark found that he himself was trembling slightly. He glanced at Delgaun and the outlanders. The Valkisian wore a look of intense satisfaction under his mask of awe. The others were almost as rapt and open-mouthed as the crowd.

Stark turned his head slightly and looked down at the litter. One white hand was already drawing the curtains, so that the scarlet silk appeared to shake with silent laughter.

The serving girl beside it had not moved. Still she looked up at Kynon, and there was nothing in her eyes but hate.

---

[2] Celestial, heavenly, or divine.

pt. ends next p.

After that there was bedlam, the rush and trample of the crowd, the beating of drums, the screaming of pipes, deafening uproar. The crowns and the crystal rod were wrapped again and taken away. Kynon raised up the boy and struck off the chains of captivity. He mounted, with the boy beside him. Delgaun walked before him through the streets, and so did the outlanders.

The body of the old man was disregarded, except by some of Kynon's barbarians who wrapped it in a white cloth and took it away.

Kynon of Shun came in triumph to Delgaun's palace. Standing beside the litter, he gave his hand to the woman, who stepped out and walked beside him through the bronze door.

The women of Shun are tall and strong, bred to stand beside their men in war as well as love, and this red-haired daughter of the Drylands was enough to stop a man's heart with her proud step and her white shoulders, and her eyes that were the color of smoke. Stark's gaze followed her from a distance.

Presently in the council room were gathered Delgaun and the outlanders, Kynon and his bright-haired queen—and no other Martians but those three.

Kynon sprawled out in the high seat at the head of the table. His face was beaming. He wiped the sweat off it, and then filled a goblet with wine, looking around the room with his bright blue eyes.

"Fill up, gentlemen. I'll give you a toast." He lifted the goblet. "Here's to the secret of the Ramas, and the gift of life!"

Stark put down his goblet, still empty. He stared directly at Kynon.

"You have no secret," said Stark deliberately.

Kynon sat perfectly still, except that, very slowly, he put his own goblet down. Nobody else moved.

Stark's voice sounded loud in the stillness.

"Furthermore," he said, "that demonstration in the square was a lie from beginning to end."

Part 4

Stark's words had the effect of an electric shock on the listeners. Delgaun's black brows went up, and the woman came forward a little to stare at the Earthman with profound interest.

Kynon asked a question, of nobody in particular. "Who," he demanded, "is this great black ape?"

Delgaun told him.

"Ah, yes," said Kynon. "Eric John Stark, the wild man from Mercury." He scowled threateningly. "Very well—explain how I lied in the square!"

"Certainly. First of all, the Earth boy was a prisoner. He was told what he had to do to save his neck, and then was carefully coached in his part. Secondly, the crystal rod and the crowns are a fake. You used a simple Purcell unit in the rod to produce an electronic brush discharge. That made the blue light. Thirdly, you gave the old man poison, probably by means of a sharp point on the crown. I saw him wince when you put it on him."

Stark paused. "The old man died. The boy went through his sham. And that was that."

Again there was a flat silence. Luhar crouched over the table, his face avid with hope. The woman's eyes dwelt on Stark and did not turn away.

Then, suddenly, Kynon laughed. He roared with it until the tears ran.

"It was a good show, though," he said at last. "Damned good. You'll have to admit that. The crowd swallowed it, horns, hoofs, and hide."

He got up and came round to Stark, clapping him on the shoulder, a blow that would have laid a lesser man flat.

"I like you, wild man. Nobody else here had the guts to speak out, but I'll give you odds they were all thinking the same thing."

Stark said, "Just where were you, Kynon, during those years you were supposed to be suffering alone in the desert?"

"Curious, aren't you? Well, I'll let you in on a secret." Kynon lapsed abruptly into perfectly good colloquial English. "I was on Terra,[1] learning about things like the Purcell electronic discharge."

Reaching over, he poured wine for Stark and held it out to him. "Now you know. Now we all know. So let's wash the dust out of our throats and get down to business."

Stark said, "No."

Kynon looked at him. "What now?"

"You're lying to your people," Stark said flatly. "You're making false promises, to lead them into war."

Kynon was genuinely puzzled by Stark's anger. "But of course!" he said. "Is there anything new or strange in that?"

Luhar spoke up, his voice acid with hate. "Watch out for him, Kynon. He'll sell you out, he'll cut your throat, if he thinks it best for the barbarians."

Delgaun said, "Stark's reputation is known all over the system. There's no need to tell us that again."

"No." Kynon shook his head, looking very candidly at Stark. "We sent for you, didn't we, knowing that? All right."

---

[1] Another name for Earth in classic science fiction.

He stepped back a little, so that the others were included in what he was going to say.

"My people have a just cause for war. They go hungry and thirsty, while the City-States along the Dryland Border hog all the water sources and grow fat. Do you know what it means to watch your children die crying for water on a long march, to come at last to the oasis and find the well sanded in by a storm, and go on again, trying to save your people and your herd? Well, I do! I was born and bred in the Drylands, and many a time I've cursed the border states with a tongue like a dry stick.

"Stark, you should know the workings of the barbarian mind as well as I do. The men of Kesh and Shun are traditional enemies. Raiding and thieving, open warfare over water and grass. I had to give them a rallying point—a faith strong enough to unite them. Resurrecting the Rama legend was the only hope I had.

"And it has worked. The tribes are one people now. They can go on and take what belongs to them—the right to live. I'm not really so far out in my promises, at that. Now do you understand?"

*

Stark studied him, with his cold cat-eyes. "Where do the men of Valkis come in—the men of Jekkara and Barrakesh? Where do *we* come in, the hired bravoes?"[2]

Kynon smiled. It was a perfectly sincere smile, and it had no humor in it, only a great pride and a cheerful cruelty.

"We're going to build an empire," he said softly. "The City-States are disorganized, too starved or too fat to fight. And Earth is taking us over. Before long, Mars will be hardly more than another Luna.

"We're going to fight that. Drylander and Low-Canaller together, we're going to build a power out of dust and blood—and there will be loot in plenty to go round."

---

[2] Daring villains, bandits, assassins, or murderers.

pt. ends p. 28

"That's where my men come in," said Delgaun, and laughed. "We Low-Canallers live by rapine."[3]

"And you," said Kynon, "the 'hired bravoes', are in it to help. I need you and the Venusian, Stark, to train my men, to plan campaigns, to give me all you know of guerrilla fighting. Knighton has a fast cruiser. He'll bring us supplies from outside. Walsh is a genius, they tell me, at fashioning weapons. Themis is a mechanic, and also the cleverest thief this side of hell—saving your presence, Delgaun! Arrod organized and bossed the Brotherhood of the Little Worlds, which had the Space Patrol going mad for years. He can do the same for us. So there you have it. Now, Stark, what do you say?"

The Earthman answered slowly, "I'll go along with you—as long as no harm comes to the tribes."

Kynon laughed. "No need to worry about that."

"Just one more question," Stark said. "What's going to happen when the people find out that this Rama stuff is just a myth?"

"They won't," said Kynon. "The crowns will be destroyed in battle, and it will be very tragic, but very final. No one knows how to make more of them. Oh, I can handle the people! They'll be happy enough, with good land and water."

He looked around then and said plaintively, "And now can we sit down and drink like civilized men?"

They sat. The wine went round, and the vultures of Valkis drank to each other's luck and loot, and Stark learned that the woman's name was Berild.

Kynon was happy. He had made his point with the people, and he was celebrating. But Stark noticed that though his tongue grew thick, it did not loosen.

Luhar grew steadily more morose and silent, glancing covertly across the table at Stark. Delgaun toyed with his goblet, and his yellow gaze which gave nothing away moved restlessly between Berild and Stark.

---

[3] Violent seizure and pillaging of other's property.

Berild drank not at all. She sat a little apart, with her face in shadow, and her red mouth smiled. Her thoughts, too, were her own secret. But Stark knew that she was still watching him, and he knew that Delgaun was aware of it.

Presently Kynon said, "Delgaun and I have some talking to do, so I'll bid you gentlemen farewell for the present. You, Stark, and Luhar—I'm going back into the desert at midnight, and you're going with me, so you'd better get some sleep."

Stark nodded. He rose and went out, with the others.

An attendant showed him to his quarters, in the north wing. Stark had not rested for twenty-four hours, and he was glad of the chance to sleep.

He lay down. The wine spun in his head, and Berild's smile mocked him. Then his thoughts turned to Ashton, and his promise. Presently he slept, and dreamed.

*

He was a boy on Mercury again, running down a path that led from a cave mouth to the floor of a valley. Above him the mountains rose into the sky and were lost beyond the shallow atmosphere. The rocks danced in the terrible heat, but the soles of his feet were like iron, and trod them lightly. He was quite naked.

The blaze of the sun between the valley walls was like the shining heart of Hell. It did not seem to the boy N'Chaka that it could ever be cold again, yet he knew that when darkness came there would be ice on the shallows of the river. The gods were constantly at war.

He passed a place, ruined by earthquake. It was a mine, and N'Chaka remembered dimly that he had once lived there, with several white-skinned creatures shaped like himself. He went on without a second glance.

He was searching for Tika. When he was old enough, he would

pt. ends p. 28

mate with her. He wanted to hunt with her now, for she was fleet[4] and as keen as he at scenting out the great lizards.

He heard her voice calling his name. There was terror in it, and N'Chaka began to run. He saw her, crouched between two huge boulders, her light fur stained with blood.

A vast black-winged shadow swooped down upon him. It glared at him with its yellow eyes, and its long beak tore at him. He thrust his spear at it, but talons hooked into his shoulder, and the golden eyes were close to him, bright and full of death.

He knew those eyes. Tika screamed, but the sound faded, everything faded but those eyes. He sprang up, grappling with the thing . . .

A man's voice yelling, a man's hands thrusting him away. The dream receded. Stark came back to reality, dropping the scared attendant who had come to waken him.

The man cringed away from him. "Delgaun sent me. He wants you—in the council room." Then he turned and fled.

*

Stark shook himself. The dream had been terribly real. He went down to the council room. It was dusk now, and the torches were lighted.

Delgaun was waiting, and Berild sat beside him at the table. They were alone there. Delgaun looked up, with his golden eyes.

"I have a job for you, Stark," he said. "You remember the captain of Kynon's men, in the square today?"

"I do."

"His name is Freka, and he's a good man, but he's addicted to a certain vice. He'll be up to his ears in it by now, and somebody has to get him back by the time Kynon leaves. Will you see to it?"

Stark glanced at Berild. It seemed to him that she was amused, whether at him or at Delgaun he could not tell. He asked,

---

[4] Fast and nimble in movement.

"Where will I find him?"

"There's only one place where he can get his particular poison—Kala's, out on the edge of Valkis. It's in the old city, beyond the lower quays." Delgaun smiled. "You may have to be ready with your fists, Stark. Freka may not want to come."

Stark hesitated. Then, "I'll do my best," he said, and went out into the dusky streets of Valkis.

He crossed a square, heading away from the palace. A twisting lane swallowed him up. And quite suddenly, someone took his arm and said rapidly,

"Smile at me, and then turn aside into the alley."

The hand on his arm was small and brown, the voice very pretty with its accompaniment of little chiming bells. He smiled, as she had bade him, and turned aside into the alley, which was barely more than a crack between two rows of houses.

Swiftly, he put his hands against the wall, so that the girl was prisoned between them. A green-eyed girl, with golden bells braided in her black hair, and impudent breasts bare above a jeweled girdle. A handsome girl, with a proud look to her.

The serving girl who had stood beside the litter in the square, and had watched Kynon with such bleak hatred.

"Well," said Stark. "And what do you want with me, little one?"

She answered, "My name is Fianna. And I do not intend to kill you, neither will I run away."

Stark let his hands drop. "Did you follow me, Fianna?"

"I did. Delgaun's palace is full of hidden ways, and I know them all. I was listening behind the panel in the council room. I heard you speak out against Kynon, and I heard Delgaun's order, just now."

"So?"

"So, if you meant what you said about the tribes, you had better get away now, while you have the chance. Kynon lied to you. He will use you, and then kill you, as he will use and then destroy his own people." Her voice was hot with bitter fury.

pt. ends next p.

Stark gave her a slow smile that might have meant anything, or nothing.

"You're a Valkisian, Fianna. What do you care what happens to the barbarians?"

Her slightly tilted green eyes looked scornfully into his.

"I'm not trying to trap you, Earthman. I hate Kynon. And my mother was a woman of the desert."

She paused, then went on somberly, "Also, I serve the lady Berild, and I have learned many things. There is trouble coming, greater trouble than Kynon knows." She asked, suddenly, "What do you know of the Ramas?"

"Nothing," he answered, "except that they don't exist now, if they ever did."

Fianna gave him an odd look. "Perhaps they don't. Will you listen to me, Earthman from Mercury? Will you get away, now that you know you're marked for death?"

Stark said, "No."

"Even if I tell you that Delgaun has set a trap for you at Kala's?"

"No. But I will thank you for your warning, Fianna."

He bent and kissed her, because she was very young and honest. Then he turned and went on his way.

Part 5

Night came swiftly. Stark left behind him the torches and the laughter and the sounding harps, coming into the streets of the old city where there was nothing but silence and the light of the low moons.

He saw the lower quays, great looming shapes of marble rounded and worn by time, and went toward them. Presently he found that he was following a faint but definite path, threaded between the ancient houses. It was very still, so that the dry whisper of the drifting dust was audible.

He passed under the shadow of the quays, and turned into a broadway that had once led up from the harbor. A little way ahead, on the other side, he saw a tall building half fallen in ruin. Its windows were shuttered, barred with light, and from it came the sound of voices and a thin thread of music, very reedy and evil.

Stark approached it, slipping through the ragged shadows as though he had no more weight to him than a drift of smoke. Once a door banged and a man came out of Kala's and passed by, going down to Valkis. Stark saw his face in the moonlight. It was the face of a beast, rather than a man. He muttered to himself as he went, and once he laughed, and Stark felt a loathing in him.

He waited until the sound of footsteps had died away. The ruined houses gave no sign of danger. A lizard rustled between the stones, and that was all. The moonlight lay bright and still on Kala's door.

Stark found a little shard of rock and tossed it, so that it made a sharp snicking sound against the shadowed wall beyond him. Then he held his breath, listening.

No one, nothing, stirred. Only the dry wind sighed in the empty houses.

Stark went out, across the open space, and nothing happened. He flung open the door of Kala's dive.

Yellow light spilled out, and a choking wave of hot and stuffy air. Inside, there were tall lamps with quartz lenses, each of which poured down a beam of throbbing, gold-orange light. And in the little pools of radiance, on filthy furs and cushions on the floor, lay men and women whose faces were slack and bestial.

Stark realized now what secret vice Kala sold here. Shanga—the going-back—the radiation that caused temporary artificial atavism[1] and let men wallow for a time in beasthood. It was supposed to have been stamped out when the Lady Fand's dark Shanga ring had been destroyed. But it still persisted, in places like this outside the law.

He looked for Freka, and recognized the tall barbarian. He was sprawled under one of the Shanga-lamps, eyes closed, face brutish, growling and twitching in sleep like the beast he had temporarily become.

A voice spoke from behind Stark's shoulder. "I am Kala. What do you wish, Outlander?"

He turned. Kala might have been beautiful once, a thousand years ago as you reckon sin. She wore still the sweet chiming bells in her hair, and Stark thought of Fianna. The woman's ravaged face turned him sick. It was like the reedy, piping music, woven out of the very heart of evil.

---

[1] In this context, a reversion to an ancestral and more primitive type.

Yet her eyes were shrewd, and he knew that she had not missed his searching look around the room, nor his interest in Freka. There was a note of warning in her voice.

He did not want trouble, yet. Not until he found some hint of the trap Fianna had told him of.

He said, "Bring me wine."

"Will you try the lamp of Going-back, Outlander? It brings much joy."

"Perhaps later. Now, I wish wine."

*

She went away, clapping her hands for a slatternly wench who came between the sprawled figures with an earthen mug. Stark sat down beside a table, where his back was to the wall and he could see both the door and the whole room.

Kala had returned to her own heap of furs by the door, but her basilisk[2] eyes were alert.

Stark made a pretense of drinking, but his mind was very busy, very cold.

Perhaps this, in itself, was the trap. Freka was temporarily a beast. He would fight, and Kala would shriek, and the other dull-eyed brutes would rise and fight also.

But he would have needed no warning about that—and Delgaun himself had said there would be trouble.

No. There was something more.

He let his gaze wander over the room. It was large, and there were other rooms off of it, the openings hung with ragged curtains. Through the rents, Stark could see others of Kala's customers sprawled under Shanga-lamps, and some of these had gone so far back from humanity that they were hideous to behold. But still there was no sign of danger to himself.

[2] A basilisk is a mythical reptile who causes death to those who look into its eyes.

pt. ends p. 35

There was only one odd thing. The room nearest to where Freka sat was empty, and its curtains were only partly drawn.

Stark began to brood on the emptiness of that room.

He beckoned Kala to him. "I will try the lamp," he said. "But I wish privacy. Have it brought to that room, there."

Kala said, "That room is taken."

"But I see no one!"

"It is taken, it is paid for, and no one may enter. I will have your lamp brought here."

"No," said Stark. "The hell with it. I'm going."

He flung down a coin and went out. Moving swiftly outside, he placed his eye to a crack in the nearest shutter, and waited.

Luhar of Venus came out of the empty room. His face was worried, and Stark smiled. He went back and stood flat against the wall beside the door.

In a moment it opened and the Venusian came out, drawing his gun as he did so.

Stark jumped him.

Luhar let out one angry cry. His gun went off a vicious streak of flame across the moonlight, and then Stark's great hand crushed the bones of his wrist together so that he dropped it clashing on the stones. He whirled around, raking Stark's face with his nails as he clawed for the Earthman's eyes, and Stark hit him. Luhar fell, rolling over, and before he could scramble up again Stark had picked up the gun and thrown it away into the ruins across the street.

Luhar came up from the pavement in one catlike spring. Stark fell with him, back through Kala's door, and they rolled together among the foul furs and cushions. Luhar was built of spring steel, with no softness in him anywhere, and his long fingers were locked around Stark's throat.

Kala screamed with fury. She caught a whip from among her cushions—a traditional weapon along the Low-Canals—and began to lash the two men impartially, her hair flying in tangled locks across her face. The bestial figures under the lamps shambled to their feet, and growled.

The long lash ripped Stark's shirt and the flesh of his back beneath it. He snarled and staggered to his feet, with Luhar still clinging to the death grip on his throat. He pushed Luhar's face away from him with both hands and threw himself forward, over a table, so that Luhar was crushed beneath him.

The Venusian's breath left him with a whistling grunt. His fingers relaxed. Stark struck his hands away. He rose and bent over Luhar and picked him up, gripping him cruelly so that he turned white with the pain, and raised him high and flung him bodily into the growling, beast-faced men who were shambling toward him.

Kala leaped at Stark, cursing, striking him with the coiling lash. He turned. The thin veneer of civilization was gone from Stark now, erased in a second by the first hint of battle. His eyes blazed with a cold light. He took the whip out of Kala's hand and laid his palm across her evil face, and she fell and lay still.

He faced the ring of bestial, Shanga-sodden men who walled him off from what he had been sent to do. There was a reddish tinge to his vision, partly blood, partly sheer rage. He could see Freka standing erect in the corner, his head weaving from side to side brutishly.

Stark raised the whip and strode into the ring of men who were no longer quite men.

*

Hands struck and clawed him. Bodies reeled and fell away. Blank eyes glittered, and red mouths squealed, and there was a mingling of snarls and bestial laughter in his ears. The bloodlust had spread to these creatures now. They swarmed upon Stark and bore him down with the weight of their writhing bodies.

They bit him and savaged him in a blind way, and he fought his

pt. ends next p.

way up again, shaking them off with his great shoulders, trampling them under his boots. The lash hissed and sang, and the smell of blood rose on the choking air.

Freka's dazed, brutish face swam before Stark. The Martian growled and flung himself forward. Stark swung the loaded butt of the whip. It cracked solidly on the Shunni's temple, and he sagged into Stark's arms.

Out of the corner of his eyes, Stark saw Luhar. He had risen and crept around the edge of the fight. He was behind Stark now, and there was a knife in his hand.

Hampered by Freka's weight, Stark could not leap aside. As Luhar rushed in, he crouched and went backward, his head and shoulders taking the Venusian low in the belly. He felt the hot kiss of the blade in his flesh, but the wound was glancing, and before Luhar could strike again, Stark twisted like a great cat and struck down. Luhar's skull rang on the flagging. The Earthman's fist rose and fell twice. After that, Luhar did not move.

Stark got to his feet. He stood with his knees bent and his shoulders flexed, looking from side to side, and the sound that came out of his throat was one of pure savagery.

He moved forward a step or two, half naked, bleeding, towering like a dark colossus over the lean Martians, and the brutish throng gave back from him. They had taken more mauling than they liked, and there was something about the Outlander's simple desire to rend[3] them apart that penetrated even their Shanga-clouded minds.

Kala sat up on the floor, and snarled, "Get out."

Stark stood a moment or two longer, looking at them. Then he lifted Freka to his feet and laid him over his shoulder like a sack of meal and went out, moving neither fast nor slow, but in a straight line, and way was made for him.

He carried the Shunni down through the silent streets, and into the twisting, crowded ways of Valkis. There, too, the people

[3] Violently rip or tear.

stared at him and drew back, out of his path. He came to Delgaun's palace. The guards closed in behind him, but they did not ask that he stop.

Delgaun was in the council room, and Berild was still with him. It seemed that they had been waiting, over their wine and their private talk. Delgaun rose to his feet as Stark came in, so sharply that his goblet fell and spilled a red pool of wine at his feet.

Stark let the Shunni drop to the floor.

"I have brought Freka," he said. "Luhar is still at Kala's."

He looked into Delgaun's eyes, golden and cruel, the eyes of his dream. It was hard not to kill.

Suddenly the woman laughed, very clear and ringing, and her laughter was all for Delgaun.

"Well done, wild man," she said to Stark. "Kynon is lucky to have such a captain. One word for the future, though—watch out for Freka. He won't forgive you this."

Stark said thickly, looking at Delgaun, "This hasn't been a night for forgiveness." Then he added, "I can handle Freka."

Berild said, "I like you, wild man." Her eyes dwelt on Stark's face, curious, compelling. "Ride beside me when we go. I would know more about you."

And she smiled.

A dark flush crept over Delgaun's face. In a voice tight with fury he said, "Perhaps you've forgotten something, Berild. There is nothing for you in this barbarian, this creature of an hour!"

He would have said more in his anger, but Berild said sharply, "We will not speak of time. Go now, Stark. Be ready at midnight."

Stark went. And as he went, his brow was furrowed deep by a strange doubt.

Part 6

At midnight, in the great square of the slave market, Kynon's caravan formed again and went out of Valkis with thundering drums and skirling pipes. Delgaun was there to see them go, and the cheering of the people rang after them on the desert wind.

Stark rode alone. He was in a brooding mood and wanted no company, least of all that of the Lady Berild. She was beautiful, she was dangerous, and she belonged to Kynon, or to Delgaun, or perhaps to both of them. In Stark's experience, women like that were sudden death, and he wanted no part of her. At any rate, not yet.

Luhar rode ahead with Kynon. He had come dragging into the square at the mounting, his face battered and swollen, an ugly look in his eyes. Kynon gave one quick look from him to Stark, who had his own scars, and said harshly,

"Delgaun tells me there's a blood feud between you two. I want no more of it, understand? After you're paid off you can kill each other and welcome, but not until then. Is that clear?"

Stark nodded, keeping his mouth shut. Luhar muttered assent, and they had not looked at each other since.

Freka rode in his customary place by Kynon, which put him

near to Luhar. It seemed to Stark that their beasts swung close together more often than was necessary from the roughness of the track.

The big barbarian captain sat rigidly erect in his saddle, but Stark had seen his face in the torchlight, sick and sweating, with the brute look still clouding his eyes. There was a purple mark on his temple, but Stark was quite sure that Berild had spoken the truth—Freka would not forgive him either the indignity or the hangover of his unfinished wallow under the lamps of Shanga.

The dead sea bottom widened away under the black sky. As they left the lights of Valkis behind, winding their way over the sand and the ribs of coral, dropping lower with every mile into the vast basin, it was hard to believe that there could be life anywhere on a world that could produce such cosmic desolation.

The little moons fled away, trailing their eerie shadows over rock formations tortured into impossible shapes by wind and water, peering into clefts that seemed to have no bottom, turning the sand white as bone. The iron stars blazed, so close that the wind seemed edged with their frosty light. And in all that endless space nothing moved, and the silence was so deep that the coughing howl of a sand-cat far away to the east made Stark jump with its loudness.

Yet Stark was not oppressed by the wilderness. Born and bred to the wild and barren places, this desert was more kin to him than the cities of men.

After a while there was a jangling of brazen bangles behind him and Fianna came up. He smiled at her, and she said rather sullenly,

"The Lady Berild sent me, to remind you of her wish."

Stark glanced to where the scarlet-curtained litter rocked along, and his eyes glinted.

"She's not one to let go of a thing, is she?"

"No." Fianna saw that no one was within earshot, and then said quietly, "Was it as I said, at Kala's?"

Stark nodded. "I think, little one, that I owe you my life. Luhar would have killed me as soon as I tackled Freka."

pt. ends p. 43

He reached over and touched her hand where it lay on the bridle. She smiled, a young girl's smile that seemed very sweet in the moonlight, honest and comradely.

It was odd to be talking of death with a pretty girl in the moonlight.

Stark said, "Why does Delgaun want to kill me?"

"He gave no reason, when he spoke to the man from Venus. But perhaps I can guess. He knows that you're as strong as he is, and so he fears you. Also, the Lady Berild looked at you in a certain way."

"I thought Berild was Kynon's woman."

"Perhaps she is—for the time," answered Fianna enigmatically. Then she shook her head, glancing around with what was almost fear. "I have risked much already. Please—don't let it be known that I've spoken to you, beyond what I was sent to say."

Her eyes pleaded with him, and Stark realized with a shock that Fianna, too, stood on the edge of a quicksand.

"Don't be afraid," he said, and meant it. "We'd better go."

She swung her beast around, and as she did so she whispered, "Be careful, Eric John Stark!"

Stark nodded. He rode behind her, thinking that he liked the sound of his name on her lips.

*

The Lady Berild lay among her furs and cushions, and even then there was no indolence[1] about her. She was relaxed as a cat is, perfectly at ease and yet vibrant with life. In the shadows of the litter her skin showed silver-white and her loosened hair was a sweet darkness.

"Are you stubborn, wild man?" she asked. "Or do you find me distasteful?"

He had not realized before how rich and soft her voice was. He looked down at the magnificent supple length of her, and said,

[1] Laziness.

"I find you most damnably attractive—and that's why I'm stubborn."

"Afraid?"

"I'm taking Kynon's pay. Should I take his woman also?"

She laughed, half scornfully. "Kynon's ambitions leave no room for me. We have an agreement, because a king must have a queen—and he finds my counsel useful. You see, I am ambitious, too! Apart from that, there is nothing."

Stark looked at her, trying to read her smoke-gray eyes in the gloom. "And Delgaun?"

"He wants me, but . . . " She hesitated, and then went on, in a tone quite different from before, her voice low and throbbing with a secret pleasure as vast and elemental as the star-shot sky.

"I belong to no one," she said. "I am my own."

Stark knew that for the moment she had forgotten him.

He rode for a time in silence, and then he said slowly, repeating Delgaun's words,

"Perhaps you have forgotten something, Berild. There is nothing for you in me, the creature of an hour."

He saw her start, and for a moment her eyes blazed and her breath was sharply drawn. Then she laughed, and said,

"The wild man is also a parrot. And an hour can be a long time—as long as eternity, if one wills it so."

"Yes," said Stark, "I have often thought so, waiting for death to come at me out of a crevice in the rocks. The great lizard stings, and his bite is fatal."

He leaned over in the saddle, his shoulders looming above hers, naked in the biting wind.

"My hours with women are short ones," he said. "They come after the battle, when there is time for such things. Perhaps then I'll come and see you."

He spurred away and left her without a backward look, and the skin of his back tingled with the expectancy of a flying knife. But the only thing that followed him was a disturbing echo of laughter down the wind.

pt. ends p. 43

Dawn came. Kynon beckoned Stark to his side, and pointed out at the cruel waste of sand, with here and there a reef of basalt[2] black against the burning white.

"This is the country you will lead your men over. Learn it." He was speaking to Luhar as well. "Learn every waterhole, every vantage point, every trail that leads toward the Border. There are no better fighters than the Dryland men when they're well led, and you must prove to them that you can lead. You'll work with their own chieftains—Freka, and the others you'll meet when we reach Sinharat."

Luhar said, "Sinharat?"

"My headquarters. It's about seven days' march—an island city, old as the moons. The Rama cult was strong there, legend has it, and it's a sort of holy place to the tribesmen. That's why I picked it."

He took a deep breath and smiled, looking out over the dead sea bottom toward the Border, and his eyes held the same pitiless light as the sun that baked the desert.

"Very soon, now," he said, more to himself than the others. "Only a handful of days before we drown the Border states in their own blood. And after that . . . "

He laughed, very softly, and said no more. Stark could believe that what Berild said of him was true. There was a flame of ambition in Kynon that would let nothing stand in its way.

He measured the size and the strength of the tall barbarian, the eagle look of his face and the iron that lay beneath his joviality. Then Stark, too, stared off toward the Border and wondered if he would ever see Tarak or hear Simon Ashton's voice again.

For three days they marched without incident. At noon they made a dry camp and slept away the blazing hours, and then went on again under a darkening sky, a long line of tall men and rangy beasts, with the scarlet litter blooming like a strange flower in the midst of it. Jingling bridles and dust, and padded hoofs trampling the bones of the sea, toward the island city of Sinharat.

---

[2] A dark, dense, fine-grained rock that sometimes displays a column-like structure and formed when volcanic lava becomes solid.

Stark did not speak again to Berild, nor did she send for him. Fianna would pass him in the camp, and smile sidelong, and go on. For her sake, he did not stop her.

Neither Luhar nor Freka came near him. They avoided him pointedly, except when Kynon called them all together to discuss some point of strategy. But the two seemed to have become friends, and drank together from the same bottle of wine.

Stark slept always beside his mount, his back guarded and his gun loose. The hard lessons learned in his childhood had stayed with him, and if there was a footfall near him in the dust he woke often before the beast did.

*

Toward morning of the fourth night the wind, that never seemed to falter from its steady blowing, began to drop. At dawn it was dead still, and the rising sun had a tinge of blood. The dust rose under the feet of the beasts and fell again where it had risen.

Stark began to sniff the air. More and more often he looked toward the north, where there was a long slope as flat as his palm that stretched away farther than he could see.

A restless unease grew within him. Presently he spurred ahead to join Kynon.

"There is a storm coming," he said, and turned his head northward again.

Kynon looked at him curiously.

"You even have the right direction," he said. "One might think you were a native." He, too, gazed with brooding anger at the long sweep of emptiness.

"I wish we were closer to the city. But one place is as bad as another when the khamsin[3] blows, and the only thing to do is keep moving. You're a dead dog if you stop—dead and buried."

[3] An oppressively hot southerly wind originating in the Sahara that blows across Egypt and over the Red Sea from late March to early May.

pt. ends next p.

He swore, with a curious admixture[4] of blunt Anglo-Saxon in his Martian profanity, as though the storm were a personal enemy.

"Pass the word along to force it—dump whatever they have to to lighten the loads. And get Berild out of that damned litter. Stick by her, will you, Stark? I've got to stay here, at the head of the line. And don't get separated. Above all, *don't get separated!*"

Stark nodded and dropped back. He got Berild mounted, and they left the litter there, a bright patch of crimson on the sand, its curtains limp in the utter stillness.

Nobody talked much. The beasts were urged on to the top of their speed. They were nervous and fidgety, inclined to break out of line and run for it. The sun rose higher.

One hour.

The windless air shimmered. The silence lay upon the caravan with a crushing hand. Stark went up and down the line, lending a hand to the sweating drovers with the pack animals that now carried only water-skins and a bare supply of food. Fianna rode close beside Berild.

Two hours.

For the first time that day there was a sound in the desert.

It came from far off, a moaning wail like the cry of a giantess in travail. It rushed closer, rising as it did so to a dry and bitter shriek that filled the whole sky, shook it, and tore it open, letting in all the winds of Hell.

It struck swiftly. One moment the air was clear and motionless. The next, it was blind with dust and screaming as it fled, tearing with demoniac[5] fury at everything in its path.

Stark spurred toward the women, who were only a few feet away but already hidden by the veil of mingled dust and sand.

Someone blundered into him in the murk. Long hair whipped across his face and he reached out, crying "Fianna! Fianna!" A

[4] A mixture of ingredients.

[5] Demonic; like a demon.

woman's hand caught his, and a voice answered, but he could not hear the words.

Then, suddenly, his beast was crowded by other scaly bodies. The woman's grip had broken. Hard masculine hands clawed at him. He could make out, dimly, the features of two men, close to his.

Luhar, and Freka.

His beast gave a great lurch, and sprang forward. Stark was dragged from the saddle, to fall backward into the raging sand.

Part 7

He lay half-stunned for a moment, his breath knocked out of him. There was a terrible reptilian screaming sounding thin through the roar of the wind. Vague shapes bolted past him, and twice he was nearly crushed by their trampling hoofs.

Luhar and Freka must have waited their chance. It was so beautifully easy. Leave Stark alone and afoot, and the storm and the desert between them would do the work, with no blame attaching to any man.

Stark got to his feet, and a human body struck him at the knees so that he went down again. He grappled with it, snarling, before he realized that the flesh between his hands was soft and draped in silken cloth. Then he saw that he was holding Berild.

"It was I," she gasped, "and not Fianna."

Her words reached him very faintly, though he knew she was yelling at the top of her lungs. She must have been knocked from her own mount when Luhar thrust between them.

Gripping her tightly, so that she should not be blown away, Stark struggled up again. With all his strength, it was almost impossible to stand.

Blinded, deafened, half strangled, he fought his way forward a few paces, and suddenly one of the pack beasts loomed shadow-like beside him, going by with a rush and a squeal.

By the grace of Providence[1] and his own swift reflexes, he caught its pack lashings, clinging with the tenacity of a man determined not to die. It floundered about, dragging them, until Berild managed to grasp its trailing halter rope. Between them, they fought the creature down.

Stark clung to its head while the woman clambered to its back, twisting her arm through the straps of the pad. A silken scarf whipped toward him. He took it and tied it over the head of the beast so it could breathe, and after that it was quieter.

There was no direction, no sight of anything, in that howling inferno. The caravan seemed to have been scattered like a drift of autumn leaves. Already, in the few brief moments he had stood still, Stark's legs were buried to the knees in a substratum of sand that rolled like water. He pulled himself free and started on, going nowhere, remembering Kynon's words.

Berild ripped her thin robe apart and gave him another strip of silk for himself. He bound it over his nose and eyes, and some of the choking and the blindness abated.

Stumbling, staggering, beaten by the wind as a child is beaten by a strong man, Stark went on, hoping desperately to find the main body of the caravan, and knowing somehow that the hope was futile.

The hours that followed were nightmare. He shut his mind to them, in a way that a civilized man would have found impossible. In his childhood there had been days, and nights, and the problems had been simple ones—how to survive one span of light that one might then struggle to survive the span of darkness that came after. One thing, one danger, at a time.

Now there was a single necessity. Keep moving. Forget tomorrow, or what happened to the caravan, or where the little Fianna with her bright eyes may be. Forget thirst, and the pain of breathing, and the fiery lash of sand on naked skin. Only don't stand still.

---

[1] The protective care of God.

pt. ends p. 48

It was growing dark when the beast fell against a half-buried boulder and snapped its foreleg. Stark gave it a quick and merciful death. They took the straps from the pad and linked themselves together. Each took as much food as he could carry, and Stark shouldered the single skin of water that fortune had vouchsafed[2] them.

They staggered on, and Berild did not whimper.

Night came, and still the khamsin blew. Stark wondered at the woman's strength, for he had to help her only when she fell. He had lost all feeling himself. His body was merely a thing that continued to move only because it had been ordered not to stop.

The haze in his own mind had grown as thick as the black obscurity of the night. Berild had ridden all day, but he had walked, and there was an end even to his strength. He was approaching it now, and was too weary even to be afraid.

He became aware at some indeterminate time that Berild had fallen and was dragging her weight against the straps. He turned blindly to help her up. She was saying something, crying his name, striking at him so that he should hear her words and understand.

At last he did. He pulled the wrappings from his face and breathed clean air. The wind had fallen. The sky was growing clear.

He dropped in his tracks and slept, with the exhausted woman half dead beside him.

*

Thirst brought them both awake in the early dawn. They drank from the skin, and then sat for a time looking at the desert, and at each other, thinking of what lay ahead.

"Do you know where we are?" Stark asked.

"Not exactly." Berild's face was shadowed with weariness. It had changed, and somehow, to Stark, it had grown more beautiful, because there was no weakness in it.

---

[2] Given; granted; bestowed.

She thought a minute, looking at the sun. "The wind blew from the north," she said. "Therefore we have come south from the track. Sinharat lies that way, across the waste they call the Belly of Stones." She pointed to the north and east.

"How far?"

"Seven, eight days, afoot."

Stark measured their supply of water and shook his head. "It'll be dry walking."

He rose and took up the skin, and Berild came beside him without a word. Her red hair hung loose over her shoulders. The rags of her silken robe had been torn away by the wind, leaving her only the loose skirt of the desert women, and her belt and collar of jewels.

She walked erect with a steady, swinging stride, and it was almost impossible for Stark to remember her as she had been, riding like a lazy queen in her scarlet litter.

There was no way to shelter themselves from the midday sun. The sun of Mars at its worst, however, was only a pale candle beside the sun of Mercury, and it did not bother Stark. He made Berild lie in the shadow of his own body, and he watched her face, relaxed and unfamiliar in sleep.

For the first time, then, he was conscious of a strangeness in her. He had seen so little of her before, in Valkis, and almost nothing on the trail. Now, there was little of her mind or heart that she could conceal from him.

Or was there? There were moments, while she slept, when the shadows of strange dreams crossed her face. Sometimes, in the unguarded moment of waking, he would see in her eyes a look he could not read, and his primitive senses quivered with a vague ripple of warning.

Yet all through those blazing days and frosty nights, tortured with thirst and weary to exhaustion, Berild was magnificent. Her white skin was darkened by the sun and her hair became a wild red mane, but she smiled and set her feet resolutely by his, and Stark thought she was the most beautiful creature he had ever seen.

pt. ends next p.

On the fourth day they climbed a scarp of limestone worn in ages past by the sea, and looked out over the place called the Belly of Stones.

The sea bottom curved downward below them into a sort of gigantic basin, the farther rim of which was lost in shimmering waves of heat. Stark thought that never, even on Mercury, had he seen a place more cruel and utterly forsaken of gods or men.

It seemed as though some primal glacier must have met its death here in the dim dawn of Mars, hollowing out its own grave. The body of the glacier had melted away, but its bones were left.

Bones of basalt, of granite and marble and porphyry,[3] of every conceivable color and shape and size, picked up by the ice as it marched southward from the pole and dropped here as a cairn[4] to mark its passing.

The Belly of Stones. Stark thought that its other name was Death . . .

For the first time, Berild faltered. She sat down and bent her head over her hands.

"I am tired," she said. "Also, I am afraid."

Stark asked, "Has it ever been crossed?"

"Once. But they were a war party, mounted and well supplied."

Stark looked out across the stones. "We will cross it," he said.

Berild raised her head. "Somehow I believe you." She rose slowly and put her hands on his breast, over the strong beating of his heart.

"Give me your strength, wild man," she whispered. "I shall need it."

He drew her to him and kissed her, and it was a strange and painful kiss, for their lips were cracked and bleeding from their terrible thirst. Then they went down together into the place called the Belly of Stones.

---

[3] A hard reddish-purple rock, anciently quarried in Egypt.

[4] A mound of stones erected as a memorial, monument, or marker.

Part 8

The desert had been a pleasant and kindly place. Stark looked back upon it with longing. And yet this inferno of blazing rock was so like the valleys of his boyhood that it did not occur to him to lie down and die.

They rested for a time in the sheltered crevice under a great leaning slab of blood-red stone, moistening their swollen tongues with a few drops of stinking water from the skin. At nightfall they drank the last of it, but Berild would not let him throw the skin away.

Darkness, and a lunar silence. The chill air sucked the day's heat out of the rocks and the iron frost came down, so that Stark and the red-haired woman must keep moving or freeze.

Stark's mind grew clouded. He spoke from time to time, in a croaking whisper, dropping back into the harsh mother-tongue of the Twilight Belt. It seemed to him that he was hunting, as he had so many times before, in the waterless places—for the blood of the great lizard would save him from thirst.

But nothing lived in the Belly of Stones. Nothing, but the two who crept and staggered across it under the low moons.

Berild fell, and could not rise again. Stark crouched beside her. Her face stared up at him, white in the moonlight, her eyes burning and strange.

"I will not die!" she whispered, not to him, but to the gods. "*I will not die!*"

And she clawed the sand and the bitter rocks, dragging herself onward. It was uncanny, the madness that she had for life.

Stark raised her up and carried her. His breath came in deep sobbing gasps. After a while he, too, fell. He went on like a beast on all fours, dragging the woman.

He knew dimly that he was climbing. There was a glimmering of dawn in the sky. His hands slipped on a lip of sand and he went rolling down a smooth slope. At length he stopped and lay on his back like a dead thing.

The sun was high when consciousness returned to him. He saw Berild lying near him and crawled to her, shaking her until her eyes opened. Her hands moved feebly and her lips formed the same four words. *I will not die*.

Stark strained his eyes to the horizon, praying for a glimpse of Sinharat, but there was nothing, only emptiness and sand. With great difficulty he got the woman to her feet, supporting her.

He tried to tell her that they must go on, but he could no longer form the words. He could only gesture and urge her forward, in the direction of the city.

But she refused to go. "Too far . . . die . . . without water . . . "

He knew that she was right, but still he was not ready to give up.

She began to move away from him, toward the south, and he thought that she had gone mad and was wandering. Then he saw that she was peering with awful intensity at the line of the scarp that formed this wall of the Belly of Stones. It rose into a great ridge, serrated like the backbone of a whale, and some three miles away a long dorsal fin of reddish rock curved out into the desert.

Berild made a little sobbing noise in her throat. She began to plod toward the distant promontory.

Stark caught up with her. He tried to stop her, but she would not be stopped, turning a feral glare upon him.

She croaked, "Water!" and pointed.

He was sure now that she was mad. He told her so, forcing the painful words out of his throat, reminding her of Sinharat and that she was going away from any possible help.

She said again, quite sanely, "Too far. Two—three days without water." She pointed. "Monastery—old well—a chance . . . "

Stark decided that he had little to lose by trusting her. He nodded and went with her toward the curve of rock.

The three miles might have been three hundred. At last they came up under the ragged cliffs—and there was nothing there but sand.

Stark looked at the woman. A great rage and a deep sense of futility came over him. They were indeed lost.

But Berild had gone a few steps farther. With a hoarse cry, she bent over what had seemed merely a slab of stone fallen from the cliff, and Stark saw that it was a carven pillar, half buried. Now he was able to make out the mounded shape of a ruin, of which only the foundations and a few broken columns were left.

For a long while Berild stood by the pillar, her eyes closed. Stark got the uncanny feeling that she was visualizing the place as it had been, though the wall must have been dust a thousand years ago. Presently she moved. He followed her, and it was strange to see her, on the naked sand, treading the arbitrary patterns of vanished corridors.

She came to a halt, in a broad flat space that might once have been a central courtyard. There she fell on her knees and began to dig.

Stark got down beside her. They scrabbled like a pair of dogs in the yielding sand. Stark's nails slipped across something hard, and there was a yellow glint through the dusty ocher.[1] Within a few minutes they had bared a golden cover six feet across, very massive and wonderfully carved with the symbols of some lost god of the sea.

---

[1] A variety of fine clay containing iron, varying from light yellow to brown or red.

pt. ends next p.

Stark struggled to lift the thing away. He could not move it. Then Berild pressed a hidden spring and the cover slid back of itself. Beneath it, sweet and cold, protected through all these ages, water stirred gently against mossy stones.

*

An hour later, Stark and Berild lay sleeping, soaked to the skin, their very hair dripping with the blessed dampness.

That night, when the low moons roved over the desert, they sat by the well, drowsy with an animal sense of rest and repletion. And Stark looked at the woman and said,

"I know you now."

"What do you know, wild man?"

Stark said quietly, "You are a Rama."

She did not answer at once. Then she said, "I was bred in these deserts. Is it so strange that I should know of this well?"

"Strange that you didn't mention it before. You were afraid, weren't you, that if you led me here your secret would come out? But it was that, or die."

He leaned forward, studying her.

"If you had led me straight to the well, I might not have wondered. But you had to stop and remember, how the halls were built and where the doorways were that led to the inner court. You lived in this place when it was whole. And no one, not even Kynon himself, knows of it but you."

"You dream, wild man. The moon is in your eyes."

Stark shook his head slowly. "I know."

She laughed, and stretched her arms wide on the sand.

"But I am young," she said. "And men have told me I am beautiful. It is good to be young, for youth has nothing to do with ashes and empty skulls."

She touched his arm, and little darts of fire went through his flesh, warm from his fingertips.

"Forget your dreams, wild man. They're madness, gone with the morning."

He looked down at her in the clear pale light, and she was young, and beautifully made, and her lips were smiling.

He bent his head. Her arms went round him. Her hair blew soft against his cheek. Then, suddenly, she set her teeth cruelly into his lip. He cried out and thrust her away, and she sat back on her heels, mocking him.

"That," she said, "is because you called Fianna's name instead of mine, when the storm broke."

Stark cursed her. There was a taste of blood in his mouth. He reached out and caught her, and again she laughed, a peculiarly sweet, wicked sound.

The wind blew over them, sighing, and the desert was very still.

For two days they remained among the ruins. At evening of the second day Stark filled the water skin, and Berild replaced the golden cover on the well. They began the last long march toward Sinharat.

Part 9

Stark saw it rising against the morning sky—a city of gold and marble, high on an island of rose-red coral laid bare by the vanished sea. Sinharat, the Ever-Living.

Yet it had died. As he came closer to it, plodding slowly through the sand, he saw that the place was no more than a beautiful corpse, the lovely towers broken, the roofless palaces open to the sky. Whatever life Kynon and his armies might have foisted[1] upon Sinharat was no more than the fleeting passage of ants across the perfect bones of the dead.

"What was it like before?" he asked, "with the blue water around it, and the banners flying?"

Berild turned a dark, calculating look upon him.

"I told you before to forget that madness. If you talk it, no one will believe you."

"No one?"

"You had best not anger me, wild man," she said quietly. "I may be your only hope of life, before this is over."

---

[1] Imposed.

They did not speak again, going with slow weary steps toward the city.

In the desert below the coral cliffs the armies of Kynon were encamped. The tall warriors of Kesh and Shun waiting, with their women and their beasts and their shining spears, for the pipers to cry them over the Border. The skin tents and the long picket lines were too many to count. In the distance, a convertible Kallman spacer that Stark recognized as Knighton's made an ugly, jarring incongruity.

Lookouts sighted the two toiling figures in the distance. Men and women and children began to stream out across the sand, and presently a great cheering arose. Where he had looked on emptiness for days, Stark was smothered now by the press of thousands. Berild was picked up and carried on the shoulders of two chiefs, and men would have carried Stark also, but he fought them off.

Broad flights of steps were cut in the coral. The throng flowed upward along them. Ahead of them all went Eric John Stark, and he was smiling. From time to time he asked a question, and men drew back from that question, and his smile.

Up the steps and into the streets of Sinharat he went, with a slow, restless stride, asking,

"Where is Luhar of Venus?"

Every man there read death in his face, but they did not try to stop him.

People came out of the graceful ruins, drawn by the clamor, and the tide rolled down the broadways, the rose-red streets of coral, until it spread out in the square before a great palace of gold and ivory and white marble blinding in the sun.

Luhar of Venus came down the terraced steps, fresh from sleep, his pale hair tumbled, his eyes still drowsy.

Others came through the door behind him. Stark did not see them. They did not matter. Berild didn't matter, calling his name from where she sat on the shoulders of the chiefs. Nothing, no one mattered, but himself and Luhar.

He crossed the square, not hurrying, a dark ravaged giant in

pt. ends p. 61

rags. He saw Luhar pause on the bottom step. He saw the sleep and the vagueness go out of the Venusian's eyes as they rested first on the red-haired woman, then on himself. He saw the fear come into them, and the undying hate.

Someone got between him and Luhar. Stark lifted the man and flung him aside without breaking his stride, and went on. Luhar half turned. He would have run away, back into the palace, but there were too many now between him and the door. He crouched and drew his gun.

Stark sprang.

He came like a great black panther leaping, and he struck low. Luhar's shot went over his back. After that there was no more shooting. There was a moment, terribly short and silent, in which the two men lay entangled, straining against each other in a sort of stasis. Then Luhar screamed.

*

Stark knew dimly that there were hands, many of them, trying to drag him away. He clung growling to the Venusian until he was torn loose by main force. He struggled against his captors, and through a red haze he saw Kynon's face, close to his and very angry. Luhar was not yet dead.

"I warned you, Stark!" said Kynon furiously. "I warned you."

Men were bending over Luhar. Knighton, Walsh, Themis, Arrod. Stark saw that Delgaun was among them. He did not question at the time how word had gone back to Valkis and sent Delgaun racing across the dead sea bottom with his hired bravoes to search for the red-haired woman. It was right that Delgaun should be there.

In short ragged sentences, Stark told how Luhar and Freka had tried to kill him, and how Berild had been lost with him.

Kynon turned to the Venusian. Death was already glazing

the cloud-gray eyes, but it had not quenched the hatred and the venom.

"He lies," whispered Luhar. "I saw him—he tried to run away and take the woman with him."

Luhar of Venus, taking vengeance with his last breath.

Freka pushed forward, transparently eager to pick up his cue. "It is so," he said. "I was with Luhar. I saw it also."

Delgaun laughed. Cruel, silent laughter. He stood up, and looked at Berild.

Berild's eyes were blazing. She ignored Delgaun and spoke to Kynon.

"You fool. Can't you see that they hate him? What Stark says is true. And I would have died in the desert because of them, if Stark hadn't been a better man than all of you."

"Strange words," said Delgaun, "coming from a man's own mate. Perhaps Luhar did lie, after all. Perhaps it was not Stark who tried to run away, but you."

She cursed him, with an ancient curse, and Kynon looked at her sullenly. He said to the men who held Stark, "Chain him below, in the dungeons." Then he took Berild's arm and went with her into the palace.

Stark fought until someone behind him knocked him on the head with the butt of a spear. The last thing he saw was the face of Fianna, standing out from the crowd, wide-eyed with pity and love.

He came to in a place of cold, dry stone. There was an iron collar around his neck, and a five-foot chain ran from it to a ring in the wall. The cell was small. A gate of iron bars closed the single entrance. Beyond was an open well, with other cell doors around it, and above were thick stone gratings open to the sky. He guessed that the place was built beneath some inner court of the palace.

There were no other prisoners. But there was a guard, a thick-shouldered barbarian who sat on the execution block in the center of the well, with a sword and a jug of wine. A guard who watched the captive Stark smiled.

pt. ends p. 61

Freka.

When he saw that Stark was awake, Freka lifted up the jug and laughed. "Here's to Death," he said. "For no one else comes here!"

He drank, and after that he did not speak, only sat and smiled.

Stark said nothing either. He waited, with the same unhuman patience he had shown when he waited for his captors under the tor.

The dim daylight faded from the gratings. Darkness came, and the pale glimmer of the moons. Freka became a silvered statue of a man, sitting on the block. Stark's eyes glowed.

The empty jug dropped and broke. Freka rose. He took the naked sword in his hand and crossed the open space to the cell. He lifted the outer bar away. It fell with a great echoing clang, and Freka entered.

"Stand up, Outlander," he said. "Stand up and face the steel. After that you'll sleep in a coral pit, and not even the worms will find you."

"Beast of Shanga!" Stark said contemptuously, and set his back against the wall, to give himself all the slack of the chain.

He saw the bright steel glimmer in the air, up and down again, but when the blow fell he had leaped aside, and the point struck ringing against the stone. Stark darted in to grapple.

His fingers slipped on hard muscle, and Freka wrenched away. He was a fighting man, and no weakling. The iron collar dug painfully into the Earthman's throat and the heavy chain threw him backward. Freka laughed, deep in his chest. The sword glinted hungrily.

*

Then, as though she had taken shape suddenly from the shadows, Fianna was in the doorway. The little gun in her hand made a hissing spurt of flame. Freka screamed once, and fell. He did not move again.

"The swine," Fianna said, without emotion. "Delgaun ordered him to wait, until it was sure that Kynon would not come down to talk to you. Then the story was to be that you had escaped somehow, with Berild's aid."

She stepped over the body and unlocked the iron collar with a key she took from her girdle.

Stark took her slender shoulders gently between his hands. "Are you a witch-girl, that you know all things and always come when I need you?"

She gave him a deep, strange look. In the dusk, her proud young face was unfamiliar, touched with something fey[2] and sad. He wished that he could see her eyes more clearly.

"I know all things because I must," she told him wearily. "And I think that you are my only hope—perhaps the only hope of Mars."

He drew her to him, and kissed her, and stroked her dark head. "You're too young to concern yourself with the destinies of worlds."

He felt her tremble. "The youth of the body is only illusion, when the mind is old."

"And is yours old, little one?"

"Old," she whispered. "As old as Berild's."

He felt her tears warm against his skin, and she was like a child in his arms.

"Then you know about her," said Stark.

"Yes."

He paused. "And Delgaun?"

"Delgaun also."

"I thought so," Stark said. He nodded, scowling at the barred moonlight in the well. "There are things I must know, myself—but we'd best get out of here. Did Berild send you?"

"Yes—as soon as she could get the key from Kynon. She is waiting for you." She stirred Freka's body with her foot. "Bring that. We'll hide it in the pit he meant for you."

Stark heaved the body over his shoulder and followed the girl

---

[2] Doomed.

pt. ends next p.

through a twisting maze of corridors, some pitch dark, some feebly lighted by the moons. Fianna moved as surely as though she were in the main square at high noon. There was the silence of death in these cold tunnels, and the dry faint smell of eternity.

At length Fianna whispered. "Here. Be careful."

She put out a hand to guide him, but Stark's eyes were like a cat's in the dark. He made out a space where the rock with which the ancient builders had faced these subterranean ways gave place to the original coral.

Ragged black mouths opened in the coral, entrances to some unguessed catacombs beneath. Stark consigned Freka to the nearest pit, and then reluctantly threw his sword in after him.

"You won't need it," Fianna told him, "and besides, it would be recognized. This will be a bitter night enough, without rousing the men of Shun over Freka's death."

Stark listened to the distant sliding echoes from the pit, and shivered. He had so nearly finished there himself. He was glad to follow Fianna away from that place of darkness and silent death.

He stopped her in a place where a bar of moonlight came splashing through a great crack in the tunnel roof.

"Now," he said, "we will talk."

She nodded. "Yes. The time has come for that."

"There are lies everywhere," said Stark. "I am tangled up in lies. You know the truth that is behind this war of Kynon's. Tell me."

"Kynon's truth is simple," she answered, speaking slowly, choosing her words. "He wants land and power, conquest. He will pour out the blood of his people for that, and after that he plans to use the men of the Low-Canals under Delgaun to keep the tribesmen in line. It may be true, as he said, that they would be satisfied with grazing land and water—but they would lose their freedom, and their pride, and I think he has judged them wrongly. I think they would revolt."

She looked up at Stark. "He planned to use your knowledge, and then destroy you if you became troublesome."

"I guessed that. What about the others?"

"The outlanders? Use them, keep them as subordinates, or pay them off. Kill them, if necessary."

"Now," said Stark. "What of Delgaun and Berild?"

Fianna said softly, "Their truth, too, is simple. They took Kynon's idea of empire, and stretched it further. It was Delgaun's idea to bring the strangers in. They would use Kynon and the tribes until the victory was won. Then they would do away with Kynon and rule themselves—with the outlanders and their ships and their powerful weapons to oppress Low-Canaller and Dry-lander alike.

"That way, they could rape a world. More outland vultures would come, drawn by the smell of loot. The Martian men would fight as long as there was the hope of plunder—after that, they would be slaves to hold the empire. Their masters would grow fat on tribute from the City-States and from the men of Earth who have built here, or who wish to build. An evil plan—but profitable."

Stark thought about Knighton and Walsh of Terra, Themis of Mercury, Arrod of Callisto Colony. He thought of others like them, and what they would do, with their talons hooked in the heart of Mars. He thought of Delgaun's yellow eyes.

He thought of Berild, and he was sick with loathing.

Fianna came close to him, speaking in a different tone that had care and anxiety only for him.

"I have told you this, because I know what Berild plans. Tonight—oh, tonight is a black and evil time, and death waits in Sinharat! It is very close to me, I know. And you must follow your own heart, Eric John Stark. I cannot tell you more."

He kissed her again, because she was sweet and very brave. Then she led him on through the dark labyrinth, to where Berild was waiting, with her dangerous beauty and all the evil of the ages in her soul.

Part 10

They came out of the darkness so suddenly that Stark blinked in the unaccustomed light of torches set in great silver sconces on the walls.

The floor had been artificially smoothed, but otherwise this crypt was as the eroding action of the sea had shaped it out of the coral reef. It was not large, and it was like a cavern in a fairy tale, walled and roofed with the fantastic wreathing shapes of the rose-red coral. At one end there was a golden coffer[1] set with flaming jewels.

Berild was there. Her wonderful hair was dressed and shining, and her body was clothed all in white, her arms and shoulders warm bronze from the kiss of the desert sun.

Kynon was there, also. He stood motionless and silent, and he did not so much as turn his head when Fianna and Stark came in. His eyes were wide open and blank as a blind man's.

"I have been waiting," said Berild, "and the time is short."

She seemed angry and impatient, and Stark said, "Freka is dead. It was necessary to hide his body."

---

[1] A chest or strongbox for storing money or valuables.

She nodded and turned to the girl. "Go now, Fianna."

Fianna bent her head and went away. She did not look at Stark. It was as though she had no interest in anything that happened.

Stark looked at Kynon, who had not moved or spoken.

"He is safe enough," said Berild, answering Stark's unspoken question. "I drugged his wine so that his mind was opened to mine, and he is my creature as long as I will it."

Hypnosis, Stark thought. His nerves were beginning to do strange things. He wished desperately that he were back in the cell facing Freka's sword, which at least would deal with him openly and without guile or subterfuge.

Berild set her hands on Stark's shoulders, and smiled as she had done that night by the ancient well.

"I offer you three things tonight, wild man," she said. Her eyes challenged him, and the scent of her hair was sweet and maddening.

"Your life—and power—and myself."

Stark let his hands slip lightly down from her shoulders to her waist. "And how will you do this thing?" he asked.

"Easily," she said, and laughed. She was very proud, and sure of her strength, and glad to be alive. "Oh, very easily. You guessed the truth about me—I am of the Twice-Born, the Ramas. I hold the secret of the Sending-on of Minds, which this great ox Kynon pretended to have. I can give you life now—and forever. Remember, wild man—forever!"

He bent his dark face to hers, so that their lips touched, and murmured, "Would I have you forever, Berild?"

"Until you tire of me—or I of you." She kissed him, and then added mockingly, "Delgaun has had me for a thousand years, and I am weary of him. So very weary!"

"A thousand years is a long time," said Stark, "and I am not Delgaun."

"No. You're a beast, a savage, a most magnificent cold-eyed animal, and that is why I love you." She touched the muscle of his

pt. ends p. 66

breast, and then his throat, and added, "It's a pity there will never be another body like this one. We must keep it as long as we can."

"What is your plan?" Stark asked her.

"Simply this. I will place your mind in Kynon's body. You will *be* Kynon, with all his power. You will be able then to keep Delgaun in check—later, you can destroy him, but not until after the battle is won, for we need the men of Valkis and Jekkara. You can keep your own body safe from him, and at the worst, if by some chance he should succeed in slaying the man he believes to be you, *you* will still be alive."

"And after the battle," said Stark softly. "What then, Berild?"

"We will rule together." She held his palms against hers. "You have strong hands, wild man. Would you not like to hold a world between them—and me?"

She looked up at him, her eyes suddenly shrewd and probing. "Or do you still believe the nonsense you talked to Kynon, about the tribes?"

*

Stark smiled. "It's easy to have principles when there's no gain involved. No. I am as my name says—a man without a tribe. I have no loyalties. And if I had, would I remember them now?"

He held her, as she had said, between his hands, and they were very strong.

But even then, Berild could warn him.

"Keep faith with me, then! My wisdom is greater than yours, and I have powers you don't dream of. What I give, I can take away."

For answer, Stark silenced her mouth with his own.

When she drew away, she said rather breathlessly, "Let us hurry. The tribes are gathered, and Kynon was to have given the signal for war at dawn. There is much I must teach you between now and then."

She paused with her hand on the lid of the golden coffer. "This is a secret place," she said quietly. "Since before the ocean died, it has been secret. Not even Kynon knew of it. I think only Delgaun and I, the last of the Twice-Born, knew—and now you."

"What about Fianna?"

Berild shrugged. "She is only my servant. To her, this is only a little cavern where I keep my private wealth."

She pressed a series of patterned bosses[2] in intricate sequence, and there was the sharp click of an opening lock. A shiver ran up along Stark's spine. The beast in him longed to run, to be away from this whole business that smelled of evil. But the man in him knelt at Berild's wish, and waited, and did not flinch when the blank-eyed Kynon came like a moving corpse beside him.

Berild raised the golden lid. And there was a great silence.

On the slave block of Valkis, Kynon had brought forth two crowns of shining crystal, and a rod of flame. As glass is to diamond, as the pallid moon to the light of the sun, were those things to the reality.

In her two hands Berild held the ancient crowns of the Ramas, the givers of life. Twin circlets of glorious fire, dimming the shallow glare of the torches, putting a nimbus of light around the white-clad woman so that she was like a goddess walking in a cloud of stars. Stark's whole being contracted to a point of icy pain at the beauty and the wonder and the terror of them.

She set one crown on Kynon's head, and even the drugged automaton[3] shivered and sighed at its touch.

Stark's mind veered away from the incredible thing that was about to happen. It spoke words to him, hurried desperate words of sanity, about the electrical patterns of the mind, and the sensitivity of crystals, and conductors, and electromagnetic impulses. But that was only the top of his brain. At base it was still the brain of N'Chaka that believed in gods and demons and all the

[2] A boss is a protruding knob, stud, or ornament.

[3] One who acts or responds in a mechanical way, much like a robot.

pt. ends next p.

sorceries of darkness. Only pride kept him from cowering abjectly at Berild's feet.

She stood above him, a creature of dreams in the unearthly light. She smiled and whispered, "Do not fear,"—and she placed the second crown upon his head.

A strange, shuddering fire swept through him. It was as though some chip of the primal heart of all creation had been set by an unguessed magic into the cells of the crystal. The force that shaped the universe and scattered forth the stars, and set the great suns to spinning. There was something awesome about it, something almost holy.

And yet he was afraid. Most shockingly afraid.

His brain was set free, in some strange fashion. The walls of his skull vanished. His mind floated in a dim vastness. It was like a tiny sun, glowing, spinning, swelling . . .

Berild lifted a crystal rod from the coffer, a wand of sorcerous fire. And now Stark's thoughts had lost all track of science. A cloud of misty darkness flowed around him, thickened . . .

A great leaping flare of light, a distant echo of a cry that he did not recognize as his own, and then . . .

Nothing.

Part II

He was lying on his face, his cheek pressed against the cool coral. He opened his eyes, his mind groping for the shreds of some remembered terror. He saw, vaguely at first and then with terrible clarity as his vision became clear, a man lying close beside him.

A tall man, very strongly built, with skin burned almost to blackness by exposure. A man who looked at him with eyes that were startlingly light in his dark face . . .

His own eyes. His own face.

He cried out and struggled to his feet, trembling, staggering, and his body felt strange to him. He looked down upon the strangeness of another man's limbs, the alien shaping of flesh and sinew upon alien bones.

The face of the dark giant who lay upon the coral mocked him. It watched, but did not see. The eyes were blank, empty, without soul or intelligence.

The mind of Eric John Stark fought, in its alien prison, for sanity.

Berild's voice spoke to him. Her hand was on his shoulder—Kynon's shoulder . . .

"All is well, wild man. Do not fear. Kynon's mind is in your body, still sleeping at my command. And you are Kynon now."

It was not an easy thing to accept, but he knew that it was so, and he knew that he had wished it to be so. It was easier to be calm after he turned his back on *the other*.

Berild took him in her arms and held him until he had stopped shuddering, oddly like a mother with a frightened child. Then she kissed him, smiling, and said,

"The first time is hard. I can remember—and that was very long ago." She shook him gently. "Now come. We'll take your body to a place of safety. And then I must tell you all of Kynon's plans for those outside."

She spoke to the thing that lay upon the coral, saying, "Get up," and it rose obediently and followed where Berild led, to a tiny barred niche in a side passage. It made no protest when it was left, locked safely in.

"Only I can give it back to you," said Berild softly. "Remember that."

Stark said, "I will remember."

He went with Berild to Kynon's quarters in the palace. He sat among Kynon's possessions, clothed in Kynon's flesh, and learned how Kynon's mind had planned to loose a red tide upon the peaceful cities of the Border.

Only a small part of his mind was attentive to this. The rest of it was concerned with the redness of Berild's hair and the warmth of her lips, and with the heady knowledge that it was possible to be alive and young forever.

Never to lose the pride of strength, never to know the dimming sight and failing mind of age. To go on, like a child in an endless playground, with no fear of tomorrow.

It was nearly dawn.

Berild rose. She had told him much, but not the things Fianna had told him, of the secret treachery she had planned with Delgaun. She helped Stark to clothe Kynon's body in the harness of war, with the longsword and the shield and the shining spear.

Then she set her lips to his so that his borrowed heart threatened to choke him with its pounding, and her eyes were wondrously bright and beautiful.

"It is time," she whispered.

She walked beside him, as he had seen her beside Kynon in Valkis, stepping like a queen.

They came out of the palace, onto the steps where Luhar had died. There were beasts waiting, trapped for war, and an escort of tall chiefs, with pipers and drummers and link-boys to light the way.

Stark mounted Kynon's beast. It sensed the wrongness in him, hissing and rearing, but he held it down, and imperiously raised his hand.

Throbbing drums and skirling pipes, tossing flames where the link-boys ran with the torches, a clash of metal and a cheer, and Kynon of Shun rode down through the streets of Sinharat to the coral cliffs, with the red-haired woman at his side.

They were waiting.

*

The men of Kesh and the men of Shun were gathered below the cliffs, waiting. Stark led the way, as Berild had told him to, onto a ledge of coral above them. Delgaun was there, with the outlanders and a handful of Valkisians. He looked tired and ill-tempered. Stark knew that he had been busy for hours with last-minute preparations.

The first pale rays of dawn broke across the desert. A vast ringing cry went up from the gathered armies. After that there was silence, a taut expectant hush.

There was no fear in Stark now. He was past that. Fear was too small an emotion for what was about to be.

He saw Delgaun's golden eyes, hot with a cruel excitement. He saw Berild's secret triumph in her smile. He looked down upon the

pt. ends next p.

warriors, and let the magnificent voice of Kynon ring out across the soundless air.

"There will be no war," he said. "You have been betrayed."

In the moment that was left to him, he confessed the lie of the Rama crowns. And then Berild, who was behind him now, had moved like a red-haired fury to drive her dagger into his heart.

In his own body, Stark might have escaped the blow. But the reflexes of Kynon were not as his. They were swift enough to postpone death—the blade bit deep, but not where Berild had wished it. He turned and caught her by the wrists, and said to Delgaun,

"She has betrayed you, too. Freka lies in a coral pit—and I am not Kynon."

Berild tore away from him. She spurred her beast toward the Valkisian. She would have broken past him, through the escort, and up the cliffs to safety in the tunnels under Sinharat. But Delgaun was too quick.

One hand caught in the masses of her hair. She was dragged screaming from the saddle, and even then her screams were not of fear, but of fury. She clawed at Delgaun, and he fell with her to the ground.

The tall chieftains of the escort came forward, but they were dazed, and confused by the anger that was rising in them. Delgaun's wiry body arched. He flung the woman over the ledge, and what happened to her after that Stark did not see, nor wish to see.

He was shouting again to the barbarians, the tale of Delgaun's treachery.

Behind him on the ledge there was turmoil where Delgaun ran on foot between the beasts, and the outlanders made their try for safety. Below him in the desert, where there had been silence, a great deep muttering was growing, like the first growling of a storm, and the ranks of spears rippled like wheat before the wind.

And Stark felt the slow running out of Kynon's blood inside him, where Berild's dagger stood out from his back.

They had headed Delgaun away from the path up the cliff. The two loose mounts had been caught and held. They had tried to catch Delgaun, but he was light and fast and slipped away from them. Now he broke back, toward Kynon's great beast.

Knock the dying man from the saddle, charge through the milling chieftains, who were hampered by their own numbers in that narrow space . . .

He leaped. And the arms of Kynon, driven by the will of Eric John Stark, encircled him and held him and would not let him go.

The two men crashed to the ledge. Stark let out one harsh cry of agony, and then was still, his hands locked around the Valkisian's throat, his eyes intent and strange.

Men came up, and he gasped, "He is mine," and they let him be.

Delgaun did not die easily. He managed to get his dagger out, and gashed the other's side until the naked ribs showed through. But once again Stark's mind was free in some dark immensity of its own. He was living again the dream he had in Valkis, and this was the end of the dream. N'Chaka had a grip at last on the demon with yellow eyes that hungered for his life, and he would not let go.

The yellow eyes widened. They blazed, and then they slowly dimmed until the last flicker of life was gone. The strength went out of N'Chaka's hands. He fell forward, over his prey.

Below, on the sand, Berild lay, and her outspread hair was as red as blood in the fiery dawn.

The men of Kesh and the men of Shun flowed in a resistless tide up over the coral cliffs. The chieftains and the pipers and the link-boys joined them, hunting the outlanders and the wolves of Valkis through the streets of Sinharat.

Unnoticed, a dark-haired girl ran down the path to the ledge. She bent over the body of Kynon, pressing her hand to its heart. Tears ran down and mingled with the blood.

A low, faint moan came from the man's lips. Weeping like a child, Fianna drew a tiny vial from her girdle and poured three drops of pale liquid on the unresponsive tongue.

Part 12

He had come a long way. He had been down in the deep black valleys of the Place of Darkness, and the iron frost was in his bones. He had climbed the bitter mountains where no creature of the Twilight Belt might go and live.

There was light, now. He had been lost and wandering, but he had won back to the light. His tribe, his people would be waiting for him. But he knew that he would never see them.

He remembered, then, with the old terrible loneliness, that they were not truly his people. They had raised him, but they were not of his blood.

And he remembered also that they were dead, slain by the miners who had needed all the water of the valley for themselves. Slain by the miners who had taken N'Chaka and put him in a cage.

With a start of terror, he thought he was again in that cage, with the leering bearded faces peering in at him. But in the blinding dazzle of light he could see no bars.

There was only one face. The anxious, pitying face of a girl.

Fianna.

His brain began to clear. Memory returned bit by bit, the fragments fitting themselves gradually into place.

Kynon. Delgaun. Berild. Sinharat, the Ever-Living.

He remembered now with perfect clarity that he was dying, and it seemed a terrible thing to die in the body of another man. For the first time, fully, he felt the separation from his own flesh. It seemed a blasphemous thing, more terrible than death.

Fianna was weeping. She stroked his hair, and whispered, "I am so glad. I was afraid—afraid you would never wake."

He was touched, because he knew that she loved him and would be sad. He lifted his hand to touch her face, to comfort her.

He saw the fingers of that hand, dark against her cheek. Dark . . .

His own fingers. His own hand.

He was not on the ledge. He was back in the coral crypt beneath the palace. The light that had dazzled his eyes was not the sun, but only the flare of torches.

He sat up, his heart pounding wildly.

Kynon of Shun lay beside him on the coral. He was quite dead, his head encircled by a crown of fire, his side open to the white bone where Delgaun's blade had struck.

The wound that Kynon himself had never felt.

The golden coffer was open. The second crown lay near Fianna, with the rod beside it.

Stark looked at her, deep into her eyes. Very softly he said, "I would not have dreamed it."

"You will understand, now—many things," she said. "And I was glad of my power today, because I could truly give you life!"

She rose, and he saw that she was very tired. Her voice was dull, as though it counted over old things that no longer mattered.

"You see why I was afraid. If *they* had ever suspected that I, too, was of the Twice-Born . . . Berild or Delgaun, each alone, I might have destroyed, but I could not destroy both of them. And if I had, there was still Kynon. You did what I could not, Eric John Stark."

"Why were you against them, Fianna? How were you proof against the poison that made them what they were?"

She answered angrily, "Because I am weary of evil, of scheming

pt. ends next p.

for power and shedding the blood of men as though they were sheep! I am no better than Berild was. I, too, have lived a long time, and my hands are not clean. But perhaps, by what you helped me do, I have made up a little for my sins."

She paused, her thoughts turned darkly inward, and it was strange to see the shadow of age touching her sweet young face. Then she said, very slowly, like an old, old woman speaking,

"I am weary of living. No matter where I go, I am a stranger. You can understand that, though not so well as I. There is an end to pleasure, and after that only loneliness is left.

"I have remembered that I was human once. That is why I set myself against their plan of empire. After all these ages I have come round full circle to the starting point, and things seem to me now as they seemed then, before I was tempted by the Sending-on of Minds.

"It is a wicked thing!" she cried suddenly. "Against nature and the gods, and it has never brought anything but evil!"

She caught up the rod and held it in her hands.

"This is the last," she said. "Cities die, and nations perish, and material things, even such as these, are destroyed. One by one the Twice-Born have perished also, through accident or swift disease or murder, as Berild would have slain Delgaun. Now only this, and I, are left."

Quite suddenly, she flung the rod against the coral, and it broke in a cloudy flame and a tinkling of crystal shards. Then, one by one, she broke the crowns.

She stood still for a long moment. Then she whispered, "Now only I am left."

Again there was silence, and Stark was shaken by the magnitude of the thing that she had done. Her slim girl's body somehow took on the stature of a goddess.

After a while he went to her and said awkwardly, “I have not thanked you, Fianna. You brought me here, you saved me . . . ”

“Kiss me once, then,” she answered, and raised her lips to his. “For I love you, Eric John Stark—and that is the pity of it. Because I am not for you, nor for any man.”

He kissed her, very tenderly, and there was the bitter taste of tears on her soft lips.

“Now come,” she whispered, and took his hand.

She led him back through the labyrinth, into the palace, and then out again into the streets of Sinharat. Stark saw that it was sunset, and that the city was deserted. The tribes of Kesh and Shun had broken camp and gone.

There was a beast ready for him, supplied with food and water. Fianna asked him where he wished to go, and pointed the way to Tarak.

“And you?” he asked. “Where will you go, little one?”

“I have not thought.” She lifted her head, and the wind played with her dark hair. She did not smile, and yet suddenly Stark knew that she was happy.

“I am free of a great burden,” she whispered. “I shall stay here for a while, and think, and after that I shall know what to do. But whatever it is there will be no evil in it, and in the end I shall rest.”

He mounted, and she looked up at him, with a look that wrung his heart although it was not sad.

“Go now,” she said, “and the gods go with you.”

“And with you.” He bent and kissed her once again, and then rode away, down to the coral cliffs.

Far out on the desert he turned and looked back, once, at the white towers of Sinharat rising against the larger moon.

Leigh Brackett

Black Amazon of Mars

A Stark Tale

Grimly Eric John Stark slogged toward that ancient Martian city—with every step he cursed the talisman of Ban Cruach that flamed in his blood-stained belt. Behind him screamed the hordes of Ciaran, hungering for that magic jewel—ahead lay the dread abode of the Ice Creatures—at his side stalked the whispering specter of Ban Cruach, urging him on to a battle Stark knew he must lose!

Black Amazon of Mars

Part 1

Through all the long cold hours of the Norland night the Martian had not moved nor spoken. At dusk of the day before Eric John Stark had brought him into the ruined tower and laid him down, wrapped in blankets, on the snow. He had built a fire of dead brush, and since then the two men had waited, alone in the vast wasteland that girdles the polar cap of Mars.

Now, just before dawn, Camar the Martian spoke.

"Stark."

"Yes?"

"I am dying."

"Yes."

"I will not reach Kushat."

"No."

Camar nodded. He was silent again.

The wind howled down from the northern ice, and the broken walls rose up against it, brooding, gigantic, roofless now but so huge and sprawling that they seemed less like walls than cliffs of ebon[1] stone. Stark would not have gone near them but for

[1] Ebony or black in color.

Camar. They were wrong, somehow, with a taint of forgotten evil still about them.

The big Earthman glanced at Camar, and his face was sad. "A man likes to die in his own place," he said abruptly. "I am sorry."

"The Lord of Silence is a great personage," Camar answered. "He does not mind the meeting place. No. It was not for that I came back into the Norlands."

He was shaken by an agony that was not of the body. "And I shall not reach Kushat!"

Stark spoke quietly, using the courtly High Martian almost as fluently as Camar.

"I have known that there was a burden heavier than death upon my brother's soul."

He leaned over, placing one large hand on the Martian's shoulder. "My brother has given his life for mine. Therefore, I will take his burden upon myself, if I can."

He did not want Camar's burden, whatever it might be. But the Martian had fought beside him through a long guerilla campaign among the harried tribes of the nearer moon. He was a good man of his hands, and in the end had taken the bullet that was meant for Stark, knowing quite well what he was doing. They were friends.

That was why Stark had brought Camar into the bleak north country, trying to reach the city of his birth. The Martian was driven by some secret demon. He was afraid to die before he reached Kushat.

And now he had no choice.

"I have sinned, Stark. I have stolen a holy thing. You're an outlander, you would not know of Ban Cruach, and the talisman that he left when he went away forever beyond the Gates of Death."

Camar flung aside the blankets and sat up, his voice gaining a febrile[2] strength.

"I was born and bred in the Thieves' Quarter under the Wall. I was proud of my skill. And the talisman was a challenge. It was

[2] In this context, nervous energy or excitement.

a treasured thing—so treasured that hardly a man has touched it since the days of Ban Cruach who made it. And that was in the days when men still had the luster on them, before they forgot that they were gods.

"'Guard well the Gates of Death,' he said, 'that is the city's trust. And keep the talisman always, for the day may come when you will need its strength. Who holds Kushat holds Mars—and the talisman will keep the city safe.'

"I was a thief, and proud. And I stole the talisman."

His hands went to his girdle, a belt of worn leather with a boss of battered steel. But his fingers were already numb.

"Take it, Stark. Open the boss—there, on the side, where the beast's head is carved . . . "

*

Stark took the belt from Camar and found the hidden spring. The rounded top of the boss came free. Inside it was something wrapped in a scrap of silk.

"I had to leave Kushat," Camar whispered. "I could never go back. But it was enough—to have taken that."

He watched, shaken between awe and pride and remorse, as Stark unwrapped the bit of silk.

Stark had discounted most of Camar's talk as superstition, but even so he had expected something more spectacular than the object he held in his palm.

It was a lens, some four inches across—man-made, and made with great skill, but still only a bit of crystal. Turning it about, Stark saw that it was not a simple lens, but an intricate interlocking of many facets. Incredibly complicated, hypnotic if one looked at it too long.

"What is its use?" he asked of Camar.

"We are as children. We have forgotten. But there is a legend, a belief—that Ban Cruach himself made the talisman as a sign

pt. ends p. 85

that he would not forget us, and would come back when Kushat is threatened. Back through the Gates of Death, to teach us again the power that was his!"

"I do not understand," said Stark. "What are the Gates of Death?"

Camar answered, "It is a pass that opens into the black mountains beyond Kushat. The city stands guard before it—why, no man remembers, except that it is a great trust."

His gaze feasted on the talisman.

Stark said, "You wish me to take this to Kushat?"

"Yes. Yes! And yet . . . " Camar looked at Stark, his eyes filling suddenly with tears. "No. The North is not used to strangers. With me, you might have been safe. But alone . . . No, Stark. You have risked too much already. Go back, out of the Norlands, while you can."

He lay back on the blankets. Stark saw that a bluish pallor had come into the hollows of his cheeks.

"Camar," he said. And again, "Camar!"

"Yes?"

"Go in peace, Camar. I will take the talisman to Kushat."

The Martian sighed, and smiled, and Stark was glad that he had made the promise.

"The riders of Mekh are wolves," said Camar suddenly. "They hunt these gorges. Look out for them."

"I will."

Stark's knowledge of the geography of this part of Mars was vague indeed, but he knew that the mountain valleys of Mekh lay ahead and to the north, between him and Kushat. Camar had told him of these upland warriors. He was willing to heed the warning.

Camar had done with talking. Stark knew that he had not long to wait. The wind spoke with the voice of a great organ. The moons had set and it was very dark outside the tower, except for the white glimmering of the snow. Stark looked up at the brooding walls, and shivered. There was a smell of death already in the air.

To keep from thinking, he bent closer to the fire, studying the lens. There were scratches on the bezel, as though it had been held sometime in a clamp, or setting, like a jewel. An ornament, probably, worn as a badge of rank. Strange ornament for a barbarian king, in the dawn of Mars. The firelight made tiny dancing sparks in the endless inner facets. Quite suddenly, he had a curious feeling that the thing was alive.

A pang of primitive and unreasoning fear shot through him, and he fought it down. His vision was beginning to blur, and he shut his eyes, and in the darkness it seemed to him that he could see and hear . . .

*

He started up, shaken now with an eerie terror, and raised his hand to hurl the talisman away. But the part of him that had learned with much pain and effort to be civilized made him stop, and think.

He sat down again. An instrument of hypnosis? Possibly. And yet that fleeting touch of sight and sound had not been his own, out of his own memories.

He was tempted now, fascinated, like a child that plays with fire. The talisman had been worn somehow. Where? On the breast? On the brow?

He tried the first, with no result. Then he touched the flat surface of the lens to his forehead.

The great tower of stone rose up monstrous to the sky. It was whole, and there were pallid lights within that stirred and flickered, and it was crowned with a shimmering darkness.

He lay outside the tower, on his belly, and he was filled with fear and a great anger, and a loathing such as turns the bones to water. There was no snow. There was ice everywhere, rising to half the tower's height, sheathing the ground.

Ice. Cold and clear and beautiful—and deadly.

He moved. He glided snakelike, with infinite caution, over

pt. ends next p.

the smooth surface. The tower was gone, and far below him was a city. He saw the temples and the palaces, the glittering lovely city beneath him in the ice, blurred and fairylike and strange, a dream half glimpsed through crystal.

He saw the Ones that lived there, moving slowly through the streets. He could not see them clearly, only the vague shining of their bodies, and he was glad.

He hated them, with a hatred that conquered even his fear, which was great indeed.

He was not Eric John Stark. He was Ban Cruach.

The tower and the city vanished, swept away on a reeling tide.

He stood beneath a scarp of black rock, notched with a single pass. The cliffs hung over him, leaning out their vast bulk as though to crush him, and the narrow mouth of the pass was full of evil laughter where the wind went by.

He began to walk forward, into the pass. He was quite alone.

The light was dim and strange at the bottom of that cleft. Little veils of mist crept and clung between the ice and the rock, thickened, became more dense as he went farther and farther into the pass. He could not see, and the wind spoke with many tongues, piping in the crevices of the cliffs.

All at once there was a shadow in the mist before him, a dim gigantic shape that moved toward him, and he knew that he looked at death. He cried out . . .

It was Stark who yelled in blind atavistic fear, and the echo of his own cry brought him up standing, shaking in every limb. He had dropped the talisman. It lay gleaming in the snow at his feet, and the alien memories were gone—and Camar was dead.

After a time he crouched down, breathing harshly. He did not want to touch the lens again. The part of him that had learned to fear strange gods and evil spirits with every step he took, the primitive aboriginal that lay so close under the surface of his mind, warned him to leave it, to run away, to desert this place of death and ruined stone.

He forced himself to take it up. He did not look at it. He

wrapped it in the bit of silk and replaced it inside the iron boss, and clasped the belt around his waist. Then he found the small flask that lay with his gear beside the fire and took a long pull, and tried to think rationally of the thing that had happened.

Memories. Not his own, but the memories of Ban Cruach, a million years ago in the morning of a world. Memories of hate, a secret war against unhuman beings that dwelt in crystal cities cut in the living ice, and used these ruined towers for some dark purpose of their own.

Was that the meaning of the talisman, the power that lay within it? Had Ban Cruach, by some elder and forgotten science, imprisoned the echoes of his own mind in the crystal?

Why? Perhaps as a warning, as a reminder of ageless, alien danger beyond the Gates of Death?

Suddenly one of the beasts tethered outside the ruined tower started up from its sleep with a hissing snarl.

Instantly Stark became motionless.

They came silently on their padded feet, the rangy mountain brutes moving daintily through the sprawling ruin. Their riders too were silent—tall men with fierce eyes and russet hair, wearing leather coats and carrying each a long, straight spear.

There were a score of them around the tower in the windy gloom. Stark did not bother to draw his gun. He had learned very young the difference between courage and idiocy.

He walked out toward them, slowly lest one of them be startled into spearing him, yet not slowly enough to denote fear. And he held up his right hand and gave them greeting.

They did not answer him. They sat their restive mounts and stared at him, and Stark knew that Camar had spoken the truth. These were the riders of Mekh, and they were wolves.

Part 2

Stark waited, until they should tire of their own silence.

Finally one demanded, "Of what country are you?"

He answered, "I am called N'Chaka, the Man-Without-a-Tribe."

It was the name they had given him, the half-human aboriginals who had raised him in the blaze and thunder and bitter frosts of Mercury.

"A stranger," said the leader, and smiled. He pointed at the dead Camar and asked, "Did you slay him?"

"He was my friend," said Stark, "I was bringing him home to die."

Two riders dismounted to inspect the body. One called up to the leader, "He was from Kushat, if I know the breed, Thord! And he has not been robbed." He proceeded to take care of that detail himself.

"A stranger," repeated the leader, Thord. "Bound for Kushat, with a man of Kushat. Well. I think you will come with us, stranger."

Stark shrugged. And with the long spears pricking him, he did not resist when the tall Thord plundered him of all he owned except his clothes—and Camar's belt, which was not worth the stealing. His gun Thord flung contemptuously away.

One of the men brought Stark's beast and Camar's from where

they were tethered, and the Earthman mounted—as usual, over the violent protest of the creature, which did not like the smell of him. They moved out from under the shelter of the walls, into the full fury of the wind.

For the rest of that night, and through the next day and the night that followed it they rode eastward, stopping only to rest the beasts and chew on their rations of jerked meat.

To Stark, riding a prisoner, it came with full force that this was the North country, half a world away from the Mars of spaceships and commerce and visitors from other planets. The future had never touched these wild mountains and barren plains. The past held pride enough.

To the north, the horizon showed a strange and ghostly glimmer where the barrier wall of the polar pack reared up, gigantic against the sky. The wind blew, down from the ice, through the mountain gorges, across the plains, never ceasing. And here and there the cryptic towers rose, broken monoliths of stone. Stark remembered the vision of the talisman, the huge structure crowned with eerie darkness. He looked upon the ruins with loathing and curiosity. The men of Mekh could tell him nothing.

Thord did not tell Stark where they were taking him, and Stark did not ask. It would have been an admission of fear.

In mid-afternoon of the second day they came to a lip of rock where the snow was swept clean, and below it was a sheer drop into a narrow valley. Looking down, Stark saw that on the floor of the valley, up and down as far as he could see, were men and beasts and shelters of hide and brush, and fires burning. By the hundreds, by the several thousand, they camped under the cliffs, and their voices rose up on the thin air in a vast deep murmur that was deafening after the silence of the plains.

A war party, gathered now, before the thaw. Stark smiled. He became curious to meet the leader of this army.

They found their way single file along a winding track that dropped down the cliff face. The wind stopped abruptly, cut off by the valley walls. They came in among the shelters of the camp.

pt. ends p. 93

Here the snow was churned and soiled and melted to slush by the fires. There were no women in the camp, no sign of the usual cheerful rabble that follows a barbarian army. There were only men—hillmen and warriors all, tough-handed killers with no thought but battle.

They came out of their holes to shout at Thord and his men, and stare at the stranger. Thord was flushed and jovial with importance.

"I have no time for you," he shouted back. "I go to speak with the Lord Ciaran."

Stark rode impassively, a dark giant with a face of stone. From time to time he made his beast curvet,[1] and laughed at himself inwardly for doing it.

They came at length to a shelter larger than the others, but built exactly the same and no more comfortable. A spear was thrust into the snow beside the entrance, and from it hung a black pennant with a single bar of silver across it, like lightning in a night sky. Beside it was a shield with the same device. There were no guards.

Thord dismounted, bidding Stark to do the same. He hammered on the shield with the hilt of his sword, announcing himself.

"Lord Ciaran! It is Thord—with a captive."

A voice, toneless and strangely muffled, spoke from within.

"Enter, Thord."

Thord pushed aside the hide curtain and went in, with Stark at his heels.

*

The dim daylight did not penetrate the interior. Cressets[2] burned, giving off a flickering brilliance and a smell of strong oil. The floor of packed snow was carpeted with furs, much worn. Otherwise there was no adornment, and no furniture but a chair

---

[1] A low or light leap by a horse, in which all four legs leave the ground.

[2] Pole-mounted metal containers of oil, grease, wood, or coal burned as torches.

and a table, both dark with age and use, and a pallet of skins in one shadowy corner with what seemed to be a heap of rags upon it.

In the chair sat a man.

He seemed very tall, in the shaking light of the cressets. From neck to thigh his lean body was cased in black link mail, and under that a tunic of leather, dyed black. Across his knees he held a sable axe, a great thing made for the shearing of skulls, and his hands lay upon it gently, as though it were a toy he loved.

His head and face were covered by a thing that Stark had seen before only in very old paintings—the ancient war-mask of the inland Kings of Mars. Wrought of black and gleaming steel, it presented an unhuman visage of slitted eyeholes and a barred slot for breathing. Behind, it sprang out in a thin, soaring sweep, like a dark wing edge-on in flight.

The intent, expressionless scrutiny of that mask was bent, not upon Thord, but upon Eric John Stark.

The hollow voice spoke again, from behind the mask. "Well?"

"We were hunting in the gorges to the south," said Thord. "We saw a fire . . . " He told the story, of how they had found the stranger and the body of the man from Kushat.

"Kushat!" said the Lord Ciaran softly. "Ah! And why, stranger, were you going to Kushat?"

"My name is Stark. Eric John Stark, Earthman, out of Mercury." He was tired of being called stranger. Quite suddenly, he was tired of the whole business.

"Why should I not go to Kushat? Is it against some law, that a man may not go there in peace without being hounded all over the Norlands? And why do the men of Mekh make it their business? They have nothing to do with the city."

Thord held his breath, watching with delighted anticipation.

The hands of the man in armor caressed the axe. They were slender hands, smooth and sinewy—small hands, it seemed, for such a weapon.

"We make what we will our business, Eric John Stark." He spoke

pt. ends p. 93

with a peculiar gentleness. "I have asked you. Why were you going to Kushat?"

"Because," Stark answered with equal restraint, "my comrade wanted to go home to die."

"It seems a long, hard journey, just for dying." The black helm bent forward, in an attitude of thought. "Only the condemned or banished leave their cities, or their clans. Why did your comrade flee Kushat?"

A voice spoke suddenly from out of the heap of rags that lay on the pallet in the shadows of the corner. A man's voice, deep and husky, with the harsh quaver of age or madness in it.

"Three men beside myself have fled Kushat, over the years that matter. One died in the spring floods. One was caught in the moving ice of winter. One lived. A thief named Camar, who stole a certain talisman."

Stark said, "My comrade was called Greshi." The leather belt weighed heavy about him, and the iron boss seemed hot against his belly. He was beginning, now, to be afraid.

*

The Lord Ciaran spoke, ignoring Stark. "It was the sacred talisman of Kushat. Without it, the city is like a man without a soul."

As the Veil of Tanit was to Carthage, Stark thought, and reflected on the fate of that city after the Veil was stolen.

"The nobles were afraid of their own people," the man in armor said. "They did not dare to tell that it was gone. But we know."

"And," said Stark, "you will attack Kushat before the thaw, when they least expect you."

"You have a sharp mind, stranger. Yes. But the great wall will be hard to carry, even so. If I came, bearing in *my* hands the talisman of Ban Cruach . . . "

He did not finish, but turned instead to Thord. "When you plundered the dead man's body, what did you find?"

"Nothing, Lord. A few coins, a knife, hardly worth the taking."

"And you, Eric John Stark. What did you take from the body?"

With perfect truth he answered, "Nothing."

"Thord," said the Lord Ciaran, "search him."

Thord came smiling up to Stark and ripped his jacket open.

With uncanny swiftness, the Earthman moved. The edge of one broad hand took Thord under the ear, and before the man's knees had time to sag Stark had caught his arm. He turned, crouching forward, and pitched Thord headlong through the door flap.

He straightened and turned again. His eyes held a feral glint. "The man has robbed me once," he said. "It is enough."

He heard Thord's men coming. Three of them tried to jam through the entrance at once, and he sprang at them. He made no sound. His fists did the talking for him, and then his feet, as he kicked the stunned barbarians back upon their leader.

"Now," he said to the Lord Ciaran, "will we talk as men?"

The man in armor laughed, a sound of pure enjoyment. It seemed that the gaze behind the mask studied Stark's savage face, and then lifted to greet the sullen Thord who came back into the shelter, his cheeks flushed crimson with rage.

"Go," said the Lord Ciaran. "The stranger and I will talk."

"But Lord," he protested, glaring at Stark, "it is not safe . . . "

"My dark mistress looks after my safety," said Ciaran, stroking the axe across his knees. "Go."

Thord went.

The man in armor was silent then, the blind mask turned to Stark, who met that eyeless gaze and was silent also. And the bundle of rags in the shadows straightened slowly and became a tall old man with rusty hair and beard, through which peered craggy juts of bone and two bright, small points of fire, as though some wicked flame burned within him.

He shuffled over and crouched at the feet of the Lord Ciaran, watching the Earthman. And the man in armor leaned forward.

"I will tell you something, Eric John Stark. I am a bastard, but I come of the blood of kings. My name and rank I must make with

pt. ends next p.

my own hands. But I will set them high, and my name will ring in the Norlands!

"I will take Kushat. Who holds Kushat, holds Mars—and the power and the riches that lie beyond the Gates of Death!"

"I have seen them," said the old man, and his eyes blazed. "I have seen Ban Cruach the mighty. I have seen the temples and the palaces glitter in the ice. I have seen *Them*, the shining ones. Oh, I have seen them, the beautiful, hideous ones!"

He glanced sidelong at Stark, very cunning. "That is why Otar is mad, stranger. *He has seen*."

A chill swept Stark. He too had seen, not with his own eyes but with the mind and memories of Ban Cruach, of a million years ago. Then it had been no illusion, the fantastic vision opened to him by the talisman now hidden in his belt! If this old madman had seen . . .

"What beings lurk beyond the Gates of Death I do not know," said Ciaran. "But my dark mistress will test their strength—and I think my red wolves will hunt them down, once they get a smell of plunder."

"The beautiful, terrible ones," whispered Otar. "And oh, the temples and the palaces, and the great towers of stone!"

"Ride with me, Stark," said the Lord Ciaran abruptly. "Yield up the talisman, and be the shield at my back. I have offered no other man that honor."

Stark asked slowly, "Why do you choose me?"

"We are of one blood, Stark, though we be strangers."

The Earthman's cold eyes narrowed. "What would your red wolves say to that? And what would Otar say? Look at him, already stiff with jealousy, and fear lest I answer, 'Yes.'"

"I do not think you would be afraid of either of them."

"On the contrary," said Stark, "I am a prudent man." He paused. "There is one other thing. I will bargain with no man until I have looked into his eyes. Take off your helm, Ciaran—and then perhaps we will talk!"

Otar's breath made a snakelike hissing between his toothless gums, and the hands of the Lord Ciaran tightened on the haft of the axe.

"No!" he whispered. "That I can never do."

Otar rose to his feet, and for the first time Stark felt the full strength that lay in this strange old man.

"Would you look upon the face of destruction?" he thundered. "Do you ask for death? Do you think a thing is hidden behind a mask of steel without a reason, that you demand to see it?"

He turned. "My Lord," he said. "By tomorrow the last of the clans will have joined us. After that, we must march. Give this Earthman to Thord, for the time that remains—and you will have the talisman."

The blank, blind mask was unmoving, turned toward Stark, and the Earthman thought that from behind it came a faint sound that might have been a sigh.

Then . . .

"Thord!" cried the Lord Ciaran, and lifted up the axe.

Part 3

The flames leaped high from the fire in the windless gorge. Men sat around it in a great circle, the wild riders out of the mountain valleys of Mekh. They sat with the curbed and shivering eagerness of wolves around a dying quarry. Now and again their white teeth showed in a kind of silent laughter, and their eyes watched.

"He is strong," they whispered, one to the other. "He will live the night out, surely!"

On an outcrop of rock sat the Lord Ciaran, wrapped in a black cloak, holding the great axe in the crook of his arm. Beside him, Otar huddled in the snow.

Close by, the long spears had been driven deep and lashed together to make a scaffolding, and upon this frame was hung a man. A big man, iron-muscled and very lean, the bulk of his shoulders filling the space between the bending shafts. Eric John Stark of Earth, out of Mercury.

He had already been scourged without mercy. He sagged of his own weight between the spears, breathing in harsh sobs, and the trampled snow around him was spotted red.

Thord was wielding the lash. He had stripped off his own coat, and his body glistened with sweat in spite of the cold. He cut his victim with great care, making the long lash sing and crack. He was proud of his skill.

Stark did not cry out.

Presently Thord stepped back, panting, and looked at the Lord Ciaran. And the black helm nodded.

Thord dropped the whip. He went up to the big dark man and lifted his head by the hair.

"Stark," he said, and shook the head roughly. "Stranger!"

Eyes opened and stared at him, and Thord could not repress a slight shiver. It seemed that the pain and indignity had wrought some evil magic on this man he had ridden with, and thought he knew. He had seen exactly the same gaze in a big snow-cat caught in a trap, and he felt suddenly that it was not a man he spoke to, but a predatory beast.

"Stark," he said. "Where is the talisman of Ban Cruach?"

The Earthman did not answer.

Thord laughed. He glanced up at the sky, where the moons rode low and swift.

"The night is only half gone. Do you think you can last it out?"

The cold, cruel, patient eyes watched Thord. There was no reply.

Some quality of pride in that gaze angered the barbarian. It seemed to mock him, who was so sure of his ability to loosen a reluctant tongue.

"You think I cannot make you talk, don't you? You don't know me, stranger! You don't know Thord, who can make the rocks speak out if he will!"

He reached out with his free hand and struck Stark across the face.

It seemed impossible that anything so still could move so quickly. There was an ugly flash of teeth, and Thord's wrist was caught above the thumb-joint. He bellowed, and the iron jaws closed down, worrying the bone.

Quite suddenly, Thord screamed. Not for pain, but for panic. And the rows of watching men swayed forward, and even the Lord Ciaran rose up, startled.

pt. ends p. 101

"*Hark!*" ran the whispering around the fire. "Hark how he growls!"

Thord had let go of Stark's hair and was beating him about the head with his clenched fist. His face was white.

"Werewolf!" he screamed. "Let me go, beast-thing! Let me go!"

But the dark man clung to Thord's wrist, snarling, and did not hear. After a bit there came the dull crack of bone.

Stark opened his jaws. Thord ceased to strike him. He backed off slowly, staring at the torn flesh. Stark had sunk down to the length of his arms.

With his left hand, Thord drew his knife. The Lord Ciaran stepped forward. "Wait, Thord!"

"It is a thing of evil," whispered the barbarian. "Warlock. Werewolf. Beast."

He sprang at Stark.

*

The man in armor moved, very swiftly, and the great axe went whirling through the air. It caught Thord squarely where the cords of his neck ran into the shoulder—caught, and shore on through.

There was a silence in the valley.

The Lord Ciaran walked slowly across the trampled snow and took up his axe again.

"I will be obeyed," he said. "And I will not stand for fear, not of god, man, nor devil." He gestured toward Stark. "Cut him down. And see that he does not die."

He strode away, and Otar began to laugh.

From a vast distance, Stark heard that shrill, wild laughter. His mouth was full of blood, and he was mad with a cold fury.

A cunning that was purely animal guided his movements then. His head fell forward, and his body hung inert against the thongs. He might almost have been dead.

A knot of men came toward him. He listened to them. They

were hesitant and afraid. Then, as he did not move, they plucked up courage and came closer, and one prodded him gently with the point of his spear.

"Prick him well," said another. "Let us be sure!"

The sharp point bit a little deeper. A few drops of blood welled out and joined the small red streams that ran from the weals[1] of the lash. Stark did not stir.

The spearman grunted. "He is safe enough now."

Stark felt the knife blades working at the thongs. He waited. The rawhide snapped, and he was free.

He did not fall. He would not have fallen then if he had taken a death wound. He gathered his legs under him and sprang.

He picked up the spearman in that first rush and flung him into the fire. Then he began to run toward the place where the scaly mounts were herded, leaving a trail of blood behind him on the snow.

A man loomed up in front of him. He saw the shadow of a spear and swerved, and caught the haft[2] in his two hands. He wrenched it free and struck down with the butt of it, and went on. Behind him he heard voices shouting and the beginning of turmoil.

The Lord Ciaran turned and came back, striding fast.

There were men before Stark now, many men, the circle of watchers breaking up because there had been nothing more to watch. He gripped the long spear. It was a good weapon, better than the flint-tipped stick with which the boy N'Chaka had hunted the giant lizard of the rocks.

His body curved into a half crouch. He voiced one cry, the challenging scream of a predatory killer, and went in among the men.

He did slaughter with that spear. They were not expecting attack. They were not expecting anything. Stark had sprung to life too quickly. And they were afraid of him. He could smell the

[1] Red swollen marks.

[2] Handle.

pt. ends p. 101

fear on them. Fear not of a man like themselves, but of a creature less and more than man.

He killed, and was happy.

They fell away from him, the wild riders of Mekh. They were sure now that he was a demon. He raged among them with the bright spear, and they heard again that sound that should not have come from a human throat, and their superstitious terror rose and sent them scrambling out of his path, trampling on each other in childish panic.

He broke through, and now there was nothing between him and escape but two mounted men who guarded the herd.

Being mounted, they had more courage. They felt that even a warlock could not stand against their charge. They came at him as he ran, the padded feet of their beasts making a muffled drumming in the snow.

Without breaking stride, Stark hurled his spear.

*

It drove through one man's body and tumbled him off, so that he fell under his comrade's mount and fouled its legs. It staggered and reared up, hissing, and Stark fled on.

Once he glanced over his shoulder. Through the milling, shouting crowd of men he glimpsed a dark, mailed figure with a winged mask, going through the ruck with a loping stride and bearing a sable axe raised high for the throwing.

Stark was close to the herd now. And they caught his scent.

The Norland brutes had never liked the smell of him, and now the reek of blood upon him was enough in itself to set them wild. They began to hiss and snarl uneasily, rubbing their reptilian flanks together as they wheeled around, staring at him with lambent[3] eyes.

He rushed them, before they should quite decide to break. He

[3] Glowing or gleaming.

was quick enough to catch one by the fleshy comb that served it for a forelock,[4] held it with savage indifference to its squealing, and leaped to its back. Then he let it bolt, and as he rode it he yelled, a shrill brute cry that urged the creatures on to panic.

The herd broke, stampeding outward from its center like a bursting shell.

Stark was in the forefront. Clinging low to the scaly neck, he saw the men of Mekh scattered and churned and tramped into the snow by the flying pads. In and out of the shelters, kicking the brush walls down, lifting up their harsh reptilian voices, they went racketing through the camp, leaving behind them wreckage as of a storm. And Stark went with them.

He snatched a cloak from off the shoulders of some petty chieftain as he went by, and then, twisting cruelly on the fleshy comb, beating with his fist at the creature's head, he got his mount turned in the way he wanted it to go, down the valley.

He caught one last glimpse of the Lord Ciaran, fighting to hold one of the creatures long enough to mount, and then a dozen striving bodies surged around him, and Stark was gone.

The beast did not slacken pace. It was as though it thought it could outrun the alien, bloody thing that clung to its back. The last fringes of the camp shot by and vanished in the gloom, and the clean snow of the lower valley lay open before it. The creature laid its belly to the ground and went, the white spray spurting from its heels.

Stark hung on. His strength was gone now, run out suddenly with the battle-madness. He became conscious now that he was sick and bleeding, that his body was one cruel pain. In that moment, more than in the hours that had gone before, he hated the black leader of the clans of Mekh.

That flight down the valley became a sort of ugly dream. Stark was aware of rock walls reeling past, and then they seemed to

[4] The portion of a horse's mane that falls forward between the ears.

pt. ends next p.

widen away and the wind came out of nowhere like the stroke of a great hammer, and he was on the open moors again.

The beast began to falter and slow down. Presently it stopped.

Stark scooped up snow to rub on his wounds. He came near to fainting, but the bleeding stopped and after that the pain was numbed to a dull ache. He wrapped the cloak around him and urged the beast to go on, gently this time, patiently, and after it had breathed it obeyed him, settling into the shuffling pace it could keep up for hours.

He was three days on the moors. Part of the time he rode in a sort of stupor, and part of the time he was feverishly alert, watching the skyline. Frequently he took the shapes of thrusting rocks for riders, and found what cover he could until he was sure they did not move. He was afraid to dismount, for the beast had no bridle. When it halted to rest he remained upon its back, shaking, his brow beaded with sweat.

The wind scoured his tracks clean as soon as he made them. Twice, in the distance, he did see riders, and one of those times he burrowed into a tall drift and stayed there for several hours.

The ruined towers marched with him across the bitter land, lonely giants fifty miles apart. He did not go near them.

He knew that he wandered a good bit, but he could not help it, and it was probably his salvation. In those tortured badlands, riven[5] by ages of frost and flood, one might follow a man on a straight track between two points. But to find a single rider lost in that wilderness was a matter of sheer luck, and the odds were with Stark.

One evening at sunset he came out upon a plain that sloped upward to a black and towering scarp,[6] notched with a single pass.

The light was level and blood-red, glittering on the frosty rock so that it seemed the throat of the pass was aflame with evil fires. To Stark's mind, essentially primitive and stripped now of all its

---

[5] Violently torn or split apart.

[6] Escarpment; steep slope.

acquired reason, that narrow cleft appeared as the doorway to the dwelling place of demons as horrible as the fabled creatures that roam the Darkside of his native world.

He looked long at the Gates of Death, and a dark memory crept into his brain. Memory of that nightmare experience when the talisman had made him seem to walk into that frightful pass, not as Stark, but as Ban Cruach.

He remembered Otar's words—*I have seen Ban Cruach the mighty*. Was he still there beyond those darkling gates, fighting his unimagined war, alone?

Again, in memory, Stark heard the evil piping of the wind. Again, the shadow of a dim and terrible shape loomed up before him . . .

He forced remembrance of that vision from his mind, by a great effort. He could not turn back now. There was no place to go.

His weary beast plodded on, and now Stark saw as in a dream that a great walled city stood guard before that awful Gate. He watched the city glide toward him through a crimson haze, and fancied he could see the ages clustered like birds around the towers.

He had reached Kushat, with the talisman of Ban Cruach still strapped in the blood-stained belt around his waist.

Part 4

He stood in a large square, lined about with huckster's stalls and the booths of wine-sellers. Beyond were buildings, streets, a city. Stark got a blurred impression of a grand and brooding darkness, bulking huge against the mountains, as bleak and proud as they, and quite as ancient, with many ruins and deserted quarters.

He was not sure how he had come there, but he was standing on his own feet, and someone was pouring sour wine into his mouth. He drank it greedily. There were people around him, jostling, chattering, demanding answers to their questions. A girl's voice said sharply, "Let him be! Can't you see he's hurt?"

Stark looked down. She was slim and ragged, with black hair and large eyes yellow as a cat's. She held a leather bottle in her hands. She smiled at him and said, "I'm Thanis. Will you drink more wine?"

"I will," said Stark, and did, and then said, "Thank you, Thanis." He put his hand on her shoulder, to steady himself. It was a supple shoulder, surprisingly strong. He liked the feel of it.

The crowd was still churning around him, growing larger, and now he heard the tramp of military feet. A small detachment of men in light armor pushed their way through.

A very young officer whose breastplate hurt the eye with brightness demanded to be told at once who Stark was and why he had come there.

"No one crosses the moors in winter," he said, as though that in itself were a sign of evil intent.

"The clans of Mekh are crossing them," Stark answered. "An army, to take Kushat—one, two days behind me."

The crowd picked that up. Excited voices tossed it back and forth, and clamored for more news. Stark spoke to the officer.

"I will see your captain, and at once."

"You'll see the inside of a prison, more likely!" snapped the young man. "What's this nonsense about the clans of Mekh?"

Stark regarded him. He looked so long and so curiously that the crowd began to snicker and the officer's beardless face flushed pink to the ears.

"I have fought in many wars," said Stark gently. "And long ago I learned to listen, when someone came to warn me of attack."

"Better take him to the captain, Lugh," cried Thanis. "It's our skins too, you know, if there is war."

The crowd began to shout. They were all poor folk, wrapped in threadbare cloaks or tattered leather. They had no love for the guards. And whether there was war or not, their winter had been long and dull, and they were going to make the most of this excitement.

"Take him, Lugh! Let him warn the nobles. Let them think how they'll defend Kushat and the Gates of Death, now that the talisman is gone!"

"That is a lie!" Lugh shouted. "And you know the penalty for telling it. Hold your tongues, or I'll have you all whipped." He gestured angrily at Stark. "See if he is armed."

One of the soldiers stepped forward, but Stark was quicker. He slipped the thong and let the cloak fall, baring his upper body.

"The clansmen have already taken everything I owned," he said. "But they gave me something, in return."

pt. ends p. 112

The crowd stared at the half healed stripes that scarred him, and there was a drawing in of breath.

The soldier picked up the cloak and laid it over the Earthman's shoulders. And Lugh said sullenly, "Come, then."

Stark's fingers tightened on Thanis' shoulder. "Come with me, little one," he whispered. "Otherwise, I must crawl."

She smiled at him and came. The crowd followed.

The captain of the guards was a fleshy man with a smell of wine about him and a face already crumbling apart though his hair was not yet gray. He sat in a squat tower above the square, and he observed Stark with no particular interest.

"You had something to tell," said Lugh. "Tell it."

*

Stark told them, leaving out all mention of Camar and the talisman. This was neither the time nor the man to hear that story. The captain listened to all he had to say about the gathering of the clans of Mekh, and then sat studying him with a bleary shrewdness.

"You have proof of all this?"

"These stripes. Their leader Ciaran ordered them laid on himself."

The captain sighed, and leaned back.

"Any wandering band of hunters could have scourged you," he said. "A nameless vagabond from the gods know where, and a lawless one at that, if I'm any judge of men—you probably deserved it."

He reached for wine, and smiled. "Look you, stranger. In the Norlands, no one makes war in the winter. And no one ever heard of Ciaran. If you hoped for a reward from the city, you overshot badly."

"The Lord Ciaran," said Stark, grimly controlling his anger, "will be battering at your gates within two days. And you will hear of him then."

"Perhaps. You can wait for him—in a cell. And you can leave

Kushat with the first caravan after the thaw. We have enough rabble[1] here without taking in more."

Thanis caught Stark by the cloak and held him back.

"*Sir*," she said, as though it were an unclean word. "I will vouch for the stranger."

The captain glanced at her. "You?"

"Sir, I am a free citizen of Kushat. According to law, I may vouch for him."

"If you scum of the Thieves' Quarter would practice the law as well as you prate[2] it, we would have less trouble," growled the captain. "Very well, take the creature, if you want him. I don't suppose you've anything to lose."

Lugh laughed.

"Name and dwelling place," said the captain, and wrote them down. "Remember, he is not to leave the Quarter."

Thanis nodded. "Come," she said to Stark. He did not move, and she looked up at him. He was staring at the captain. His beard had grown in these last days, and his face was still scarred by Thord's blows and made wolfish with pain and fever. And now, out of this evil mask, his eyes were peering with a chill and terrible intensity at the soft-bellied man who sat and mocked him.

Thanis laid her hand on his rough cheek. "Come," she said. "Come and rest."

Gently she turned his head. He blinked and swayed, and she took him around the waist and led him unprotesting to the door.

There she paused, looking back.

"Sir," she said, very meekly, "news of this attack is being shouted through the Quarter now. If it *should* come, and it were known that you had the warning and did not pass it on . . . " She made an expressive gesture, and went out.

Lugh glanced uneasily at the captain. "She's right, sir. If by chance the man did tell the truth . . . "

---

[1] A crowd of vulgar, noisy people; a mob.

[2] Talk foolishly about; prattle.

pt. ends p. 112

The captain swore. "Rot. A rogue's tale. And yet . . . " He scowled indecisively, and then reached for parchment. "After all, it's a simple thing. Write it up, pass it on, and let the nobles do the worrying."

His pen began to scratch.

Thanis took Stark by steep and narrow ways, darkling[3] now in the afterglow, where the city climbed and fell again over the uneven rock. Stark was aware of the heavy smells of spices and unfamiliar foods, and the musky undertones of a million generations swarmed together to spawn and die in these crowded catacombs of slate and stone.

There was a house, blending into other houses, close under the loom of the great Wall. There was a flight of steps, hollowed deep with use, twisting crazily around outer corners.

There was a low room, and a slender man named Balin, vaguely glimpsed, who said he was Thanis' brother. There was a bed of skins and woven cloths.

Stark slept.

*

Hands and voices called him back. Strong hands shaking him, urgent voices. He started up growling, like an animal suddenly awaked, still lost in the dark mists of exhaustion. Balin swore, and caught his fingers away.

"What is this you have brought home, Thanis? By the gods, it snapped at me!"

Thanis ignored him. "Stark," she said. "Stark! Listen. Men are coming. Soldiers. They will question you. Do you hear me?"

Stark said heavily, "I hear."

"*Do not speak of Camar!*"

Stark got to his feet, and Balin said hastily, "Peace! The thing is safe. I would not steal a death warrant!"

---

[3] Growing dark.

His voice had a ring of truth. Stark sat down again. It was an effort to keep awake. There was clamor in the street below. It was still night.

Balin said carefully, "Tell them what you told the captain, nothing more. They will kill you if they know."

A rough hand thundered at the door, and a voice cried, "Open up!"

Balin sauntered over to lift the bar. Thanis sat beside Stark, her hand touching his. Stark rubbed his face. He had been shaved and washed, his wounds rubbed with salve. The belt was gone, and his blood-stained clothing. He realized only then that he was naked, and drew a cloth around him. Thanis whispered, "The belt is there on that peg, under your cloak."

Balin opened the door, and the room was full of men.

Stark recognized the captain. There were others, four of them, young, old, intermediate, annoyed at being hauled away from their beds and their gaming tables at this hour. The sixth man wore the jeweled cuirass[4] of a noble. He had a nice, a kind face. Gray hair, mild eyes, soft cheeks. A fine man, but ludicrous in the trappings of a soldier.

"Is this the man?" he asked, and the captain nodded.

"Yes." It was his turn to say Sir.

Balin brought a chair. He had a fine flourish about him. He wore a crimson jewel in his left ear, and every line of him was quick and sensitive, instinct with mockery. His eyes were brightly cynical, in a face worn lean with years of merry sinning. Stark liked him.

He was a civilized man. They all were—the noble, the captain, the lot of them. So civilized that the origins of their culture were forgotten half an age before the first clay brick was laid in Babylon.

Too civilized, Stark thought. Peace had drawn their fangs and cut their claws. He thought of the wild clansmen coming fast across the snow, and felt a certain pity for the men of Kushat.

---

[4] A piece of armor consisting of a breastplate and backplate fastened together.

pt. ends p. 112

The noble sat down.

"This is a strange tale you bring, wanderer. I would hear it from your own lips."

Stark told it. He spoke slowly, watching every word, cursing the weariness that fogged his brain.

The noble, who was called Rogain, asked him questions. Where was the camp? How many men? What were the exact words of the Lord Ciaran, and who was he?

Stark answered, with meticulous care.

Rogain sat for some time lost in thought. He seemed worried and upset, one hand playing aimlessly with the hilt of his sword. A scholar's hand, without a callous on it.

"There is one thing more," said Rogain. "What business had you on the moors in winter?"

Stark smiled. "I am a wanderer by profession."

"Outlaw?" asked the captain, and Stark shrugged.

"Mercenary is a kinder word."

*

Rogain studied the pattern of stripes on the Earthman's dark skin. "Why did the Lord Ciaran, so-called, order you scourged?"

"I had thrashed one of his chieftains."

Rogain sighed and rose. He stood regarding Stark from under brooding brows, and at length he said, "It is a wild tale. I can't believe it—and yet, why should you lie?"

He paused, as though hoping that Stark would answer that and relieve him of worry.

Stark yawned. "The tale is easily proved. Wait a day or two."

"I will arm the city," said Rogain. "I dare not do otherwise. But I will tell you this." An astonishing unpleasant look came into his eyes. "If the attack does not come—if you have set a whole city by the ears for nothing—I will have you flayed alive and your body tumbled over the Wall for the carrion birds to feed on."

He strode out, taking his retinue[5] with him. Balin smiled. "He will do it, too," he said, and dropped the bar.

Stark did not answer. He stared at Balin, and then at Thanis, and then at the belt hanging on the peg, in a curiously blank and yet penetrating fashion, like an animal that thinks its own thoughts. He took a deep breath. Then, as though he found the air clean of danger, he rolled over and went instantly to sleep.

Balin lifted his shoulders expressively. He grinned at Thanis. "Are you positive it's human?"

"He's beautiful," said Thanis, and tucked the cloths around him. "Hold your tongue." She continued to sit there, watching Stark's face as the slow dreams moved across it. Balin laughed.

It was evening again when Stark awoke. He sat up, stretching lazily. Thanis crouched by the hearthstone, stirring something savory in a blackened pot. She wore a red kirtle[6] and a necklet[7] of beaten gold, and her hair was combed out smooth and shining.

She smiled at him and rose, bringing him his own boots and trousers, carefully cleaned, and a tunic of leather tanned fine and soft as silk. Stark asked her where she got it.

"Balin stole it—from the baths where the nobles go. He said you might as well have the best." She laughed. "He had a devil of a time finding one big enough to fit you."

She watched with unashamed interest while he dressed. Stark said, "Don't burn the soup."

She put her tongue out at him. "Better be proud of that fine hide while you have it," she said. "There's no sign of attack."

Stark was aware of sounds that had not been there before—the pacing of men on the Wall above the house, the calling of the watch. Kushat was armed and ready—and his time was running out. He hoped that Ciaran had not been delayed on the moors.

Thanis said, "I should explain about the belt. When Balin

---

[5] A group of attendants or others accompanying a high-ranking or important person.

[6] A gown or dress.

[7] A kind of rigid and close-fitting necklace.

pt. ends p. 112

undressed you, he saw Camar's name scratched on the inside of the boss. And, he can open a lizard's egg without harming the shell."

"What about you?" asked Stark.

She flexed her supple fingers. "I do well enough."

*

Balin came in. He had been seeking news, but there was little to be had.

"The soldiers are grumbling about a false alarm," he said. "The people are excited, but more as though they were playing a game. Kushat has not fought a war for centuries." He sighed. "The pity of it is, Stark, I believe your story. And I'm afraid."

Thanis handed him a steaming bowl. "Here—employ your tongue with this. Afraid, indeed! Have you forgotten the Wall? No one has carried it since the city was built. Let them attack!"

Stark was amused. "For a child, you know much concerning war."

"I knew enough to save your skin!" she flared, and Balin smiled.

"She has you there, Stark. And speaking of skins . . . " He glanced up at the belt. "Or better, speaking of talismans, which we were not. How did you come by it?"

Stark told him. "He had a sin on his soul, did Camar. And—he was my friend."

Balin looked at him with deep respect. "You were a fool," he said. "Look you. The thing is returned to Kushat. Your promise is kept. There is nothing for you here but danger, and were I you I would not wait to be flayed, or slain, or taken in a quarrel that is not yours."

"Ah," said Stark softly, "but it is mine. The Lord Ciaran made it so." He, too, glanced at the belt. "What of the talisman?"

"Return it where it came from," Thanis said. "My brother is a better thief than Camar. He can certainly do that."

"No!" said Balin, with surprising force. "We will keep it, Stark and I. Whether it has power, I do not know. But if it has—I think Kushat will need it, and in strong hands."

Stark said somberly, "It has power, the Talisman. Whether for good or evil, I don't know."

They looked at him, startled. But a touch of awe seemed to repress their curiosity.

He could not tell them. He was, somehow, reluctant to tell anyone of that dark vision of what lay beyond the Gates of Death, which the talisman of Ban Cruach had lent him.

Balin stood up. "Well, for good or evil, at least the sacred relic of Ban Cruach has come home." He yawned. "I am going to bed. Will you come, Thanis, or will you stay and quarrel with our guest?"

"I will stay," she said, "and quarrel."

"Ah, well." Balin sighed puckishly. "Good night." He vanished into an inner room. Stark looked at Thanis. She had a warm mouth, and her eyes were beautiful, and full of light.

He smiled, holding out his hand.

The night wore on, and Stark lay drowsing. Thanis had opened the curtains. Wind and moonlight swept together into the room, and she stood leaning upon the sill, above the slumbering city. The smile that lingered in the corners of her mouth was sad and far-away, and very tender.

Stark stirred uneasily, making small sounds in his throat. His motions grew violent. Thanis crossed the room and touched him.

Instantly he was awake.

"Animal," she said softly. "You dream."

Stark shook his head. His eyes were still clouded, though not with sleep. "Blood," he said, "heavy in the wind."

"I smell nothing but the dawn," she said, and laughed.

Stark rose. "Get Balin. I'm going up on the Wall."

She did not know him now. "What is it, Stark? What's wrong?"

"Get Balin." Suddenly it seemed that the room stifled him. He caught up his cloak and Camar's belt and flung open the door, standing on the narrow steps outside. The moonlight caught in his eyes, pale as frost-fire.

pt. ends next p.

Thanis shivered. Balin joined her without being called. He, too, had slept but lightly. Together they followed Stark up the rough-cut stair that led to the top of the Wall.

He looked southward, where the plain ran down from the mountains and spread away below Kushat. Nothing moved out there. Nothing marred the empty whiteness. But Stark said,

"They will attack at dawn."

Part 5

They waited. Some distance away a guard leaned against the parapet,[1] huddled in his cloak. He glanced at them incuriously. It was bitterly cold. The wind came whistling down through the Gates of Death, and below in the streets the watchfires shuddered and flared.

They waited, and still there was nothing.

Balin said impatiently, "How can you know they're coming?"

Stark shivered, a shallow rippling of the flesh that had nothing to do with cold, and every muscle of his body came alive. Phobos[2] plunged downward. The moonlight dimmed and changed, and the plain was very empty, very still.

"They will wait for darkness. They will have an hour or so, between moonset and dawn."

Thanis muttered, "Dreams! Besides, I'm cold." She hesitated, and then crept in under Balin's cloak. Stark had gone away from her. She watched him sulkily where he leaned upon the stone. He might have been part of it, as dark and unstirring.

---

[1] A low wall or railing along the edge of a balcony, roof, etc.

[2] The inner, and larger, of the two satellites of Mars.

Deimos[3] sank low toward the west.

Stark turned his head, drawn inevitably to look toward the cliffs above Kushat, soaring upward to blot out half the sky. Here, close under them, they seemed to tower outward in a curving mass, like the last wave of eternity rolling down, crested white with the ash of shattered worlds.

I have stood beneath those cliffs before. I have felt them leaning down to crush me, and I have been afraid.

He was still afraid. The mind that had poured its memories into that crystal lens had been dead a million years, but neither time nor death had dulled the terror that beset Ban Cruach in his journey through that nightmare pass.

He looked into the black and narrow mouth of the Gates of Death, cleaving the scarp like a wound, and the primitive ape-thing within him cringed and moaned, oppressed with a sudden sense of fate.

He had come painfully across half a world, to crouch before the Gates of Death. Some evil magic had let him see forbidden things, had linked his mind in an unholy bond with the long-dead mind of one who had been half a god. These evil miracles had not been for nothing. He would not be allowed to go unscathed.

He drew himself up sharply then, and swore. He had left N'Chaka behind, a naked boy running in a place of rocks and sun on Mercury. He had become Eric John Stark, a man, and civilized. He thrust the senseless premonition from him, and turned his back upon the mountains.

Deimos touched the horizon. A last gleam of reddish light tinged the snow, and then was gone.

Thanis, who was half asleep, said with sudden irritation, "I do not believe in your barbarians. I'm going home." She thrust Balin aside and went away, down the steps.

The plain was now in utter darkness, under the faint, far Northern stars.

---

[3] The outer, and smaller, of the two satellites of Mars.

Stark settled himself against the parapet. There was a sort of timeless patience about him. Balin envied it. He would have liked to go with Thanis. He was cold and doubtful, but he stayed.

Time passed, endless minutes of it, lengthening into what seemed hours.

Stark said, "Can you hear them?"

"No."

"They come." His hearing, far keener than Balin's, picked up the little sounds, the vast inchoate[4] rustling of an army on the move in stealth and darkness. Light-armed men, hunters, used to stalking wild beasts in the snow. They could move softly, very softly.

"I hear nothing," Balin said, and again they waited.

The westering stars moved toward the horizon, and at length in the east a dim pallor crept across the sky.

The plain was still shrouded in night, but now Stark could make out the high towers of the King City of Kushat, ghostly and indistinct—the ancient, proud high towers of the rulers and their nobles, set above the crowded Quarters of merchants and artisans and thieves. He wondered who would be king in Kushat by the time this unrisen sun had set.

"You were wrong," said Balin, peering. "There is nothing on the plain."

Stark said, "Wait."

*

Swiftly now, in the thin air of Mars, the dawn came with a rush and a leap, flooding the world with harsh light. It flashed in cruel brilliance from sword-blades, from spearheads, from helmets and burnished mail, from the war-harness of beasts, glistened on bare russet heads and coats of leather, set the banners of the clans to burning, crimson and gold and green, bright against the snow.

There was no sound, not a whisper, in all the land.

---

[4] Recently or just begun.

pt. ends p. 120

Somewhere a hunting horn sent forth one deep cry to split the morning. Then burst out the wild skirling of the mountain pipes and the broken thunder of drums, and a wordless scream of exultation that rang back from the Wall of Kushat like the very voice of battle. The men of Mekh began to move.

Raggedly, slowly at first, then more swiftly as the press of warriors broke and flowed, the barbarians swept toward the city as water sweeps over a broken dam.

Knots and clumps of men, tall men running like deer, leaping, shouting, swinging their great brands. Riders, spurring their mounts until they fled belly down. Spears, axes, sword-blades tossing, a sea of men and beasts, rushing, trampling, shaking the ground with the thunder of their going.

And ahead of them all came a solitary figure in black mail, riding a raking beast trapped all in black, and bearing a sable axe.

Kushat came to life. There was a swarming and a yelling in the streets, and soldiers began to pour up onto the Wall. A thin company, Stark thought, and shook his head. Mobs of citizens choked the alleys, and every rooftop was full. A troop of nobles went by, brave in their bright mail, to take up their post in the square by the great gate.

Balin said nothing, and Stark did not disturb his thoughts. From the look of him, they were dark indeed.

Soldiers came and ordered them off the Wall. They went back to their own roof, where they were joined by Thanis. She was in a high state of excitement, but unafraid.

"Let them attack!" she said. "Let them break their spears against the Wall. They will crawl away again."

Stark began to grow restless. Up in their high emplacements, the big ballistas[5] creaked and thrummed. The muted song of the bows became a wailing hum. Men fell, and were kicked off the ledges by their fellows. The blood-howl of the clans rang unceasing

[5] Large crossbows that fire spears.

on the frosty air, and Stark heard the rap of scaling ladders against stone.

Thanis said abruptly, "What is that—that sound like thunder?"

"Rams," he answered. "They are battering the gate."

She listened, and Stark saw in her face the beginning of fear.

It was a long fight. Stark watched it hungrily from the roof all that morning. The soldiers of Kushat did bravely and well, but they were as folded sheep against the tall killers of the mountains. By noon the officers were beating the Quarters for men to replace the slain.

Stark and Balin went up again, onto the Wall.

The clans had suffered. Their dead lay in windrows[6] under the Wall, amid the broken ladders. But Stark knew his barbarians. They had sat restless and chafing in the valley for many days, and now the battle-madness was on them and they were not going to be stopped.

Wave after wave of them rolled up, and was cast back, and came on again relentlessly. The intermittent thunder boomed still from the gates, where sweating giants swung the rams under cover of their own bowmen. And everywhere, up and down through the forefront of the fighting, rode the man in black armor, and wild cheering followed him.

Balin said heavily, "It is the end of Kushat."

*

A ladder banged against the stones a few feet away. Men swarmed up the rungs, fierce-eyed clansmen with laughter in their mouths. Stark was first at the head.

They had given him a spear. He spitted two men through with it and lost it, and a third man came leaping over the parapet. Stark received him into his arms.

Balin watched. He saw the warrior go crashing back, sweeping

[6] Rows or lines of hay raked together, to be rolled into heaps.

his fellows off the ladder. He saw Stark's face. He heard the sounds and smelled the blood and sweat of war, and he was sick to the marrow of his bones, and his hatred of the barbarians was a terrible thing.

Stark caught up a dead man's blade, and within ten minutes his arm was as red as a butcher's. And ever he watched the winged helm that went back and forth below, a standard to the clans.

By mid-afternoon the barbarians had gained the Wall in three places. They spread inward along the ledges, pouring up in a resistless tide, and the defenders broke. The rout became a panic.

"It's all over now," Stark said. "Find Thanis, and hide her."

Balin let fall his sword. "Give me the talisman," he whispered, and Stark saw that he was weeping. "Give it me, and I will go beyond the Gates of Death and rouse Ban Cruach from his sleep. And if he has forgotten Kushat, I will take his power into my own hands. I will fling wide the Gates of Death and loose destruction on the men of Mekh—or if the legends are all lies, then I will die."

He was like a man crazed. "Give me the talisman!"

Stark slapped him, carefully and without heat, across the face. "Get your sister, Balin. Hide her, unless you would be uncle to a red-haired brat."

He went then, like a man who has been stunned. Screaming women with their children clogged the ways that led inward from the Wall, and there was bloody work afoot on the rooftops and in the narrow alleys.

The gate was holding, still.

*

Stark forced his way toward the square. The booths of the hucksters were overthrown, the wine-jars broken and the red wine spilled. Beasts squealed and stamped, tired of their chafing harness, driven wild by the shouting and the smell of blood. The dead were heaped high where they had fallen from above.

They were all soldiers here, clinging grimly to their last foothold. The deep song of the rams shook the very stones. The iron-sheathed timbers of the gate gave back an answering scream, and toward the end all other sounds grew hushed. The nobles came down slowly from the Wall and mounted, and sat waiting.

There were fewer of them now. Their bright armor was dented and stained, and their faces had a pallor on them.

One last hammer-stroke of the rams.

With a bitter shriek the weakened bolts tore out, and the great gate was broken through.

The nobles of Kushat made their first, and final charge.

As soldiers they went up against the riders of Mekh, and as soldiers they held them until they died. Those that were left were borne back into the square, caught as in the crest of an avalanche. And first through the gates came the winged battle-mask of the Lord Ciaran, and the sable axe that drank men's lives where it hewed.

There was a beast with no rider to claim it, tugging at its head-rope. Stark swung onto the saddle pad and cut it free. Where the press[7] was thickest, a welter of struggling brutes and men fighting knee to knee, there was the man in black armor, riding like a god, magnificent, born to war. Stark's eyes shone with a strange, cold light. He struck his heels hard into the scaly flanks. The beast plunged forward.

In and over and through, making the long sword sing. The beast was strong, and frightened beyond fear. It bit and trampled, and Stark cut a path for them, and presently he shouted above the din,

"Ho, there! *Ciaran!*"

The black mask turned toward him, and the remembered voice spoke from behind the barred slot, joyously.

"The wanderer. The wild man!"

Their two mounts shocked together. The axe came down in a whistling curve, and a red sword-blade flashed to meet it. Swift,

[7] Large crowd.

pt. ends next p.

swift, a ringing clash of steel, and the blade was shattered and the axe fallen to the ground.

Stark pressed in.

Ciaran reached for his sword, but his hand was numbed by the force of that blow and he was slow, a split second. The hilt of Stark's weapon, still clutched in his own numbed grip, fetched him a stunning blow on the helm, so that the metal rang like a flawed bell.

The Lord Ciaran reeled back, only for a moment, but long enough. Stark grasped the war-mask and ripped it off, and got his hands around the naked throat.

He did not break that neck, as he had planned. And the Clansmen who had started in to save their leader stopped and did not move.

Stark knew now why the Lord Ciaran had never shown his face.

The throat he held was white and strong, and his hands around it were buried in a mane of red-gold hair that fell down over the shirt of mail. A red mouth passionate with fury, wonderful curving bone under sculptured flesh, eyes fierce and proud and tameless as the eyes of a young eagle, fire-blue, defying him, hating him . . .

"By the gods," said Stark, very softly. "By the eternal gods!"

Part 6

A woman! And in that moment of amazement, she was quicker than he.

There was nothing to warn him, no least flicker of expression. Her two fists came up together between his outstretched arms and caught him under the jaw with a force that nearly snapped his neck. He went over backward, clean out of the saddle, and lay sprawled on the bloody stones, half stunned, the wind knocked out of him.

The woman wheeled her mount. Bending low, she took up the axe from where it had fallen, and faced her warriors, who were as dazed as Stark.

"I have led you well," she said. "I have taken you Kushat. Will any man dispute me?"

They knew the axe, if they did not know her. They looked from side to side uneasily, completely at a loss, and Stark, still gasping on the ground, thought that he had never seen anything as proud and beautiful as she was then in her black mail, with her bright hair blowing and her glance like blue lightning.

The nobles of Kushat chose that moment to charge. This strange unmasking of the Mekhish lord had given them time to rally, and now they thought that the Gods had wrought a miracle to help them. They found hope, where they had lost everything but courage.

"A wench!" they cried. "A strumpet[1] of the camps. *A woman!*"

They howled it like an epithet, and tore into the barbarians.

She who had been the Lord Ciaran drove the spurs in deep, so that the beast leaped forward screaming. She went, and did not look to see if any had followed, in among the men of Kushat. And the great axe rose and fell, and rose again.

She killed three, and left two others bleeding on the stones, and not once did she look back.

The clansmen found their tongues.

"*Ciaran! Ciaran!*"

The crashing shout drowned out the sound of battle. As one man, they turned and followed her.

Stark, scrambling for his life underfoot, could not forbear[2] smiling. Their childlike minds could see only two alternatives—to slay her out of hand, or to worship her. They had chosen to worship. He thought the bards would be singing of the Lord Ciaran of Mekh as long as there were men to listen.

He managed to take cover behind a wrecked booth, and presently make his way out of the square. They had forgotten him, for the moment. He did not wish to wait, just then, until they—or she—remembered.

She.

He still did not believe it, quite. He touched the bruise under his jaw where she had struck him, and thought of the lithe, swift strength of her, and the way she had ridden alone into battle. He remembered the death of Thord, and how she had kept her red wolves tamed, and he was filled with wonder, and a deep excitement.

---

[1] Prostitute.

[2] Refrain from; resist.

He remembered what she had said to him once—*We are of one blood, though we be strangers.*

He laughed, silently, and his eyes were very bright.

The tide of war had rolled on toward the King City, where from the sound of it there was hot fighting around the castle. Eddies of the main struggle swept shrieking through the streets, but the rat-runs under the Wall were clear. Everyone had stampeded inward, the victims with the victors close on their heels. The short northern day was almost gone.

He found a hiding place that offered reasonable safety, and settled himself to wait.

Night came, but he did not move. From the sounds that reached him, the sacking of Kushat was in full swing. They were looting the richer streets first. Their upraised voices were thick with wine, and mingled with the cries of women. The reflection of many fires tinged the sky.

By midnight the sounds began to slacken, and by the second hour after the city slept, drugged with wine and blood and the weariness of battle. Stark went silently out into the streets, toward the King City.

According to the immemorial pattern of Martian city-states, the castles of the king and the noble families were clustered together in solitary grandeur. Many of the towers were fallen now, the great halls open to the sky. Time had crushed the grandeur that had been Kushat, more fatally than the boots of any conqueror.

In the house of the king, the flamboys[3] guttered low and the chieftains of Mekh slept with their weary pipers among the benches of the banquet hall. In the niches of the tall, carved portal, the guards nodded over their spears. They, too, had fought that day. Even so, Stark did not go near them.

Shivering slightly in the bitter wind, he followed the bulk of the massive walls until he found a postern[4] door, half open as

[3] Another term for flambeaux or torches.

[4] A rear or side entrance.

pt. ends p. 130

some kitchen knave had left it in his flight. Stark entered, moving like a shadow.

*

The passageway was empty, dimly lighted by a single torch. A stairway branched off from it, and he climbed that, picking his way by guess and his memories of similar castles he had seen in the past.

He emerged into a narrow hall, obviously for the use of servants. A tapestry closed the end, stirring in the chill draft that blew along the floor. He peered around it, and saw a massive, vaulted corridor, the stone walls paneled in wood much split and blackened by time, but still showing forth the wonderful carvings of beasts and men, larger than life and overlaid with gold and bright enamel.

From the corridor a single doorway opened—and Otar slept before it, curled on a pallet like a dog.

Stark went back down the narrow hall. He was sure that there must be a back entrance to the king's chambers, and he found the little door he was looking for.

From there on was darkness. He felt his way, stepping with infinite caution, and presently there was a faint gleam of light filtering around the edges of another curtain of heavy tapestry.

He crept toward it, and heard a man's slow breathing on the other side.

He drew the curtain back, a careful inch. The man was sprawled on a bench athwart[5] the door. He slept the honest sleep of exhaustion, his sword in his hand, the stains of his day's work still upon him. He was alone in the small room. A door in the farther wall was closed.

Stark hit him, and caught the sword before it fell. The man grunted once and became utterly relaxed. Stark bound him with his own harness and shoved a gag in his mouth, and went on, through the door in the opposite wall.

---

[5] Across.

The room beyond was large and high and full of shadows. A fire burned low on the hearth, and the uncertain light showed dimly the hangings and the rich stuffs that carpeted the floor, and the dark, sparse shapes of furniture.

Stark made out the lattice-work of a covered bed, let into the wall after the northern fashion.

She was there, sleeping, her red-gold hair the color of the flames.

He stood a moment, watching her, and then, as though she sensed his presence, she stirred and opened her eyes.

She did not cry out. He had known that she would not. There was no fear in her. She said, with a kind of wry humor, "I will have a word with my guards about this."

*

She flung aside the covering and rose. She was almost as tall as he, white-skinned and very straight. He noted the long thighs, the narrow loins and magnificent shoulders, the small virginal breasts. She moved as a man moves, without coquetry.[6] A long furred gown, that Stark guessed had lately graced the shoulders of the king, lay over a chair. She put it on.

"Well, wild man?"

"I have come to warn you." He hesitated over her name, and she said,

"My mother named me Ciara, if that seems better to you." She gave him her falcon's glance. "I could have slain you in the square, but now I think you did me a service. The truth would have come out sometime—better then, when they had no time to think about it." She laughed. "They will follow me now, over the edge of the world, if I ask them."

Stark said slowly, "Even beyond the Gates of Death?"

"Certainly, there. Above all, there!"

---

[6] Flirtatious behavior.

She turned to one of the tall windows and looked out at the cliffs and the high notch of the pass, touched with greenish silver by the little moons.

"Ban Cruach was a great king. He came out of nowhere to rule the Norlands with a rod of iron, and men speak of him still as half a god. Where did he get his power, if not from beyond the Gates of Death? Why did he go back there at the end of his days, if not to hide away his secret? Why did he build Kushat to guard the pass forever, if not to hoard that power out of reach of all the other nations of Mars?

"Yes, Stark. My men will follow me. And if they do not, I will go alone."

"You are not Ban Cruach. Nor am I." He took her by the shoulders. "Listen, Ciara. You're already king in the Norlands, and half a legend as you stand. Be content."

"Content!" Her face was close to his, and he saw the blaze of it, the white intensity of ambition and an iron pride. "Are you content?" she asked him. "Have you ever been content?"

He smiled. "For strangers, we do know each other well. No. But the spurs are not so deep in me."

"The wind and the fire. One spends its strength in wandering, the other devours. But one can help the other. I made you an offer once, and you said you would not bargain unless you could look into my eyes. Look now!"

He did, and his hands upon her shoulders trembled.

"No," he said harshly. "You're a fool, Ciara. Would you be as Otar, mad with what you have seen?"

"Otar is an old man, and likely crazed before he crossed the mountains. Besides—I am not Otar."

Stark said somberly, "Even the bravest may break. Ban Cruach himself . . . "

She must have seen the shadow of that horror in his eyes, for he felt her body tense.

"What of Ban Cruach? What do you know, Stark? Tell me!"

He was silent, and she went from him angrily.

"You have the talisman," she said. "That I am sure of. And if need be, I will flay you alive to get it!" She faced him across the room. "But whether I get it or not, I will go through the Gates of Death. I must wait, now, until after the thaw. The warm wind will blow soon, and the gorges will be running full. But afterward, I will go, and no talk of fears and demons will stop me."

She began to pace the room with long strides, and the full skirts of the gown made a subtle whispering about her.

"You do not know," she said, in a low and bitter voice. "I was a girl-child, without a name. By the time I could walk, I was a servant in the house of my grandfather. The two things that kept me living were pride and hate. I left my scrubbing of floors to practice arms with the young boys. I was beaten for it every day, but every day I went. I knew even then that only force would free me. And my father was a king's son, a good man of his hands. His blood was strong in me. I learned."

She held her head very high. She had earned the right to hold it so. She finished quietly,

"I have come a long way. I will not turn back now."

"Ciara." Stark came and stood before her. "I am talking to you as a fighting man, an equal. There may be power behind the Gates of Death, I do not know. But this I have seen—madness, horror, an evil that is beyond our understanding.

"I think you will not accuse me of cowardice. And yet I would not go into that pass for all the power of all the kings of Mars!"

Once started, he could not stop. The full force of that dark vision of the talisman swept over him again in memory. He came closer to her, driven by the need to make her understand.

"Yes, I have the talisman! And I have had a taste of its purpose. I think Ban Cruach left it as a warning, so that none would follow him. I have seen the temples and the palaces glitter in the ice. I have seen the Gates of Death—*not with my own eyes, Ciara, but with his. With the eyes and the memories of Ban Cruach!*"

He had caught her again, his hands strong on her strong arms.

"Will you believe me, or must you see for yourself—the

dreadful things that walk those buried streets, the shapes that rise from nowhere in the mists of the pass?"

Her gaze burned into his. Her breath was hot and sweet upon his lips, and she was like a sword between his hands, shining and unafraid.

"Give me the talisman. Let me see!"

He answered furiously, "You are mad. As mad as Otar." And he kissed her, in a rage, in a panic lest all that beauty be destroyed—a kiss as brutal as a blow, that left him shaken.

She backed away slowly, one step, and he thought she would have killed him. He said heavily:

"If you will see, you will. The thing is here."

He opened the boss and laid the crystal in her outstretched hand. He did not meet her eyes.

"Sit down. Hold the flat side against your brow."

She sat, in a great chair of carven wood. Stark noticed that her hand was unsteady, her face the color of white ash. He was glad she did not have the axe where she could reach it. She did not play at anger.

For a long moment she studied the intricate lens, the incredible depository of a man's mind. Then she raised it slowly to her forehead.

He saw her grow rigid in the chair. How long he watched beside her he never knew. Seconds, an eternity. He saw her eyes turn blank and strange, and a shadow came into her face, changing it subtly, altering the lines, so that it seemed almost a stranger was peering through her flesh.

All at once, in a voice that was not her own, she cried out terribly, "*Oh gods of Mars!*"

The talisman dropped rolling to the floor, and Ciara fell forward into Stark's arms.

He thought at first that she was dead. He carried her to the bed, in an agony of fear that surprised him with its violence, and laid her down, and put his hand over her heart.

It was beating strongly. Relief that was almost a sickness swept over him. He turned, searching vaguely for wine, and saw the talisman. He picked it up and put it back inside the boss. A jeweled flagon stood on a table across the room. He took it and started back, and then, abruptly, there was a wild clamor in the hall outside and Otar was shouting Ciara's name, pounding on the door.

It was not barred. In another moment they would burst through, and he knew that they would not stop to inquire what he was doing there.

He dropped the flagon and went out swiftly, the way he had come. The guard was still unconscious. In the narrow hall beyond, Stark hesitated. A woman's voice was rising high above the tumult in the main corridor, and he thought he recognized it.

He went to the tapestry curtain and looked for the second time around its edge.

The lofty space was full of men, newly wakened from their heavy sleep and as nervous as so many bears. Thanis struggled in the grip of two of them. Her scarlet kirtle was torn, her hair flying in wild elf-locks, and her face was the face of a mad thing. The whole story of the doom of Kushat was written large upon it.

She screamed again and again, and would not be silenced.

"Tell her, the witch that leads you! Tell her that she is already doomed to death, with all her army!"

Otar opened up the door of Ciara's room.

Thanis surged forward. She must have fled through all that castle before she was caught, and Stark's heart ached for her.

"You!" she shrieked through the doorway, and poured out all the filth of the quarter upon Ciara's name. "Balin has gone to bring doom upon you! He will open wide the Gates of Death, and then you will die!—die!—*die!*"

Stark felt the shock of a terrible dread, as he let the curtain fall.

pt. ends next p.

Mad with hatred against conquerors, Balin had fulfilled his raging promise and had gone to fling open the Gates of Death.

Remembering his nightmare vision of the shining, evil ones whom Ban Cruach had long ago prisoned beyond those gates, Stark felt a sickness grow within him as he went down the stair and out the postern door.

It was almost dawn. He looked up at the brooding cliffs, and it seemed to him that the wind in the pass had a sound of laughter that mocked his growing dread.

He knew what he must do, if an ancient, mysterious horror was not to be released upon Kushat.

I may still catch Balin before he has gone too far! If I don't—

He dared not think of that. He began to walk very swiftly through the night streets, toward the distant, towering Gates of Death.

Part 7

It was past noon. He had climbed high toward the saddle of the pass. Kushat lay small below him, and he could see now the pattern of the gorges, cut ages deep in the living rock, that carried the spring torrents of the watershed around the mighty ledge on which the city was built.

The pass itself was channeled, but only by its own snows and melting ice. It was too high for a watercourse. Nevertheless, Stark thought, a man might find it hard to stay alive if he were caught there by the thaw.

He had seen nothing of Balin. The gods knew how many hours' start he had. Stark imagined him, scrambling wild-eyed over the rocks, driven by the same madness that had sent Thanis up into the castle to call down destruction on Ciara's head.

The sun was brilliant but without warmth. Stark shivered, and the icy wind blew strong. The cliffs hung over him, vast and sheer and crushing, and the narrow mouth of the pass was before him. He would go no farther. He would turn back, now.

But he did not. He began to walk forward, into the Gates of Death.

The light was dim and strange at the bottom of that cleft. Little veils of mist crept and clung between the ice and the rock, thickened, became more dense as he went farther and farther into the pass. He could not see, and the wind spoke with many tongues, piping in the crevices of the cliffs.

The steps of the Earthman slowed and faltered. He had known fear in his life before. But now he was carrying the burden of two men's terrors—Ban Cruach's, and his own.

He stopped, enveloped in the clinging mist. He tried to reason with himself—that Ban Cruach's fears had died a million years ago, that Otar had come this way and lived, and Balin had come also.

But the thin veneer of civilization sloughed away and left him with the naked bones of truth. His nostrils twitched to the smell of evil, the subtle unclean taint[1] that only a beast, or one as close to it as he, can sense and know. Every nerve was a point of pain, raw with apprehension. An overpowering recognition of danger, hidden somewhere, mocking at him, made his very body change, draw in upon itself and flatten forward, so that when at last he went on again he was more like a four-footed thing than a man walking upright.

Infinitely wary, silent, moving surely over the ice and the tumbled rock, he followed Balin. He had ceased to think. He was going now on sheer instinct.

The pass led on and on. It grew darker, and in the dim uncanny twilight there were looming shapes that menaced him, and ghostly wings that brushed him, and a terrible stillness that was not broken by the eerie voices of the wind.

Rock and mist and ice. Nothing that moved or lived. And yet the sense of danger deepened, and when he paused the beating of his heart was like thunder in his ears.

Once, far away, he thought he heard the echoes of a man's voice crying, but he had no sight of Balin.

The pass began to drop, and the twilight deepened into a kind of sickly night.

---

[1] Unpleasant smell.

On and down, more slowly now, crouching, slinking, heavily oppressed, tempted to snarl at boulders and tear at wraiths of fog. He had no idea of the miles he had traveled. But the ice was thicker now, the cold intense.

The rock walls broke off sharply. The mist thinned. The pallid darkness lifted to a clear twilight. He came to the end of the Gates of Death.

Stark stopped. Ahead of him, almost blocking the end of the pass, something dark and high and massive loomed in the thinning mists.

It was a great cairn, and upon it sat a figure, facing outward from the Gates of Death as though it kept watch over whatever country lay beyond.

The figure of a man in antique Martian armor.

After a moment, Stark crept toward the cairn. He was still almost all savage, torn between fear and fascination.

He was forced to scramble over the lower rocks of the cairn itself. Quite suddenly he felt a hard shock, and a flashing sensation of warmth that was somehow inside his own flesh, and not in any tempering of the frozen air. He gave a startled leap forward, and whirled, looking up into the face of the mailed figure with the confused idea that it had reached down and struck him.

It had not moved, of course. And Stark knew, with no need of anyone to tell him, that he looked into the face of Ban Cruach.

*

It was a face made for battles and for ruling, the bony ridges harsh and strong, the hollows under them worn deep with years. Those eyes, dark shadows under the rusty helm, had dreamed high dreams, and neither age nor death had conquered them.

And even in death, Ban Cruach was not unarmed.

Clad as for battle in his ancient mail, he held upright between his hands a mighty sword. The pommel was a ball of crystal large as a man's fist, that held within it a spark of intense brilliance. The little, blinding flame throbbed with its own force, and the sword-blade blazed with a white, cruel radiance.

Ban Cruach, dead but frozen to eternal changelessness by the bitter cold, sitting here upon his cairn for a million years and warding forever the inner end of the Gates of Death, as his ancient city of Kushat warded the outer.

Stark took two cautious steps closer to Ban Cruach, and felt again the shock and the flaring heat in his blood. He recoiled, satisfied.

The strange force in the blazing sword made an invisible barrier across the mouth of the pass, protected Ban Cruach himself. A barrier of short waves, he thought, of the type used in deep therapy, having no heat in themselves but increasing the heat in body cells by increasing their vibration. But these waves were stronger than any he had known before.

A barrier, a wall of force, closing the inner end of the Gates of Death. A barrier that was not designed against man.

Stark shivered. He turned from the somber, brooding form of Ban Cruach and his eyes followed the gaze of the dead king, out beyond the cairn.

He looked across this forbidden land within the Gates of Death.

At his back was the mountain barrier. Before him, a handful of miles to the north, the terminus of the polar cap rose like a cliff of bluish crystal soaring up to touch the early stars. Locked in between those two titanic walls was a great valley of ice.

White and glimmering that valley was, and very still, and very beautiful, the ice shaped gracefully into curving domes and hollows. And in the center of it stood a dark tower of stone, a cyclopean bulk that Stark knew must go down an unguessable distance to its base on the bedrock. It was like the tower in which Camar had died. But this one was not a broken ruin. It loomed with alien arrogance, and within its bulk pallid lights flickered eerily, and it was crowned by a cloud of shimmering darkness.

It was like the tower of his dread vision, the tower that he had seen, not as Eric John Stark, but as Ban Cruach!

Stark's gaze dropped slowly from the evil tower to the curving ice of the valley. And the fear within him grew beyond all bounds.

He had seen that, too, in his vision. The glimmering ice, the domes and hollows of it. He had looked down through it at the city that lay beneath, and he had seen those who came and went in the buried streets.

Stark hunkered down. For a long while he did not stir.

He did not want to go out there. He did not want to go out from the grim, warning figure of Ban Cruach with his blazing sword, into that silent valley. He was afraid, afraid of what he might see if he went there and looked down through the ice, afraid of the final dread fulfillment of his vision.

But he had come after Balin, and Balin must be out there somewhere. He did not want to go, but he was himself, and he must.

*

He went, going very softly, out toward the tower of stone. And there was no sound in all that land.

The last of the twilight had faded. The ice gleamed, faintly luminous under the stars, and there was light beneath it, a soft radiance that filled all the valley with the glow of a buried moon.

Stark tried to keep his eyes upon the tower. He did not wish to look down at what lay under his stealthy feet.

Inevitably, he looked.

The temples and the palaces glittering in the ice . . .

Level upon level, going down. Wells of soft light spanned with soaring bridges, slender spires rising, an endless variation of streets and crystal walls exquisitely patterned, above and below and overlapping, so that it was like looking down through a thousand giant snowflakes. A metropolis of gossamer and frost, fragile and lovely as a dream, locked in the clear, pure vault of the ice.

pt. ends p. 138

Stark saw the people of the city passing along the bright streets, their outlines blurred by the icy vault as things are half obscured by water. The creatures of vision, vaguely shining, infinitely evil.

He shut his eyes and waited until the shock and the dizziness left him. Then he set his gaze resolutely on the tower, and crept on, over the glassy sky that covered those buried streets.

Silence. Even the wind was hushed.

He had gone perhaps half the distance when the cry rang out.

It burst upon the valley with a shocking violence. "*Stark! Stark!*" The ice rang with it, curving ridges picked up his name and flung it back and forth with eerie crystal voices, and the echoes fled out whispering *Stark! Stark!* until it seemed that the very mountains spoke.

Stark whirled about. In the pallid gloom between the ice and the stars there was light enough to see the cairn behind him, and the dim figure atop it with the shining sword.

Light enough to see Ciara, and the dark knot of riders who had followed her through the Gates of Death.

She cried his name again. "Come back! Come back!"

The ice of the valley answered mockingly, "*Come back! Come back!*" and Stark was gripped with a terror that held him motionless.

She should not have called him. She should not have made a sound in that deathly place.

A man's hoarse scream rose above the flying echoes. The riders turned and fled suddenly, the squealing, hissing beasts crowding each other, floundering wildly on the rocks of the cairn, stampeding back into the pass.

Ciara was left alone. Stark saw her fight the rearing beast she rode and then flung herself out of the saddle and let it go. She came toward him, running, clad in her black armor, the great axe swinging high.

"Behind you, Stark! Oh, gods of Mars!"

He turned then and saw them, coming out from the tower of

stone, the pale, shining creatures that move so swiftly across the ice, so fleet and swift that no man living could outrun them.

*

He shouted to Ciara to turn back. He drew his sword and over his shoulder he cursed her in a black fury because he could hear her mailed feet coming on behind him.

The gliding creatures, sleek and slender, reedlike, bending, delicate as wraiths, their bodies shaped from northern rainbows of amethyst and rose—if they should touch Ciara, if their loathsome hands should touch her . . .

Stark let out one raging catlike scream, and rushed them.

The opalescent bodies slipped away beyond his reach. The creatures watched him.

They had no faces, but they watched. They were eyeless but not blind, earless, but not without hearing. The inquisitive tendrils that formed their sensory organs stirred and shifted like the petals of ungodly flowers, and the color of them was the white frost-fire that dances on the snow.

"Go back, Ciara!"

But she would not go, and he knew that they would not have let her. She reached him, and they set their backs together. The shining ones ringed them round, many feet away across the ice, and watched the long sword and the great hungry axe, and there was something in the lissome[2] swaying of their bodies that suggested laughter.

"You fool," said Stark. "You bloody fool."

"And you?" answered Ciara. "Oh, yes, I know about Balin. That mad girl, screaming in the palace—she told me, and you were seen from the wall, climbing to the Gates of Death. I tried to catch you."

"Why?"

[2] Supple and graceful.

pt. ends next p.

She did not answer that. "They won't fight us, Stark. Do you think we could make it back to the cairn?"

"No. But we can try."

Guarding each others' backs, they began to walk toward Ban Cruach and the pass. If they could reach the barrier, they would be safe.

Stark knew now what Ban Cruach's wall of force was built against. And he began to guess the riddle of the Gates of Death.

The shining ones glided with them, out of reach. They did not try to bar the way. They formed a circle around the man and woman, moving with them and around them at the same time, an endless weaving chain of many bodies shining with soft jewel tones of color.

They drew closer and closer to the cairn, to the brooding figure of Ban Cruach and his sword. It crossed Stark's mind that the creatures were playing with him and Ciara. Yet they had no weapons. Almost, he began to hope . . .

From the tower where the shimmering cloud of darkness clung came a black crescent of force that swept across the ice-field like a sickle and gathered the two humans in.

Stark felt a shock of numbing cold that turned his nerves to ice. His sword dropped from his hand, and he heard Ciara's axe go down. His body was without strength, without feeling, dead.

He fell, and the shining ones glided in toward him.

Part 8

Twice before in his life Stark had come near to freezing. It had been like this, the numbness and the cold. And yet it seemed that the dark force had struck rather at his nerve centers than at his flesh.

He could not see Ciara, who was behind him, but he heard the metallic clashing of her mail and one small, whispered cry, and he knew that she had fallen, too.

The glowing creatures surrounded him. He saw their bodies bending over him, the frosty tendrils of their faces writhing as though in excitement or delight.

Their hands touched him. Little hands with seven fingers, deft and frail. Even his numbed flesh felt the terrible cold of their touch, freezing as outer space. He yelled, or tried to, but they were not abashed.

They lifted him and bore him toward the tower, a company of them, bearing his heavy weight upon their gleaming shoulders.

He saw the tower loom high and higher still above him. The cloud of dark force that crowned it blotted out the stars. It became too huge and high to see at all, and then there was a low flat arch of stone close above his face, and he was inside.

Straight overhead—a hundred feet, two hundred, he could not tell—was a globe of crystal, fitted into the top of the tower as a jewel is held in a setting.

The air around it was shadowed with the same eerie gloom that hovered outside, but less dense, so that Stark could see the smoldering purple spark that burned within the globe, sending out its dark vibrations.

A globe of crystal, with a heart of sullen flame. Stark remembered the sword of Ban Cruach, and the white fire that burned in its hilt.

Two globes, the bright-cored and the dark. The sword of Ban Cruach touched the blood with heat. The globe of the tower deadened the flesh with cold. It was the same force, but at opposite ends of the spectrum.

Stark saw the cryptic controls of that glooming globe—a bank of them, on a wide stone ledge just inside the tower, close beside him. There were shining ones on that ledge tending those controls, and there were other strange and massive mechanisms there too.

Flying spirals of ice climbed up inside the tower, spanning the great stone well with spidery bridges, joining icy galleries. In some of those galleries, Stark vaguely glimpsed rigid, gleaming figures like statues of ice, but he could not see them clearly as he was carried on.

He was being carried downward. He passed slits in the wall, and knew that the pallid lights he had seen through them were the moving bodies of the creatures as they went up and down these high-flung, icy bridges. He managed to turn his head to look down, and saw what was beneath him.

The well of the tower plunged down a good five hundred feet to bedrock, widening as it went. The web of ice-bridges and the spiral ways went down as well as up, and the creatures that carried him were moving smoothly along a transparent ribbon of ice no more than a yard in width, suspended over that terrible drop.

Stark was glad that he could not move just then. One

instinctive start of horror would have thrown him and his bearers to the rock below, and would have carried Ciara with them.

Down and down, gliding in utter silence along the descending spiral ribbon. The great glooming crystal grew remote above him. Ice was solid now in the slots of the walls. He wondered if they had brought Balin this way.

There were other openings, wide arches like the one they had brought their captives through, and these gave Stark brief glimpses of broad avenues and unguessable buildings, shaped from the pellucid[1] ice and flooded with the soft radiance that was like eerie moonlight.

At length, on what Stark took to be the third level of the city, the creatures bore him through one of these archways, into the streets beyond.

*

Below him now was the translucent thickness of ice that formed the floor of this level and the roof of the level beneath. He could see the blurred tops of delicate minarets,[2] the clustering roofs that shone like chips of diamond.

Above him was an ice roof. Elfin spires rose toward it, delicate as needles. Lacy battlements and little domes, buildings star-shaped, wheel-shaped, the fantastic, lovely shapes of snow-crystals, frosted over with a sparkling foam of light.

The people of the city gathered along the way to watch, a living, shifting rainbow of amethyst and rose and green, against the pure blue-white. And there was no least whisper of sound anywhere.

For some distance they went through a geometric maze of streets. And then there was a cathedral-like building all arched

[1] Translucent and clear as glass.

[2] Tall slender towers with one or more balconies, typically part of a mosque.

and spired, standing in the center of a twelve-pointed plaza. Here they turned, and bore their captives in.

Stark saw a vaulted roof, very slim and high, etched with a glittering tracery that might have been carving of an alien sort, delicate as the weavings of spiders. The feet of his bearers were silent on the icy paving.

At the far end of the long vault sat seven of the shining ones in high seats marvelously shaped from the ice. And before them, gray-faced, shuddering with cold and not noticing it, drugged with a sick horror, stood Balin. He looked around once, and did not speak.

Stark was set on his feet, with Ciara beside him. He saw her face, and it was terrible to see the fear in her eyes, that had never shown fear before.

He himself was learning why men went mad beyond the Gates of Death.

Chill, dreadful fingers touched him expertly. A flash of pain drove down his spine, and he could stand again.

The seven who sat in the high seats were motionless, their bright tendrils stirring with infinite delicacy as though they studied the three humans who stood before them.

Stark thought he could feel a cold, soft fingering of his brain. It came to him that these creatures were probably telepaths. They lacked organs of speech, and yet they must have some efficient means of communications. Telepathy was not uncommon among the many races of the Solar System, and Stark had had experience with it before.

He forced his mind to relax. The alien impulse was instantly stronger. He sent out his own questing thought and felt it brush the edges of a consciousness so utterly foreign to his own that he knew he could never probe it, even had he had the skill.

He learned one thing—that the shining faceless ones looked upon him with equal horror and loathing. They recoiled from the unnatural human features, and most of all, most strongly, they abhorred the warmth of human flesh. Even the infinitesimal amount of heat radiated by their half-frozen human bodies caused the ice-folk discomfort.

Stark marshaled his imperfect abilities and projected a mental question to the seven.

"What do you want of us?"

The answer came back, faint and imperfect, as though the gap between their alien minds was almost too great to bridge. And the answer was one word.

"*Freedom!*"

Balin spoke suddenly. He voiced only a whisper, and yet the sound was shockingly loud in that crystal vault.

"They have asked me already. Tell them no, Stark! Tell them no!"

He looked at Ciara then, a look of murderous hatred. "If you turn them loose upon Kushat, I will kill you with my own hands before I die."

Stark spoke again, silently, to the seven. "I do not understand."

*

Again the struggling, difficult thought. "We are the old race, the kings of the glacial ice. Once we held all the land beyond the mountains, outside the pass you call the Gates of Death."

Stark had seen the ruins of the towers out on the moors. He knew how far their kingdom had extended.

"We *controlled* the ice, far outside the polar cap. Our towers blanketed the land with the dark force drawn from Mars itself, from the magnetic field of the planet. That radiation bars out heat, from the Sun, and even from the awful winds that blow warm from the south. So there was never any thaw. Our cities were many, and our race was great.

"Then came Ban Cruach, from the south . . .

"He waged a war against us. He learned the secret of the crystal globes, and learned how to reverse their force and use it against

pt. ends p. 149

us. He, leading his army, destroyed our towers one by one, and drove us back . . .

"Mars needed water. The outer ice was melted, our lovely cities crumbled to nothing, so that creatures like Ban Cruach might have water! And our people died.

"We retreated at the last, to this our ancient polar citadel behind the Gates of Death. Even here, Ban Cruach followed. He destroyed even this tower once, at the time of the thaw. But this city is founded in polar ice—and only the upper levels were harmed. Even Ban Cruach could not touch the heart of the eternal polar cap of Mars!

"When he saw that he could not destroy us utterly, he set himself in death to guard the Gates of Death with his blazing sword, that we might never again reclaim our ancient dominion.

"That is what we mean when we ask for freedom. We ask that you take away the sword of Ban Cruach, so that we may once again go out through the Gates of Death!"

Stark cried aloud, hoarsely, "*No!*"

He knew the barren deserts of the south, the wastes of red dust, the dead sea bottoms—the terrible thirst of Mars, growing greater with every year of the million that had passed since Ban Cruach locked the Gates of Death.

He knew the canals, the pitiful waterways that were all that stood between the people of Mars and extinction. He remembered the yearly release from death when the spring thaw brought the water rushing down from the north.

He thought of these cold creatures going forth, building again their great towers of stone, sheathing half a world in ice that would never melt. He thought of the people of Jekkara and Valkis and Barrakesh, of the countless cities of the south, watching for the flood that did not come, and falling at last to mingle their bodies with the blowing dust.

He said again, "No. Never."

The distant thought-voice of the seven spoke, and this time the question was addressed to Ciara.

Stark saw her face. She did not know the Mars he knew, but she had memories of her own—the mountain-valleys of Mekh, the moors, the snowy gorges. She looked at the shining ones in their high seats, and said,

"If I take that sword, it will be to use it against you as Ban Cruach did!"

Stark knew that the seven had understood the thought behind her words. He felt that they were amused.

"The secret of that sword was lost a million years ago, the day Ban Cruach died. Neither you nor anyone now knows how to use it as he did. But the sword's radiations of warmth still lock us here.

"We cannot approach that sword, for its vibrations of heat slay us if we do. But you warm-bodied ones can approach it. And you will do so, and take it from its place. *One of you will take it!*"

They were very sure of that.

"We can see, a little way, into your evil minds. Much we do not understand. But—the mind of the large man is full of the woman's image, and the mind of the woman turns to him. Also, there is a link between the large man and the small man, less strong, but strong enough."

The thought-voice of the seven finished, "The large man will take away the sword for us because he must—to save the other two."

Ciara turned to Stark. "They cannot force you, Stark. Don't let them. No matter what they do to me, don't let them!"

Balin stared at her with a certain wonder. "You would die, to protect Kushat?"

"Not Kushat alone, though its people too are human," she said, almost angrily. "There are my red wolves—a wild pack, but my own. And others." She looked at Balin. "What do *you* say? Your life against the Norlands?"

Balin made an effort to lift his head as high as hers, and the red jewel flashed in his ear. He was a man crushed by the falling of his world, and terrified by what his mad passion had led him into, here beyond the Gates of Death. But he was not afraid to die.

pt. ends p. 149

He said so, and even Ciara knew that he spoke the truth.

But the seven were not dismayed. Stark knew that when their thought-voice whispered in his mind,

"It is not death alone you humans have to fear, but the manner of your dying. You shall see that, before you choose."

*

Swiftly, silently, those of the ice-folk who had borne the captives into the city came up from behind, where they had stood withdrawn and waiting. And one of them bore a crystal rod like a scepter, with a spark of ugly purple burning in the globed end.

Stark leaped to put himself between them and Ciara. He struck out, raging, and because he was almost as quick as they, he caught one of the slim luminous bodies between his hands.

The utter coldness of that alien flesh burned his hands as frost will burn. Even so, he clung on, snarling, and saw the tendrils writhe and stiffen as though in pain.

Then, from the crystal rod, a thread of darkness spun itself to touch his brain with silence, and the cold that lies between the worlds.

He had no memory of being carried once more through the shimmering streets of that elfin, evil city, back to the stupendous well of the tower, and up along the spiral path of ice that soared those dizzy hundreds of feet from bedrock to the glooming crystal globe. But when he again opened his eyes, he was lying on the wide stone ledge at ice-level.

Beside him was the arch that led outside. Close above his head was the control bank that he had seen before.

Ciara and Balin were there also, on the ledge. They leaned stiffly against the stone wall beside the control bank, and facing them was a squat, round mechanism from which projected a sort of wheel of crystal rods.

Their bodies were strangely rigid, but their eyes and minds

were awake. Terribly awake. Stark saw their eyes, and his heart turned within him.

Ciara looked at him. She could not speak, but she had no need to. *No matter what they do to me . . .*

She had not feared the swordsmen of Kushat. She had not feared her red wolves, when he unmasked her in the square. She was afraid now. But she warned him, ordered him not to save her.

They cannot force you. Stark! Don't let them.

And Balin, too, pleaded with him for Kushat.

They were not alone on the ledge. The ice-folk clustered there, and out upon the flying spiral pathway, on the narrow bridges and the spans of fragile ice, they stood in hundreds watching, eyeless, faceless, their bodies drawn in rainbow lines across the dimness of the shaft.

Stark's mind could hear the silent edges of their laughter. Secret, knowing laughter, full of evil, full of triumph, and Stark was filled with a corroding terror.

He tried to move, to crawl toward Ciara standing like a carven image in her black mail. He could not.

Again her fierce, proud glance met his. And the silent laughter of the ice-folk echoed in his mind, and he thought it very strange that in this moment, now, he should realize that there had never been another woman like her on all of the worlds of the Sun.

The fear she felt was not for herself. It was for him.

Apart from the multitudes of the ice-folk, the group of seven stood upon the ledge. And now their thought-voice spoke to Stark, saying,

"Look about you. Behold the men who have come before you through the Gates of Death!"

Stark raised his eyes to where their slender fingers pointed, and saw the icy galleries around the tower, saw more clearly the icy statues in them that he had only glimpsed before.

pt. ends next p.

*

Men, set like images in the galleries. Men whose bodies were sheathed in a glittering mail of ice, sealing them forever. Warriors, nobles, fanatics, and thieves—the wanderers of a million years who had dared to enter this forbidden valley, and had remained forever.

He saw their faces, their tortured eyes wide open, their features frozen in the agony of a slow and awful death.

"They refused us," the seven whispered. "They would not take away the sword. And so they died, as this woman and this man will die, unless you choose to save them.

"We will show you, human, how they died!"

One of the ice-folk bent and touched the squat, round mechanism that faced Balin and Ciara. Another shifted the pattern of control on the master-bank.

The wheel of crystal rods on that squat mechanism began to turn. The rods blurred, became a disc that spun faster and faster.

High above in the top of the tower the great globe brooded, shrouded in its cloud of shimmering darkness. The disc became a whirling blur. The glooming shadow of the globe deepened, coalesced. It began to lengthen and descend, stretching itself down toward the spinning disc.

The crystal rods of the mechanism drank the shadow in. And out of that spinning blur there came a subtle weaving of threads of darkness, a gossamer curtain winding around Ciara and Balin so that their outlines grew ghostly and the pallor of their flesh was as the pallor of snow at night.

And still Stark could not move.

The veil of darkness began to sparkle faintly. Stark watched it, watched the chill motes brighten, watched the tracery of frost whiten over Ciara's mail, touch Balin's dark hair with silver.

Frost. Bright, sparkling, beautiful, a halo of frost around their bodies. A dust of splintered diamond across their faces, an aureole[3] of brittle light to crown their heads.

Frost. Flesh slowly hardening in marbly whiteness, as the cold slowly increased. And yet their eyes still lived, and saw, and understood.

The thought-voice of the seven spoke again.

"You have only minutes now to decide! Their bodies cannot endure too much, and live again. Behold their eyes, and how they suffer!

"Only minutes, human! Take away the sword of Ban Cruach! Open for us the Gates of Death, and we will release these two, alive."

Stark felt again the flashing stab of pain along his nerves, as one of the shining creatures moved behind him. Life and feeling came back into his limbs.

He struggled to his feet. The hundreds of the ice-folk on the bridges and galleries watched him in an eager silence.

He did not look at them. His eyes were on Ciara's. And now, her eyes pleaded.

"Don't, Stark! Don't barter the life of the Norlands for me!"

The thought-voice beat at Stark, cutting into his mind with cruel urgency.

"Hurry, human! They are already beginning to die. Take away the sword, and let them live!"

Stark turned. He cried out, in a voice that made the icy bridges tremble:

"I will take the sword!"

He staggered out, then. Out through the archway, across the ice, toward the distant cairn that blocked the Gates of Death.

---

[3] A circle of light surrounding something, especially the head or body of a representation of a deity or holy person; a halo.

Part 9

Across the glowing ice of the valley Stark went at a stumbling run that grew swifter and more sure as his cold-numbed body began to regain its functions. And behind him, pouring out of the tower to watch, came the shining ones.

They followed after him, gliding lightly. He could sense their excitement, the cold, strange ecstasy of triumph. He knew that already they were thinking of the great towers of stone rising again above the Norlands, the crystal cities still and beautiful under the ice, all vestige of the ugly citadels of man gone and forgotten.

The seven spoke once more, a warning.

"If you turn toward us with the sword, the woman and the man will die. And you will die as well. For neither you nor any other can now use the sword as a weapon of offense."

Stark ran on. He was thinking then only of Ciara, with the frost-crystals gleaming on her marble flesh and her eyes full of mute torment.

The cairn loomed up ahead, dark and high. It seemed to Stark that the brooding figure of Ban Cruach watched him coming with those shadowed eyes beneath the rusty helm. The great sword blazed between those dead, frozen hands.

The ice-folk had slowed their forward rush. They stopped and waited, well back from the cairn.

Stark reached the edge of tumbled rock. He felt the first warm flare of the force-waves in his blood, and slowly the chill began to creep out from his bones. He climbed, scrambling upward over the rough stones of the cairn.

Abruptly, then, at Ban Cruach's feet, he slipped and fell. For a second it seemed that he could not move.

His back was turned toward the ice-folk. His body was bent forward, and shielded so, his hands worked with feverish speed.

From his cloak he tore a strip of cloth. From the iron boss he took the glittering lens, the talisman of Ban Cruach. Stark laid the lens against his brow, and bound it on.

The remembered shock, the flood and sweep of memories that were not his own. The mind of Ban Cruach thundering its warning, its hard-won knowledge of an ancient, epic war . . .

He opened his own mind wide to receive those memories. Before he had fought against them. Now he knew that they were his one small chance in this swift gamble with death. Two things only of his own he kept firm in that staggering tide of another man's memories. Two names—Ciara and Balin.

He rose up again. And now his face had a strange look, a curious duality. The features had not changed, but somehow the lines of the flesh had altered subtly, so that it was almost as though the old unconquerable king himself had risen again in battle.

He mounted the last step or two and stood before Ban Cruach. A shudder ran through him, a sort of gathering and settling of the flesh, as though Stark's being had accepted the stranger within it. His eyes, cold and pale as the very ice that sheathed the valley, burned with a cruel light.

He reached and took the sword, out of the frozen hands of Ban Cruach.

As though it were his own, he knew the secret of the metal rings that bound its hilt, below the ball of crystal. The savage throb of the invisible radiation beat in his quickening flesh. He was warm

pt. ends p. 159

again, his blood running swiftly, his muscles sure and strong. He touched the rings and turned them.

The fan-shaped aura of force that had closed the Gates of Death narrowed in, and as it narrowed it leaped up from the blade of the sword in a tongue of pale fire, faintly shimmering, made visible now by the full focus of its strength.

Stark felt the wave of horror bursting from the minds of the ice-folk as they perceived what he had done. And he laughed.

His bitter laughter rang harsh across the valley as he turned to face them, and he heard in his brain the shuddering, silent shriek that went up from all that gathered company . . .

"*Ban Cruach! Ban Cruach has returned!*"

They had touched his mind. They knew.

*

He laughed again, and swept the sword in a flashing arc, and watched the long bright blade of force strike out more terrible than steel, against the rainbow bodies of the shining ones.

They fell. Like flowers under a scythe[1] they fell, and all across the ice the ones who were yet untouched turned about in their hundreds and fled back toward the tower.

Stark came leaping down the cairn, the talisman of Ban Cruach bound upon his brow, the sword of Ban Cruach blazing in his hand.

He swung that awful blade as he ran. The force-beam that sprang from it cut through the press of creatures fleeing before him, hampered by their own numbers as they crowded back through the archway.

He had only a few short seconds to do what he had to do.

Rushing with great strides across the ice, spurning the withered

---

[1] A manual tool with a long handle and a long, curved single-edged blade that moves in a plane parallel to the ground, used for mowing, cutting, or reaping by hand.

bodies of the dead... And then, from the glooming darkness that hovered around the tower of stone, the black cold beam struck down.

Like a coiling whip it lashed him. The deadly numbness invaded the cells of his flesh, ached in the marrow of his bones. The bright force of the sword battled the chill invaders, and a corrosive agony tore at Stark's inner body where the antipathetic radiations waged war.

His steps faltered. He gave one hoarse cry of pain, and then his limbs failed and he went heavily to his knees.

Instinct only made him cling to the sword. Waves of blinding anguish racked him. The coiling lash of darkness encircled him, and its touch was the abysmal cold of outer space, striking deep into his heart.

Hold the sword close, hold it closer, like a shield. The pain is great, but I will not die unless I drop the sword.

Ban Cruach the mighty had fought this fight before.

Stark raised the sword again, close against his body. The fierce pulse of its brightness drove back the cold. Not far, for the freezing touch was very strong. But far enough so that he could rise again and stagger on.

The dark force of the tower writhed and licked about him. He could not escape it. He slashed it in a blind fury with the blazing sword, and where the forces met a flicker of lightning leaped in the air, but it would not be beaten back.

He screamed at it, a raging cat-cry that was all Stark, all primitive fury at the necessity of pain. And he forced himself to run, to drag his tortured body faster across the ice. *Because Ciara is dying, because the dark cold wants me to stop ...*

The ice-folk jammed and surged against the archway, in a panic hurry to take refuge far below in their many-leveled city. He raged at them, too. They were part of the cold, part of the pain. Because of them Ciara and Balin were dying. He sent the blade of force lancing among them, his hatred rising full tide to join the hatred of Ban Cruach that lodged in his mind.

pt. ends p. 159

Stab and cut and slash with the long terrible beam of brightness. They fell and fell, the hideous shining folk, and Stark sent the light of Ban Cruach's weapon sweeping through the tower itself, through the openings that were like windows in the stone.

Again and again, stabbing through those open slits as he ran. And suddenly the dark beam of force ceased to move. He tore out of it, and it did not follow him, remaining stationary as though fastened to the ice.

The battle of forces left his flesh. The pain was gone. He sped on to the tower.

He was close now. The withered bodies lay in heaps before the arch. The last of the ice-folk had forced their way inside. Holding the sword level like a lance, Stark leaped in through the arch, into the tower.

*

The shining ones were dead where the destroying warmth had touched them. The flying spiral ribbons of ice were swept clean of them, the arching bridges and the galleries of that upper part of the tower.

They were dead along the ledge, under the control bank. They were dead across the mechanism that spun the frosty doom around Ciara and Balin. The whirling disc still hummed.

Below, in that stupendous well, the crowding ice-folk made a seething pattern of color on the narrow ways. But Stark turned his back on them and ran along the ledge, and in him was the heavy knowledge that he had come too late.

The frost had thickened around Ciara and Balin. It encrusted them like stiffened lace, and now their flesh was overlaid with a diamond shell of ice.

Surely they could not live!

He raised the sword to smite down at the whirring disc, to smash it, but there was no need. When the full force of that concentrated beam struck it, meeting the focus of shadow that it held, there was a violent flare of light and a shattering of crystal. The mechanism was silent.

The glooming veil was gone from around the ice-shelled man and woman. Stark forgot the creatures in the shaft below him. He turned the blazing sword full upon Ciara and Balin.

It would not affect the thin covering of ice. If the woman and the man were dead, it would not affect their flesh, any more than it had Ban Cruach's. But if they lived, if there was still a spark, a flicker beneath that frozen mail, the radiation would touch their blood with warmth, start again the pulse of life in their bodies.

He waited, watching Ciara's face. It was still as marble, and as white.

Something—instinct, or the warning mind of Ban Cruach that had learned a million years ago to beware the creatures of the ice—made him glance behind him.

Stealthy, swift and silent, up the winding ways they came. They had guessed that he had forgotten them in his anxiety. The sword was turned away from them now, and if they could take him from behind, stun him with the chill force of the scepter-like rods they carried . . .

He slashed them with the sword. He saw the flickering beam go down and down the shaft, saw the bodies fall like drops of rain, rebounding here and there from the flying spans and carrying the living with them.

He thought of the many levels of the city. He thought of all the countless thousands that must inhabit them. He could hold them off in the shaft as long as he wished if he had no other need for the sword. But he knew that as soon as he turned his back they would be upon him again, and if he should once fall . . .

He could not spare a moment, or a chance.

He looked at Ciara, not knowing what to do, and it seemed to him that the sheathing frost had melted, just a little, around her face.

pt. ends p. 159

Desperately, he struck down again at the creatures in the shaft, and then the answer came to him.

He dropped the sword. The squat, round mechanism was beside him, with its broken crystal wheel. He picked it up.

It was heavy. It would have been heavy for two men to lift, but Stark was a driven man. Grunting, swaying with the effort, he lifted it and let it fall, out and down.

Like a thunderbolt it struck among those slender bridges, the spiderweb of icy strands that spanned the shaft. Stark watched it go, and listened to the brittle snapping of the ice, the final crashing of a million shards at the bottom far below.

He smiled, and turned again to Ciara, picking up the sword.

It was hours later. Stark walked across the glowing ice of the valley, toward the cairn. The sword of Ban Cruach hung at his side. He had taken the talisman and replaced it in the boss, and he was himself again.

Ciara and Balin walked beside him. The color had come back into their faces, but faintly, and they were still weak enough to be glad of Stark's hands to steady them.

At the foot of the cairn they stopped, and Stark mounted it alone.

He looked for a long moment into the face of Ban Cruach. Then he took the sword, and carefully turned the rings upon it so that the radiation spread out as it had before, to close the Gates of Death.

Almost reverently, he replaced the sword in Ban Cruach's hands. Then he turned and went down over the tumbled stones.

The shimmering darkness brooded still over the distant tower. Underneath the ice, the elfin city still spread downward. The shining ones would rebuild their bridges in the shaft, and go on as they had before, dreaming their cold dreams of ancient power.

But they would not go out through the Gates of Death. Ban Cruach in his rusty mail was still lord of the pass, the warder of the Norlands.

Stark said to the others, "Tell the story in Kushat. Tell it through the Norlands, the story of Ban Cruach and why he guards the Gates of Death. Men have forgotten. And they should not forget."

They went out of the valley then, the two men and the woman. They did not speak again, and the way out through the pass seemed endless.

Some of Ciara's chieftains met them at the mouth of the pass above Kushat. They had waited there, ashamed to return to the city without her, but not daring to go back into the pass again. They had seen the creatures of the valley, and they were still afraid.

They gave mounts to the three. They themselves walked behind Ciara, and their heads were low with shame.

They came into Kushat through the riven gate, and Stark went with Ciara to the King City, where she made Balin follow too.

"Your sister is there," she said. "I have had her cared for."

The city was quiet, with the sullen apathy that follows after battle. The men of Mekh cheered Ciara in the streets. She rode proudly, but Stark saw that her face was gaunt and strained.

He, too, was marked deep by what he had seen and done, beyond the Gates of Death.

They went up into the castle.

Thanis took Balin into her arms, and wept. She had lost her first wild fury, and she could look at Ciara now with a restrained hatred that had a tinge almost of admiration.

"You fought for Kushat," she said, unwillingly, when she had heard the story. "For that, at least, I can thank you."

She went to Stark then, and looked up at him. "Kushat, and my brother's life . . . " She kissed him, and there were tears on her lips. But she turned to Ciara with a bitter smile.

"No one can hold him, any more than the wind can be held. You will learn that."

pt. ends next p.

She went out then with Balin, and left Stark and Ciara alone, in the chambers of the king.

*

Ciara said, "The little one is very shrewd." She unbuckled the hauberk[2] and let it fall, standing slim in her tunic of black leather, and walked to the tall windows that looked out upon the mountains. She leaned her head wearily against the stone.

"An evil day, an evil deed. And now I have Kushat to govern, with no reward of power from beyond the Gates of Death. How man can be misled!"

Stark poured wine from the flagon and brought it to her. She looked at him over the rim of the cup, with a certain wry amusement.

"The little one is shrewd, and she is right. I don't know that I can be as wise as she . . . Will you stay with me, Stark, or will you go?"

He did not answer at once, and she asked him, "What hunger drives you, Stark? It is not conquest, as it was with me. What are you looking for that you cannot find?"

He thought back across the years, back to the beginning—to the boy N'Chaka who had once been happy with Old One and little Tika, in the blaze and thunder and bitter frosts of a valley in the Twilight Belt of Mercury. He remembered how all that had ended, under the guns of the miners—the men who were his own kind.

He shook his head. "I don't know. It doesn't matter." He took her between his two hands, feeling the strength and the splendor of her, and it was oddly difficult to find words.

"I want to stay, Ciara. Now, this minute, I could promise that I would stay forever. But I know myself. You belong here, you will make Kushat your own. I don't. Someday I will go."

---

[2] A long coat or tunic of chain mail.

Ciara nodded. "My neck, also, was not made for chains, and one country was too little to hold me. Very well, Stark. Let it be so."

She smiled, and let the wine-cup fall.

Leigh Brackett

Enchantress of Venus

A Stark Tale

Laughing, she cast him down into the hideous depths, beneath the seas of flaming gas, to where dead blossoms swayed, whispering, over strangely jumbled ruins . . . But there he found the secret of her power, and came surging back—up from the depths, up from the seas, the tortured swamps—to storm her forbidding shrine and seek her within, death like a gift in his hands . . .

Enchantress of Venus *Part 1*

The ship moved slowly across the Red Sea, through the shrouding veils of mist, her sail barely filled by the languid thrust of the wind. Her hull, of a thin light metal, floated without sound, the surface of the strange ocean parting before her prow[1] in silent rippling streamers of flame.

Night deepened toward the ship, a river of indigo flowing out of the west. The man known as Stark stood alone by the after rail and watched its coming. He was full of impatience and a gathering sense of danger, so that it seemed to him that even the hot wind smelled of it.

The steersman[2] lay drowsily over his sweep.[3] He was a big man, with skin and hair the color of milk. He did not speak, but Stark felt that now and again the man's eyes turned toward him, pale and calculating under half-closed lids, with a secret avarice.[4]

The captain and the two other members of the little coasting vessel's crew were forward, at their evening meal. Once or twice

---

[1] The portion of a ship's bow (front end) above water.

[2] One who steers a boat or ship.

[3] A long, heavy oar.

[4] Extreme desire for riches and wealth.

8 pp.

Stark heard a burst of laughter, half-whispered and furtive. It was as though all four shared in some private joke, from which he was rigidly excluded.

The heat was oppressive. Sweat gathered on Stark's dark face. His shirt stuck to his back. The air was heavy with moisture, tainted with the muddy fecundity[5] of the land that brooded westward behind the eternal fog.

There was something ominous about the sea itself. Even on its own world, the Red Sea is hardly more than legend. It lies behind the Mountains of White Cloud, the great barrier wall that hides away half a planet. Few men have gone beyond that barrier, into the vast mystery of Inner Venus. Fewer still have come back.

Stark was one of that handful. Three times before he had crossed the mountains, and once he had stayed for nearly a year. But he had never quite grown used to the Red Sea.

It was not water. It was gaseous, dense enough to float the buoyant hulls of the metal ships, and it burned perpetually with its deep inner fires. The mists that clouded it were stained with the bloody glow. Beneath the surface Stark could see the drifts of flame where the lazy currents ran, and the little coiling bursts of sparks that came upward and spread and melted into other bursts, so that the face of the sea was like a cosmos of crimson stars.

It was very beautiful, glowing against the blue, luminous darkness of the night. Beautiful, and strange.

There was a padding of bare feet, and the captain, Malthor, came up to Stark, his outlines dim and ghostly in the gloom.

"We will reach Shuruun," he said, "before the second glass is run."

Stark nodded. "Good."

The voyage had seemed endless, and the close confinement of the narrow deck had got badly on his nerves.

"You will like Shuruun," said the captain jovially. "Our wine,

---

[5] Richness; fertility.

our food, our women—all superb. We don't have many visitors. We keep to ourselves, as you will see. But those who do come . . . "

He laughed, and clapped Stark on the shoulder. "Ah, yes. You will be happy in Shuruun!"

It seemed to Stark that he caught an echo of laughter from the unseen crew, as though they listened and found a hidden jest in Malthor's words.

Stark said, "That's fine."

"Perhaps," said Malthor, "you would like to lodge with me. I could make you a good price."

He had made a good price for Stark's passage from up the coast. An exorbitantly good one.

Stark said, "No."

"You don't have to be afraid," said the Venusian, in a confidential tone. "The strangers who come to Shuruun all have the same reason. It's a good place to hide. We're out of everybody's reach."

He paused, but Stark did not rise to his bait. Presently he chuckled and went on, "In fact, it's such a safe place that most of the strangers decide to stay on. Now, at my house, I could give you . . . "

Stark said again, flatly, "No."

The captain shrugged. "Very well. Think it over, anyway." He peered ahead into the red, coiling mists. "Ah! See there?" He pointed, and Stark made out the shadowy loom of cliffs. "We are coming into the strait now."

Malthor turned and took the steering sweep himself, the helmsman going forward to join the others. The ship began to pick up speed. Stark saw that she had come into the grip of a current that swept toward the cliffs, a river of fire racing ever more swiftly in the depths of the sea.

*

The dark wall seemed to plunge toward them. At first Stark

could see no passage. Then, suddenly, a narrow crimson streak appeared, widened, and became a gut of boiling flame, rushing silently around broken rocks. Red fog rose like smoke. The ship quivered, sprang ahead, and tore like a mad thing into the heart of the inferno.

In spite of himself, Stark's hands tightened on the rail. Tattered veils of mist swirled past them. The sea, the air, the ship itself, seemed drenched in blood. There was no sound, in all that wild sweep of current through the strait. Only the sullen fires burst and flowed.

The reflected glare showed Stark that the Straits of Shuruun were defended. Squat fortresses brooded on the cliffs. There were ballistas,[6] and great windlasses for the drawing of nets across the narrow throat. The men of Shuruun could enforce their law, that barred all foreign shipping from their gulf.

They had reason for such a law, and such a defense. The legitimate trade of Shuruun, such as it was, was in wine and the delicate laces woven from spider-silk. Actually, however, the city lived and throve on piracy, the arts of wrecking, and a contraband trade in the distilled juice of the *vela* poppy.

Looking at the rocks and the fortresses, Stark could understand how it was that Shuruun had been able for more centuries than anyone could tell to victimize the shipping of the Red Sea, and offer a refuge to the outlaw, the wolf's-head,[7] the breaker of tabu.[8]

With startling abruptness, they were through the gut and drifting on the still surface of this all but landlocked arm of the Red Sea.

Because of the shrouding fog, Stark could see nothing of the land. But the smell of it was stronger, warm damp soil and the heavy, faintly rotten perfume of vegetation half jungle, half swamp. Once, through a rift in the wreathing vapor, he thought he glimpsed the shadowy bulk of an island, but it was gone at once.

---

[6] Ancient catapults for hurling stones or similar projectiles.

[7] Another term for outlaw.

[8] Alternate spelling of taboo.

After the terrifying rush of the strait, it seemed to Stark that the ship barely moved. His impatience and the subtle sense of danger deepened. He began to pace the deck, with the nervous, velvet motion of a prowling cat. The moist, steamy air seemed all but unbreathable after the clean dryness of Mars, from whence he had come so recently. It was oppressively still.

Suddenly he stopped, his head thrown back, listening.

The sound was borne faintly on the slow wind. It came from everywhere and nowhere, a vague dim thing without source or direction. It almost seemed that the night itself had spoken—the hot blue night of Venus, crying out of the mists with a tongue of infinite woe.

It faded and died away, only half heard, leaving behind it a sense of aching sadness, as though all the misery and longing of a world had found voice in that desolate wail.

Stark shivered. For a time there was silence, and then he heard the sound again, now on a deeper note. Still faint and far away, it was sustained longer by the vagaries of the heavy air, and it became a chant, rising and falling. There were no words. It was not the sort of thing that would have need of words. Then it was gone again.

Stark turned to Malthor. "What was that?"

The man looked at him curiously. He seemed not to have heard.

"That wailing sound," said Stark impatiently.

"Oh, that." The Venusian shrugged. "A trick of the wind. It sighs in the hollow rocks around the strait."

*

He yawned, giving place again to the steersman, and came to stand beside Stark. The Earthman ignored him. For some reason, that sound half heard through the mists had brought his uneasiness to a sharp pitch.

Civilization had brushed over Stark with a light hand. Raised

pt. ends p. 170

from infancy by half-human aboriginals, his perceptions were still those of a savage. His ear was good.

Malthor lied. That cry of pain was not made by any wind.

"I have known several Earthmen," said Malthor, changing the subject, but not too swiftly. "None of them were like you."

Intuition warned Stark to play along. "I don't come from Earth," he said. "I come from Mercury."

Malthor puzzled over that. Venus is a cloudy world, where no man has ever seen the Sun, let alone a star. The captain had heard vaguely of these things. Earth and Mars he knew of. But Mercury was an unknown word.

Stark explained. "The planet nearest the Sun. It's very hot there. The Sun blazes like a huge fire, and there are no clouds to shield it."

"Ah. That is why your skin is so dark." He held his own pale forearm close to Stark's and shook his head. "I have never seen such skin," he said admiringly. "Nor such great muscles."

Looking up, he went on in a tone of complete friendliness, "I wish you would stay with me. You'll find no better lodgings in Shuruun. And I warn you, there are people in the town who will take advantage of strangers—rob them, even slay them. Now, I am known by all as a man of honor. You could sleep soundly under my roof."

He paused, then added with a smile, "Also, I have a daughter. An excellent cook—and very beautiful."

The woeful chanting came again, dim and distant on the wind, an echo of warning against some unimagined fate.

Stark said for the third time, "No."

He needed no intuition to tell him to walk wide of the captain. The man was a rogue, and not a very subtle one.

A flint-hard, angry look came briefly into Malthor's eyes. "You're a stubborn man. You'll find that Shuruun is no place for stubbornness."

He turned and went away. Stark remained where he was. The ship drifted on through a slow eternity of time. And all down that long still gulf of the Red Sea, through the heat and the wreathing fog, the ghostly chanting haunted him, like the keening of lost souls in some forgotten hell.

Presently the course of the ship was altered. Malthor came again to the afterdeck,[9] giving a few quiet commands. Stark saw land ahead, a darker blur on the night, and then the shrouded outlines of a city.

Torches blazed on the quays and in the streets, and the low buildings caught a ruddy glow from the burning sea itself. A squat and ugly town, Shuruun, crouching witch-like on the rocky shore, her ragged skirts dipped in blood.

The ship drifted in toward the quays.

*

Stark heard a whisper of movement behind him, the hushed and purposeful padding of naked feet. He turned, with the astonishing swiftness of an animal that feels itself threatened, his hand dropping to his gun.

A belaying pin, thrown by the steersman, struck the side of his head with stunning force. Reeling, half blinded, he saw the distorted shapes of men closing in upon him. Malthor's voice sounded, low and hard. A second belaying pin whizzed through the air and cracked against Stark's shoulder.

Hands were laid upon him. Bodies, heavy and strong, bore his down. Malthor laughed.

Stark's teeth glinted bare and white. Someone's cheek brushed past, and he sank them into the flesh. He began to growl, a sound that should never have come from a human throat. It seemed to the startled Venusians that the man they had attacked had by some wizardry become a beast, at the first touch of violence.

The man with the torn cheek screamed. There was a voiceless scuffling on the deck, a terrible intensity of motion, and then the great dark body rose and shook itself free of the tangle, and was

---

[9] An open deck near the stern or rear of a ship.

pt. ends next p.

gone, over the rail, leaving Malthor with nothing but the silken rags of a shirt in his hands.

The surface of the Red Sea closed without a ripple over Stark. There was a burst of crimson sparks, a momentary trail of flame going down like a drowned comet, and then—nothing.

Part 2

Stark dropped slowly downward through a strange world. There was no difficulty about breathing, as in a sea of water. The gases of the Red Sea support life quite well, and the creatures that dwell in it have almost normal lungs.

Stark did not pay much attention at first, except to keep his balance automatically. He was still dazed from the blow, and he was raging with anger and pain.

The primitive in him, whose name was not Stark but N'Chaka, and who had fought and starved and hunted in the blazing valleys of Mercury's Twilight Belt, learning lessons he never forgot, wished to return and slay Malthor and his men. He regretted that he had not torn out their throats, for now his trail would never be safe from them.

But the man Stark, who had learned some more bitter lessons in the name of civilization, knew the unwisdom of that. He snarled over his aching head, and cursed the Venusians in the harsh, crude dialect that was his mother tongue, but he did not turn back. There would be time enough for Malthor.

It struck him that the gulf was very deep.

Fighting down his rage, he began to swim in the direction

of the shore. There was no sign of pursuit, and he judged that Malthor had decided to let him go. He puzzled over the reason for the attack. It could hardly be robbery, since he carried nothing but the clothes he stood in, and very little money.

No. There was some deeper reason. A reason connected with Malthor's insistence that he lodge with him. Stark smiled. It was not a pleasant smile. He was thinking of Shuruun, and the things men said about it, around the shores of the Red Sea.

Then his face hardened. The dim coiling fires through which he swam brought him memories of other times he had gone adventuring in the depths of the Red Sea.

He had not been alone then. Helvi had gone with him—the tall son of a barbarian kinglet[1] up-coast by Yarell. They had hunted strange beasts through the crystal forests of the sea-bottom and bathed in the welling flames that pulse from the very heart of Venus to feed the ocean. They had been brothers.

Now Helvi was gone, into Shuruun. He had never returned.

Stark swam on. And presently he saw below him in the red gloom something that made him drop lower, frowning with surprise.

There were trees beneath him. Great forest giants towering up into an eerie sky, their branches swaying gently to the slow wash of the currents.

Stark was puzzled. The forests where he and Helvi had hunted were truly crystalline, without even the memory of life. The "trees" were no more trees in actuality than the branching corals of Terra's southern oceans.

But these were real, or had been. He thought at first that they still lived, for their leaves were green, and here and there creepers had starred them with great nodding blossoms of gold and purple and waxy white. But when he floated down close enough to touch them, he realized that they were dead—trees, creepers, blossoms, all.

---

[1] A king of a small or unimportant kingdom.

They had not mummified, nor turned to stone. They were pliable, and their colors were very bright. Simply, they had ceased to live, and the gases of the sea had preserved them by some chemical magic, so perfectly that barely a leaf had fallen.

Stark did not venture into the shadowy denseness below the topmost branches. A strange fear came over him, at the sight of that vast forest dreaming in the depths of the gulf, drowned and forgotten, as though wondering why the birds had gone, taking with them the warm rains and the light of day.

He thrust his way upward, himself like a huge dark bird above the branches. An overwhelming impulse to get away from that unearthly place drove him on, his half-wild sense shuddering with an impression of evil so great that it took all his acquired common-sense to assure him that he was not pursued by demons.

*

He broke the surface at last, to find that he had lost his direction in the red deep and made a long circle around, so that he was far below Shuruun. He made his way back, not hurrying now, and presently clambered out over the black rocks.

He stood at the end of a muddy lane that wandered in toward the town. He followed it, moving neither fast nor slow, but with a wary alertness.

Huts of wattle-and-daub[2] took shape out of the fog, increased in numbers, became a street of dwellings. Here and there rush-lights glimmered through the slitted windows. A man and a woman clung together in a low doorway. They saw him and sprang apart, and the woman gave a little cry. Stark went on. He did not look back, but he knew that they were following him quietly, at a little distance.

The lane twisted snakelike upon itself, crawling now through

[2] A primitive material consisting of interwoven sticks and twigs covered with mud or clay.

pt. ends p. 177

a crowded jumble of houses. There were more lights, and more people, tall white-skinned folk of the swamp-edges, with pale eyes and long hair the color of new flax, and the faces of wolves.

Stark passed among them, alien and strange with his black hair and sun-darkened skin. They did not speak, nor try to stop him. Only they looked at him out of the red fog, with a curious blend of amusement and fear, and some of them followed him, keeping well behind. A gang of small naked children came from somewhere among the houses and ran shouting beside him, out of reach, until one boy threw a stone and screamed something unintelligible except for one word—*Lhari*. Then they all stopped, horrified, and fled.

Stark went on, through the quarter of the lacemakers, heading by instinct toward the wharves. The glow of the Red Sea pervaded all the air, so that it seemed as though the mist was full of tiny drops of blood. There was a smell about the place he did not like, a damp miasma[3] of mud and crowding bodies and wine, and the breath of the *vela* poppy. Shuruun was an unclean town, and it stank of evil.

There was something else about it, a subtle thing that touched Stark's nerves with a chill finger. Fear. He could see the shadow of it in the eyes of the people, hear its undertone in their voices. The wolves of Shuruun did not feel safe in their own kennel. Unconsciously, as this feeling grew upon him, Stark's step grew more and more wary, his eyes more cold and hard.

He came out into a broad square by the harbor front. He could see the ghostly ships moored along the quays, the piled casks of wine, the tangle of masts and cordage[4] dim against the background of the burning gulf. There were many torches here. Large low buildings stood around the square. There was laughter and the sound of voices from the dark verandas, and somewhere a woman sang to the melancholy lilting of a reed pipe.

---

[3] Unhealthy and unpleasant atmosphere.

[4] Ropes or cords of a ship's rigging.

A suffused glow of light in the distance ahead caught Stark's eye. That way the streets sloped to a higher ground, and straining his vision against the fog, he made out very dimly the tall bulk of a castle crouched on the low cliffs, looking with bright eyes upon the night, and the streets of Shuruun.

Stark hesitated briefly. Then he started across the square toward the largest of the taverns.

There were a number of people in the open space, mostly sailors and their women. They were loose and foolish with wine, but even so they stopped where they were and stared at the dark stranger, and then drew back from him, still staring.

Those who had followed Stark came into the square after him and then paused, spreading out in an aimless sort of way to join with other groups, whispering among themselves.

The woman stopped singing in the middle of a phrase.

A curious silence fell on the square. A nervous sibilance[5] ran round and round under the silence, and men came slowly out from the verandas and the doors of the wine shops. Suddenly a woman with disheveled hair pointed her arm at Stark and laughed, the shrieking laugh of a harpy.[6]

*

Stark found his way barred by three tall young men with hard mouths and crafty eyes, who smiled at him as hounds smile before the kill.

"Stranger," they said. "Earthman."

"Outlaw," answered Stark, and it was only half a lie.

One of the young men took a step forward. "Did you fly like a dragon over the Mountains of White Cloud? Did you drop from the sky?"

"I came on Malthor's ship."

---

[5] Hissing sound.

[6] A bad-tempered woman.

pt. ends next p.

A kind of sigh went round the square, and with it the name of Malthor. The eager faces of the young men grew heavy with disappointment. But the leader said sharply, "I was on the quay when Malthor docked. You were not on board."

It was Stark's turn to smile. In the light of the torches, his eyes blazed cold and bright as ice against the sun.

"Ask Malthor the reason for that," he said. "Ask the man with the torn cheek. Or perhaps," he added softly, "you would like to learn for yourselves."

The young men looked at him, scowling, in an odd mood of indecision. Stark settled himself, every muscle loose and ready. And the woman who had laughed crept closer and peered at Stark through her tangled hair, breathing heavily of the poppy wine.

All at once she said loudly, "He came out of the sea. That's where he came from. He's . . . "

One of the young men struck her across the mouth and she fell down in the mud. A burly seaman ran out and caught her by the hair, dragging her to her feet again. His face was frightened and very angry. He hauled the woman away, cursing her for a fool and beating her as he went. She spat out blood, and said no more.

"Well," said Stark to the young men. "Have you made up your minds?"

"Minds!" said a voice behind them—a harsh-timbered, rasping voice that handled the liquid vocables[7] of the Venusian speech very clumsily indeed. "They have no minds, these whelps! If they had, they'd be off about their business, instead of standing here badgering a stranger."

The young men turned, and now between them Stark could see the man who had spoken. He stood on the steps of the tavern. He was an Earthman, and at first Stark thought he was old, because his hair was white and his face deeply lined. His body was wasted with fever, the muscles all gone to knotty strings twisted over

[7] In this context, the sounds of words, irrespective of their meaning.

bone. He leaned heavily on a stick, and one leg was crooked and terribly scarred.

He grinned at Stark and said, in colloquial English, "Watch me get rid of 'em!"

He began to tongue-lash the young men, telling them that they were idiots, the misbegotten offspring of swamp-toads, utterly without manners, and that if they did not believe the stranger's story they should go and ask Malthor, as he suggested. Finally he shook his stick at them, fairly screeching.

"Go on, now. Go away! Leave us alone—my brother of Earth and I!"

The young men gave one hesitant glance at Stark's feral eyes. Then they looked at each other and shrugged, and went away across the square half sheepishly, like great loutish[8] boys caught in some misdemeanor.

The white-haired Earthman beckoned to Stark. And, as Stark came up to him on the steps he said under his breath, almost angrily, "You're in a trap."

Stark glanced back over his shoulder. At the edge of the square the three young men had met a fourth, who had his face bound up in a rag. They vanished almost at once into a side street, but not before Stark had recognized the fourth man as Malthor.

It was the captain he had branded.

With loud cheerfulness, the lame man said in Venusian, "Come in and drink with me, brother, and we will talk of Earth."

---

[8] Stupid and aggressive.

Part 3

The tavern was of the standard low-class Venusian pattern—a single huge room under bare thatch, the wall half open with the reed shutters rolled up, the floor of split logs propped up on piling out of the mud. A long low bar, little tables, mangy skins and heaps of dubious cushions on the floor around them, and at one end the entertainers—two old men with a drum and a reed pipe, and a couple of sulky, tired-looking girls.

The lame man led Stark to a table in the corner and sank down, calling for wine. His eyes, which were dark and haunted by long pain, burned with excitement. His hands shook. Before Stark had sat down he had begun to talk, his words stumbling over themselves as though he could not get them out fast enough.

"How is it there now? Has it changed any? Tell me how it is—the cities, the lights, the paved streets, the women, the Sun. Oh Lord, what I wouldn't give to see the Sun again, and women with dark hair and their clothes on!" He leaned forward, staring hungrily into Stark's face, as though he could see those things mirrored there. "For God's sake, talk to me—talk to me in English, and tell me about Earth!"

"How long have you been here?" asked Stark.

6 pp.

"I don't know. How do you reckon time on a world without a Sun, without one damned little star to look at? Ten years, a hundred years, how should I know? Forever. Tell me about Earth."

Stark smiled wryly. "I haven't been there for a long time. The police were too ready with a welcoming committee. But the last time I saw it, it was just the same."

The lame man shivered. He was not looking at Stark now, but at some place far beyond him.

"Autumn woods," he said. "Red and gold on the brown hills. Snow. I can remember how it felt to be cold. The air bit you when you breathed it. And the women wore high-heeled slippers. No big bare feet tromping in the mud, but little sharp heels tapping on clean pavement."

Suddenly he glared at Stark, his eyes furious and bright with tears.

"Why the hell did you have to come here and start me remembering? I'm Larrabee. I live in Shuruun. I've been here forever, and I'll be here till I die. There isn't any Earth. It's gone. Just look up into the sky, and you'll know it's gone. There's nothing anywhere but clouds, and Venus, and mud."

He sat still, shaking, turning his head from side to side. A man came with wine, put it down, and went away again. The tavern was very quiet. There was a wide space empty around the two Earthmen. Beyond that people lay on the cushions, sipping the poppy wine and watching with a sort of furtive expectancy.

Abruptly, Larrabee laughed, a harsh sound that held a certain honest mirth.

"I don't know why I should get sentimental about Earth at this late date. Never thought much about it when I was there."

Nevertheless, he kept his gaze averted, and when he picked up his cup his hand trembled so that he spilled some of the wine.

Stark was staring at him in unbelief. "Larrabee," he said. "You're Mike Larrabee. You're the man who got half a million credits out of the strong room of the *Royal Venus*."

Larrabee nodded. "And got away with it, right over the

Mountains of White Cloud, that they said couldn't be flown. And do you know where that half a million is now? At the bottom of the Red Sea, along with my ship and my crew, out there in the gulf. Lord knows why I lived." He shrugged. "Well, anyway, I was heading for Shuruun when I crashed, and I got here. So why complain?"

He drank again, deeply, and Stark shook his head.

"You've been here nine years, then, by Earth time," he said. He had never met Larrabee, but he remembered the pictures of him that had flashed across space on police bands. Larrabee had been a young man then, dark and proud and handsome.

Larrabee guessed his thought. "I've changed, haven't I?"

Stark said lamely, "Everybody thought you were dead."

Larrabee laughed.

*

After that, for a moment, there was silence. Stark's ears were straining for any sound outside. There was none.

He said abruptly, "What about this trap I'm in?"

"I'll tell you one thing about it," said Larrabee. "There's no way out. I can't help you. I wouldn't if I could, get that straight. But I can't, anyway."

"Thanks," Stark said sourly. "You can at least tell me what goes on."

"Listen," said Larrabee. "I'm a cripple, and an old man, and Shuruun isn't the sweetest place in the Solar System to live. But I do live. I have a wife, a slatternly[1] wench I'll admit, but good enough in her way. You'll notice some little dark-haired brats rolling in the mud. They're mine, too. I have some skill at setting bones and such, and so I can get drunk for nothing as often as I will—which is often. Also, because of this bum leg, I'm perfectly safe. So don't ask me what goes on. I take great pains not to know."

[1] Dirty and negligent.

Stark said, "Who are the Lhari?"

"Would you like to meet them?" Larrabee seemed to find something very amusing in that thought. "Just go on up to the castle. They live there. They're the Lords of Shuruun, and they're always glad to meet strangers."

He leaned forward suddenly. "Who are you anyway? What's your name, and why the devil did you come here?"

"My name is Stark. And I came here for the same reason you did."

"Stark," repeated Larrabee slowly, his eyes intent. "That rings a faint bell. Seems to me I saw a *Wanted* flash once, some idiot that had led a native revolt somewhere in the Jovian Colonies—a big cold-eyed brute they referred to colorfully as the wild man from Mercury."

He nodded, pleased with himself. "Wild man, eh? Well, Shuruun will tame you down!"

"Perhaps," said Stark. His eyes shifted constantly, watching Larrabee, watching the doorway and the dark veranda and the people who drank but did not talk among themselves. "Speaking of strangers, one came here at the time of the last rains. He was Venusian, from up-coast. A big young man. I used to know him. Perhaps he could help me."

Larrabee snorted. By now, he had drunk his own wine and Stark's too. "Nobody can help you. As for your friend, I never saw him. I'm beginning to think I should never have seen you." Quite suddenly he caught up his stick and got with some difficulty to his feet. He did not look at Stark, but said harshly, "You better get out of here." Then he turned and limped unsteadily to the bar.

Stark rose. He glanced after Larrabee, and again his nostrils twitched to the smell of fear. Then he went out of the tavern the way he had come in, through the front door. No one moved to stop him. Outside, the square was empty. It had begun to rain.

Stark stood for a moment on the steps. He was angry, and filled with a dangerous unease, the hair-trigger nervousness of a tiger that senses the beaters creeping toward him up the wind.

pt. ends next p.

He would almost have welcomed the sight of Malthor and the three young men. But there was nothing to fight but the silence and the rain.

*

He stepped out into the mud, wet and warm around his ankles. An idea came to him, and he smiled, beginning now to move with a definite purpose, along the side of the square.

The sharp downpour strengthened. Rain smoked from Stark's naked shoulders, beat against thatch and mud with a hissing rattle. The harbor had disappeared behind boiling clouds of fog, where water struck the surface of the Red Sea and was turned again instantly by chemical action into vapor. The quays and the neighboring streets were being swallowed up in the impenetrable mist. Lightning came with an eerie bluish flare, and thunder came rolling after it.

Stark turned up the narrow way that led toward the castle.

Its lights were winking out now, one by one, blotted by the creeping fog. Lightning etched its shadowy bulk against the night, and then was gone. And through the noise of the thunder that followed, Stark thought he heard a voice calling.

He stopped, half crouching, his hand on his gun. The cry came again, a girl's voice, thin as the wail of a sea-bird through the driving rain. Then he saw her, a small white blur in the street behind him, running, and even in that dim glimpse of her every line of her body was instinct with fright.

Stark set his back against a wall and waited. There did not seem to be anyone with her, though it was hard to tell in the darkness and the storm.

She came up to him, and stopped, just out of his reach, looking at him and away again with a painful irresoluteness. A bright flash showed her to him clearly. She was young, not long out of her childhood, and pretty in a stupid sort of way. Just now her mouth trembled on the edge of weeping, and her eyes were very large and scared. Her skirt clung to her long thighs, and above it her naked body, hardly fleshed into womanhood, glistened like snow in the wet. Her pale hair hung dripping over her shoulders.

Stark said gently, "What do you want with me?"

She looked at him, so miserably like a wet puppy that he smiled. And as though that smile had taken what little resolution she had out of her, she dropped to her knees, sobbing.

"I can't do it," she wailed. "He'll kill me, but I just can't do it!"

"Do what?" asked Stark.

She stared up at him. "Run away," she urged him. "Run away *now*! You'll die in the swamps, but that's better than being one of the Lost Ones!" She shook her thin arms at him. "*Run away!*"

Part 4

The street was empty. Nothing showed, nothing stirred anywhere. Stark leaned over and pulled the girl to her feet, drawing her in under the shelter of the thatched eaves.

"Now then," he said. "Suppose you stop crying and tell me what this is all about."

Presently, between gulps and hiccoughs,[1] he got the story out of her.

"I am Zareth," she said. "Malthor's daughter. He's afraid of you, because of what you did to him on the ship, so he ordered me to watch for you in the square, when you would come out of the tavern. Then I was to follow you, and . . . "

She broke off, and Stark patted her shoulder. "Go on."

But a new thought had occurred to her. "If I do, will you promise not to beat me, or . . . " She looked at his gun and shivered.

"I promise."

She studied his face, what she could see of it in the darkness, and then seemed to lose some of her fear.

"I was to stop you. I was to say what I've already said, about

[1] Hiccups.

being Malthor's daughter and the rest of it, and then I was to say that he wanted me to lead you into an ambush while pretending to help you escape, but that I couldn't do it, and would help you to escape anyhow because I hated Malthor and the whole business about the Lost Ones. So you would believe me, and follow me, and I would lead you into the ambush."

She shook her head and began to cry again, quietly this time, and there was nothing of the woman about her at all now. She was just a child, very miserable and afraid. Stark was glad he had branded Malthor.

"But I can't lead you into the ambush. I do hate Malthor, even if he is my father, because he beats me. And the Lost Ones . . . " She paused. "Sometimes I hear them at night, chanting way out there beyond the mist. It is a very terrible sound."

"It is," said Stark. "I've heard it. Who are the Lost Ones, Zareth?"

"I can't tell you that," said Zareth. "It's forbidden even to speak of them. And anyway," she finished honestly, "I don't even know. People disappear, that's all. Not our own people of Shuruun, at least not very often. But strangers like you—and I'm sure my father goes off into the swamps to hunt among the tribes there, and I'm sure he comes back from some of his voyages with nothing in his hold but men from some captured ship. Why, or what for, I don't know. Except I've heard the chanting."

"They live out there in the gulf, do they, the Lost Ones?"

"They must. There are many islands there."

"And what of the Lhari, the Lords of Shuruun? Don't they know what's going on? Or are they part of it?"

She shuddered, and said, "It's not for us to question the Lhari, nor even to wonder what they do. Those who have are gone from Shuruun, nobody knows where."

Stark nodded. He was silent for a moment, thinking. Then Zareth's little hand touched his shoulder.

"Go," she said. "Lose yourself in the swamps. You're strong, and there's something about you different from other men. You may live to find your way through."

pt. ends p. 190

"No. I have something to do before I leave Shuruun." He took Zareth's damp fair head between his hands and kissed her on the forehead. "You're a sweet child, Zareth, and a brave one. Tell Malthor that you did exactly as he told you, and it was not your fault I wouldn't follow you."

"He will beat me anyway," said Zareth philosophically, "but perhaps not quite so hard."

"He'll have no reason to beat you at all, if you tell him the truth—that I would not go with you because my mind was set on going to the castle of the Lhari."

*

There was a long, long silence, while Zareth's eyes widened slowly in horror, and the rain beat on the thatch, and fog and thunder rolled together across Shuruun.

"To the castle," she whispered. "Oh, no! Go into the swamps, or let Malthor take you—but don't go to the castle!" She took hold of his arm, her fingers biting into his flesh with the urgency of her plea. "You're a stranger, you don't know . . . Please, don't go up there!"

"Why not?" asked Stark. "Are the Lhari demons? Do they devour men?" He loosened her hands gently. "You'd better go now. Tell your father where I am, if he wishes to come after me."

Zareth backed away slowly, out into the rain, staring at him as though she looked at someone standing on the brink of hell, not dead, but worse than dead. Wonder showed in her face, and through it a great yearning pity. She tried once to speak, and then shook her head and turned away, breaking into a run as though she could not endure to look upon Stark any longer. In a second she was gone.

Stark looked after her for a moment, strangely touched. Then he stepped out into the rain again, heading upward along the steep path that led to the castle of the Lords of Shuruun.

The mist was blinding. Stark had to feel his way, and as he climbed higher, above the level of the town, he was lost in the sullen redness. A hot wind blew, and each flare of lighting turned the crimson fog to a hellish purple. The night was full of a vast hissing where the rain poured into the gulf. He stopped once to hide his gun in a cleft between the rocks.

At length he stumbled against a carven pillar of black stone and found the gate that hung from it, a massive thing sheathed in metal. It was barred, and the pounding of his fists upon it made little sound.

Then he saw the gong, a huge disc of beaten gold beside the gate. Stark picked up the hammer that lay there, and set the deep voice of the gong rolling out between the thunderbolts.

A barred slit opened and a man's eyes looked out at him. Stark dropped the hammer.

"Open up!" he shouted. "I would speak with the Lhari!"

From within he heard an echo of laughter. Scraps of voices came to him on the wind, and then more laughter, and then, slowly, the great valves of the gate creaked open, wide enough only to admit him.

He stepped through, and the gateway shut behind him with a ringing clash.

He stood in a huge open court. Enclosed within its walls was a village of thatched huts, with open sheds for cooking, and behind them were pens for the stabling of beasts, the wingless dragons of the swamps that can be caught and broken to the goad.[2]

He saw this only in vague glimpses, because of the fog. The men who had let him in clustered around him, thrusting him forward into the light that streamed from the huts.

"He would speak with the Lhari!" one of them shouted, to the women and children who stood in the doorways watching. The words were picked up and tossed around the court, and a great burst of laughter went up.

---

[2] A phrase meaning they can be tamed or domesticated.

pt. ends p. 190

Stark eyed them, saying nothing. They were a puzzling breed. The men, obviously, were soldiers and guards to the Lhari, for they wore the harness of fighting men. As obviously, these were their wives and children, all living behind the castle walls and having little to do with Shuruun.

But it was their racial characteristics that surprised him. They had interbred with the pale tribes of the Swamp-Edges that had peopled Shuruun, and there were many with milk-white hair and broad faces. Yet even these bore an alien stamp. Stark was puzzled, for the race he would have named was unknown here behind the Mountains of White Cloud, and almost unknown anywhere on Venus at Sea-level, among the sweltering marshes and the eternal fogs.

They stared at him even more curiously, remarking on his skin and his black hair and the unfamiliar modeling of his face. The women nudged each other and whispered, giggling, and one of them said aloud, "They'll need a barrel-hoop to collar that neck!"

The guards closed in around him. "Well, if you wish to see the Lhari, you shall," said the leader, "but first we must make sure of you."

Spear-points ringed him round. Stark made no resistance while they stripped him of all he had, except for his shorts and sandals. He had expected that, and it amused him, for there was little enough for them to take.

"All right," said the leader. "Come on."

The whole village turned out in the rain to escort Stark to the castle door. There was about them the same ominous interest that the people of Shuruun had had, with one difference. They knew what was supposed to happen to him, knew all about it, and were therefore doubly appreciative of the game.

The great doorway was square and plain, and yet neither crude nor ungraceful. The castle itself was built of the black stone, each block perfectly cut and fitted, and the door itself was sheathed in the same metal as the gate, darkened but not corroded.

The leader of the guard cried out to the warder, "Here is one who would speak with the Lhari!"

The warder laughed. "And so he shall! Their night is long, and dull."

He flung open the heavy door and cried the word down the hallway. Stark could hear it echoing hollowly within, and presently from the shadows came servants clad in silks and wearing jeweled collars, and from the guttural sound of their laughter Stark knew that they had no tongues.

Stark faltered, then. The doorway loomed hollowly before him, and it came to him suddenly that evil lay behind it and that perhaps Zareth was wiser than he when she warned him from the Lhari.

Then he thought of Helvi, and of other things, and lost his fear in anger. Lightning burned the sky. The last cry of the dying storm shook the ground under his feet. He thrust the grinning warder aside and strode into the castle, bringing a veil of the red fog with him, and did not listen to the closing of the door, which was stealthy and quiet as the footfall of approaching Death.

Torches burned here and there along the walls, and by their smoky glare he could see that the hallway was like the entrance—square and unadorned, faced with the black rock. It was high, and wide, and there was about the architecture a calm reflective dignity that had its own beauty, in some ways more impressive than the sensuous loveliness of the ruined palaces he had seen on Mars.

There were no carvings here, no paintings nor frescoes. It seemed that the builders had felt that the hall itself was enough, in its massive perfection of line and the somber gleam of polished stone. The only decoration was in the window embrasures.[3] These were empty now, open to the sky with the red fog wreathing

---

[3] Small openings in a parapet.

pt. ends next p.

through them, but there were still scraps of jewel-toned panes clinging to the fretwork,[4] to show what they had once been.

A strange feeling swept over Stark. Because of his wild upbringing, he was abnormally sensitive to the sort of impressions that most men receive either dully or not at all.

Walking down the hall, preceded by the tongueless creatures in their bright silks and blazing collars, he was struck by a subtle *difference* in the place. The castle itself was only an extension of the minds of its builders, a dream shaped into reality. Stark felt that that dark, cool, curiously timeless dream had not originated in a mind like his own, nor like that of any man he had ever seen.

Then the end of the hall was reached, the way barred by low broad doors of gold fashioned in the same chaste simplicity.

A soft scurrying of feet, a shapeless tittering from the servants, a glancing of malicious, mocking eyes. The golden doors swung open, and Stark was in the presence of the Lhari.

---

[4] Ornamental designs in wood.

Part 5

They had the appearance in that first glance, of creatures glimpsed in a fever-dream, very bright and distant, robed in a misty glow that gave them an illusion of unearthly beauty.

The place in which the Earthman now stood was like a cathedral for breadth and loftiness. Most of it was in darkness, so that it seemed to reach without limit above and on all sides, as though the walls were only shadowy phantasms of the night itself. The polished black stone under his feet held a dim translucent gleam, depthless as water in a black tarn. There was no substance anywhere.

Far away in this shadowy vastness burned a cluster of lamps, a galaxy of little stars to shed a silvery light upon the Lords of Shuruun.

There had been no sound in the place when Stark entered, for the opening of the golden doors had caught the attention of the Lhari and held it in contemplation of the stranger. Stark began to walk toward them in this utter stillness.

Quite suddenly, in the impenetrable gloom somewhere to his right, there came a sharp scuffling and a scratching of reptilian claws, a hissing and a sort of low angry muttering, all magnified and distorted by the echoing vault into a huge demoniac whispering that swept all around him.

Stark whirled around, crouched and ready, his eyes blazing and his body bathed in cold sweat. The noise increased, rushing toward him. From the distant glow of the lamps came a woman's tinkling laughter, thin crystal broken against the vault. The hissing and snarling rose to hollow crescendo, and Stark saw a blurred shape bounding at him.

His hands reached out to receive the rush, but it never came. The strange shape resolved itself into a boy of about ten, who dragged after him on a bit of rope a young dragon, new and toothless from the egg, and protesting with all its strength.

Stark straightened up, feeling let down and furious—and relieved. The boy scowled at him through a forelock of silver curls. Then he called him a very dirty word and rushed away, kicking and hauling at the little beast until it raged like the father of all dragons and sounded like it, too, in that vast echo chamber.

A voice spoke. Slow, harsh, sexless, it rang thinly through the vault. Thin—but a steel blade is thin, too. It speaks inexorably, and its word is final.

The voice said, "Come here, into the light."

Stark obeyed the voice. As he approached the lamps, the aspect of the Lhari changed and steadied. Their beauty remained, but it was not the same. They had looked like angels. Now that he could see them clearly, Stark thought that they might have been the children of Lucifer himself.

There were six of them, counting the boy. Two men, about the same age as Stark, with some complicated gambling game forgotten between them. A woman, beautiful, gowned in white silk, sitting with her hands in her lap, doing nothing. A woman, younger, not so beautiful perhaps, but with a look of stormy and bitter vitality. She wore a short tunic of crimson, and a stout leather glove on her left hand, where perched a flying thing of prey with its fierce eyes hooded.

The boy stood beside the two men, his head poised arrogantly.

From time to time he cuffed the little dragon, and it snapped at him with its impotent jaws. He was proud of himself for doing that. Stark wondered how he would behave with the beast when it had grown its fangs.

Opposite him, crouched on a heap of cushions, was a third man. He was deformed, with an ungainly body and long spidery arms, and in his lap a sharp knife lay on a block of wood, half formed into the shape of an obese creature half woman, half pure evil. Stark saw with a flash of surprise that the face of the deformed young man, of all the faces there, was truly human, truly beautiful. His eyes were old in his boyish face, wise, and very sad in their wisdom. He smiled upon the stranger, and his smile was more compassionate than tears.

They looked at Stark, all of them, with restless, hungry eyes. They were the pure breed, that had left its stamp of alienage on the pale-haired folk of the swamps, the serfs who dwelt in the huts outside.

They were of the Cloud People, the folk of the High Plateaus, kings of the land on the farther slopes of the Mountains of White Cloud. It was strange to see them here, on the dark side of the barrier wall, but here they were. How they had come, and why, leaving their rich cool plains for the fetor[1] of these foreign swamps, he could not guess. But there was no mistaking them—the proud fine shaping of their bodies, their alabaster skin, their eyes that were all colors and none, like the dawn sky, their hair that was pure warm silver.

They did not speak. They seemed to be waiting for permission to speak, and Stark wondered which one of them had voiced that steely summons.

Then it came again. "Come here—come closer." And he looked

[1] A putrid and offensive smell or odor.

beyond them, beyond the circle of lamps into the shadows again, and saw the speaker.

She lay upon a low bed, her head propped on silken pillows, her vast, her incredibly gigantic body covered with a silken pall.[2] Only her arms were bare, two shapeless masses of white flesh ending in tiny hands. From time to time she stretched one out and took a morsel of food from the supply laid ready beside her, snuffling and wheezing with the effort, and then gulped the tidbit down with a horrible voracity.

Her features had long ago dissolved into a shaking formlessness, with the exception of her nose, which rose out of the fat curved and cruel and thin, like the bony beak of the creature that sat on the girl's wrist and dreamed its hooded dreams of blood. And her eyes . . .

Stark looked into her eyes and shuddered. Then he glanced at the carving half formed in the cripple's lap, and knew what thought had guided the knife.

Half woman, half pure evil. And strong. Very strong. Her strength lay naked in her eyes for all to see, and it was an ugly strength. It could tear down mountains, but it could never build.

He saw her looking at him. Her eyes bored into his as though they would search out his very guts and study them, and he knew that she expected him to turn away, unable to bear her gaze. He did not. Presently he smiled and said, "I have out-stared a rock-lizard, to determine which of us should eat the other. And I've out-stared the very rock while waiting for him."

She knew that he spoke the truth. Stark expected her to be angry, but she was not. A vague mountainous rippling shook her and emerged at length as a voiceless laughter.

"You see that?" she demanded, addressing the others. "You whelps of the Lhari—not one of you dares to face me down, yet here is a great dark creature from the gods know where who can stand and shame you."

---

[2] A cloth cover, usually black, spread over a coffin or tomb.

She glanced again at Stark. "What demon's blood brought you forth, that you have learned neither prudence nor fear?"

Stark answered somberly, "I learned them both before I could walk. But I learned another thing also—a thing called anger."

"And you are angry?"

"Ask Malthor if I am, and why!"

He saw the two men start a little, and a slow smile crossed the girl's face.

"Malthor," said the hulk upon the bed, and ate a mouthful of roast meat dripping with fat. "That is interesting. But rage against Malthor did not bring you here. I am curious, Stranger. Speak."

"I will."

*

Stark glanced around. The place was a tomb, a trap. The very air smelled of danger. The younger folk watched him in silence. Not one of them had spoken since he came in, except the boy who had cursed him, and that was unnatural in itself. The girl leaned forward, idly stroking the creature on her wrist so that it stirred and ran its knife-like talons in and out of their bony sheathes with sensuous pleasure. Her gaze on Stark was bold and cool, oddly challenging. Of them all, she alone saw him as a man. To the others he was a problem, a diversion—something less than human.

Stark said, "A man came to Shuruun at the time of the last rains. His name was Helvi, and he was son of a little king by Yarell. He came seeking his brother, who had broken tabu and fled for his life. Helvi came to tell him that the ban was lifted, and he might return. Neither one came back."

The small evil eyes were amused, blinking in their tallowy creases. "And so?"

"And so I have come after Helvi, who is my friend."

Again there was the heaving of that bulk of flesh, the explosion

pt. ends p. 200

of laughter that hissed and wheezed in snakelike echoes through the vault.

"Friendship must run deep with you, Stranger. Ah, well. The Lhari are kind of heart. You shall find your friend."

And as though that were the signal to end their deferential silence, the younger folk burst into laughter also, until the vast hall rang with it, giving back a sound like demons laughing on the edge of Hell.

The cripple only did not laugh, but bent his bright head over his carving, and sighed.

The girl sprang up. "Not yet, Grandmother! Keep him awhile."

The cold, cruel eyes shifted to her. "And what will you do with him, Varra? Haul him about on a string, like Bor with his wretched beast?"

"Perhaps—though I think it would need a stout chain to hold him." Varra turned and looked at Stark, bold and bright, taking in the breadth and the height of him, the shaping of the great smooth muscles, the iron line of the jaw. She smiled. Her mouth was very lovely, like the red fruit of the swamp tree that bears death in its pungent sweetness.

"Here is a man," she said. "The first man I have seen since my father died."

The two men at the gaming table rose, their faces flushed and angry. One of them strode forward and gripped the girl's arm roughly.

"So I am not a man," he said, with surprising gentleness. "A sad thing, for one who is to be your husband. It's best that we settle that now, before we wed."

Varra nodded. Stark saw that the man's fingers were cutting savagely into the firm muscle of her arm, but she did not wince.

"High time to settle it all, Egil. You have borne enough from me. The day is long overdue for my taming. I must learn now to bend my neck, and acknowledge my lord."

For a moment Stark thought she meant it, the note of mockery in her voice was so subtle. Then the woman in white, who all this time had not moved nor changed expression, voiced again the thin, tinkling laugh he had heard once before. From that, and the dark suffusion of blood in Egil's face, Stark knew that Varra was only casting the man's own phrases back at him. The boy let out one derisive bark, and was cuffed into silence.

Varra looked straight at Stark. "Will you fight for me?" she demanded.

Quite suddenly, it was Stark's turn to laugh. "No!" he said.

Varra shrugged. "Very well, then. I must fight for myself."

"Man," snarled Egil. "I'll show you who's a man, you scapegrace[3] little vixen!"

He wrenched off his girdle with his free hand, at the same time bending the girl around so he could get a fair shot at her. The creature of prey, a Terran[4] falcon, clung to her wrist, beating its wings and screaming, its hooded head jerking.

*

With a motion so quick that it was hardly visible, Varra slipped the hood and flew the creature straight for Egil's face.

He let go, flinging up his arms to ward off the talons and the tearing beak. The wide wings beat and hammered. Egil yelled. The boy Bor got out of range and danced up and down shrieking with delight.

Varra stood quietly. The bruises were blackening on her arm, but she did not deign[5] to touch them. Egil blundered against the gaming table and sent the ivory pieces flying. Then he tripped over a cushion and fell flat, and the hungry talons ripped his tunic to ribbons down the back.

Varra whistled, a clear peremptory call. The creature gave a

[3] An archaic term meaning an idle and mischievous or wayward person, especially a young person or child.

[4] From Earth.

[5] Do something considered below one's dignity.

pt. ends p. 200

last peck at the back of Egil's head and flopped sullenly back to its perch on her wrist. She held it, turning toward Stark. He knew from the poise of her that she was on the verge of launching her pet at him. But she studied him and then shook her head.

"No," she said, and slipped the hood back on. "You would kill it."

Egil had scrambled up and gone off into the darkness, sucking a cut on his arm. His face was black with rage. The other man looked at Varra.

"If you were pledged to me," he said, "I'd have that temper out of you!"

"Come and try it," answered Varra.

The man shrugged and sat down. "It's not my place. I keep the peace in my own house." He glanced at the woman in white, and Stark saw that her face, hitherto blank of any expression, had taken on a look of abject fear.

"You do," said Varra, "and, if I were Arel, I would stab you while you slept. But you're safe. She had no spirit to begin with."

Arel shivered and looked steadfastly at her hands. The man began to gather up the scattered pieces. He said casually, "Egil will wring your neck some day, Varra, and I shan't weep to see it."

All this time the old woman had eaten and watched, watched and eaten, her eyes glittering with interest.

"A pretty brood, are they not?" she demanded of Stark. "Full of spirit, quarreling like young hawks in the nest. That's why I keep them around me, so—they are such sport to watch. All except Treon there." She indicated the crippled youth. "He does nothing. Dull and soft-mouthed, worse than Arel. What a grandson to be cursed with! But his sister has fire enough for two." She munched a sweet, grunting with pride.

Treon raised his head and spoke, and his voice was like music, echoing with an eerie liveliness in that dark place.

"Dull I may be, Grandmother, and weak in body, and without hope. Yet I shall be the last of the Lhari. Death sits waiting on the towers, and he shall gather you all before me. I know, for the winds have told me."

He turned his suffering eyes upon Stark and smiled, a smile of such woe and resignation that the Earthman's heart ached with it. Yet there was a thankfulness in it too, as though some long waiting was over at last.

"You," he said softly, "Stranger with the fierce eyes. I saw you come, out of the darkness, and where you set foot there was a bloody print. Your arms were red to the elbows, and your breast was splashed with the redness, and on your brow was the symbol of death. Then I knew, and the wind whispered into my ear, 'It is so. This man shall pull the castle down, and its stones shall crush Shuruun and set the Lost Ones free.'"

He laughed, very quietly. "Look at him, all of you. For he will be your doom!"

There was a moment's silence, and Stark, with all the superstitions of a wild race thick within him, turned cold to the roots of his hair. Then the old woman said disgustedly, "Have the winds warned you of this, my idiot?"

And with astonishing force and accuracy she picked up a ripe fruit and flung it at Treon.

"Stop your mouth with that," she told him. "I am weary to death of your prophecies."

*

Treon looked at the crimson juice trickling slowly down the breast of his tunic, to drip upon the carving in his lap. The half formed head was covered with it. Treon was shaking with silent mirth.

"Well," said Varra, coming up to Stark, "what do you think of the Lhari? The proud Lhari, who would not stoop to mingle their blood with the cattle of the swamps. My half-witted brother, my worthless cousins, that little monster Bor who is the last twig of the tree—do you wonder I flew my falcon at Egil?"

She waited for an answer, her head thrown back, the silver curls

pt. ends next p.

framing her face like wisps of storm-cloud. There was a swagger about her that at once irritated and delighted Stark. A hellcat, he thought, but a mighty fetching one, and bold as brass. Bold—and honest. Her lips were parted, midway between anger and a smile.

He caught her to him suddenly and kissed her, holding her slim strong body as though she were a doll. He was in no hurry to set her down. When at last he did, he grinned and said, "Was that what you wanted?"

"Yes," answered Varra. "That was what I wanted." She spun about, her jaw set dangerously. "Grandmother . . . "

She got no farther. Stark saw that the old woman was attempting to sit upright, her face purpling with effort and the most terrible wrath he had ever seen.

"You," she gasped at the girl. She choked on her fury and her shortness of breath, and then Egil came soft-footed into the light, bearing in his hand a thing made of black metal and oddly shaped, with a blunt, thick muzzle.

"Lie back, Grandmother," he said. "I had a mind to use this on Varra—"

Even as he spoke he pressed a stud, and Stark in the act of leaping for the sheltering darkness, crashed down and lay like a dead man. There had been no sound, no flash, nothing, but a vast hand that smote him suddenly into oblivion.

Egil finished—"but I see a better target."

Part 6

Red. Red. Red. The color of blood. Blood in his eyes. He was remembering now. The quarry had turned on him, and they had fought on the bare, blistering rocks.

Nor had N'Chaka killed. The Lord of the Rocks was very big, a giant among lizards, and N'Chaka was small. The Lord of the Rocks had laid open N'Chaka's head before the wooden spear had more than scratched his flank.

It was strange that N'Chaka still lived. The Lord of the Rocks must have been full fed. Only that had saved him.

N'Chaka groaned, not with pain, but with shame. He had failed. Hoping for a great triumph, he had disobeyed the tribal law that forbids a boy to hunt the quarry of a man, and he had failed. Old One would not reward him with the girdle and the flint spear of manhood. Old One would give him to the women for the punishment of little whips. Tika would laugh at him, and it would be many seasons before Old One would grant him permission to try the Man's Hunt.

Blood in his eyes.

He blinked to clear them. The instinct of survival was prodding him. He must arouse himself and creep away, before the Lord of the Rocks returned to eat him.

The redness would not go away. It swam and flowed, strangely sparkling. He blinked again, and tried to lift his head, and could not, and fear struck down upon him like the iron frost of night upon the rocks of the valley.

It was all wrong. He could see himself clearly, a naked boy dizzy with pain, rising and clambering over the ledges and the shale to the safety of the cave. He could see that, and yet he could not move.

All wrong. Time, space, the universe, darkened and turned.

A voice spoke to him. A girl's voice. Not Tika's and the speech was strange.

Tika was dead. Memories rushed through his mind, the bitter things, the cruel things. Old One was dead, and all the others . . .

The voice spoke again, calling him by a name that was not his own.

Stark.

Memory shattered into a kaleidoscope of broken pictures, fragments, rushing, spinning. He was adrift among them. He was lost, and the terror of it brought a scream into his throat.

Soft hands touching his face, gentle words, swift and soothing. The redness cleared and steadied, though it did not go away, and quite suddenly he was himself again, with all his memories where they belonged.

*

He was lying on his back, and Zareth, Malthor's daughter, was looking down at him. He knew now what the redness was. He had seen it too often before not to know. He was somewhere at the bottom of the Red Sea—that weird ocean in which a man can breathe.

And he could not move. That had not changed, nor gone away. His body was dead.

The terror he had felt before was nothing to the agony that filled him now. He lay entombed in his own flesh, staring up at Zareth, wanting an answer to a question he dared not ask.

She understood, from the look in his eyes.

"It's all right," she said, and smiled. "It will wear off. You'll be all right. It's only the weapon of the Lhari. Somehow it puts the body to sleep, but it will wake again."

Stark remembered the black object that Egil had held in his hands. A projector of some sort, then, beaming a current of high-frequency vibration that paralyzed the nerve centers. He was amazed. The Cloud People were barbarians themselves, though on a higher scale than the swamp-edge tribes, and certainly had no such scientific proficiency. He wondered where the Lhari had got hold of such a weapon.

It didn't really matter. Not just now. Relief swept over him, bringing him dangerously close to tears. The effect would wear off. At the moment, that was all he cared about.

He looked up at Zareth again. Her pale hair floated with the slow breathing of the sea, a milky cloud against the spark-shot crimson. He saw now that her face was drawn and shadowed, and there was a terrible hopelessness in her eyes. She had been alive when he first saw her—frightened, not too bright, but full of emotion and a certain dogged courage. Now the spark was gone, crushed out.

She wore a collar around her white neck, a ring of dark metal with the ends fused together for all time.

"Where are we?" he asked.

And she answered, her voice carrying deep and hollow in the dense substance of the sea, "We are in the place of the Lost Ones."

Stark looked beyond her, as far as he could see, since he was unable to turn his head. And wonder came to him.

Black walls, black vault above him, a vast hall filled with the wash of the sea that slipped in streaks of whispering flame through the high embrasures. A hall that was twin to the vault of shadows where he had met the Lhari.

pt. ends p. 207

"There is a city," said Zareth dully. "You will see it soon. You will see nothing else until you die."

Stark said, very gently, "How do you come here, little one?"

"Because of my father. I will tell you all I know, which is little enough. Malthor has been slaver to the Lhari for a long time. There are a number of them among the captains of Shuruun, but that is a thing that is never spoken of—so I, his daughter, could only guess. I was sure of it when he sent me after you."

She laughed, a bitter sound. "Now I'm here, with the collar of the Lost Ones on my neck. But Malthor is here, too." She laughed again, ugly laughter to come from a young mouth. Then she looked at Stark, and her hand reached out timidly to touch his hair in what was almost a caress. Her eyes were wide, and soft, and full of tears.

"Why didn't you go into the swamps when I warned you?"

Stark answered stolidly, "Too late to worry about that now." Then, "You say Malthor is here, a slave?"

"Yes." Again, that look of wonder and admiration in her eyes. "I don't know what you said or did to the Lhari, but the Lord Egil came down in a black rage and cursed my father for a bungling fool because he could not hold you. My father whined and made excuses, and all would have been well—only his curiosity got the better of him and he asked the Lord Egil what had happened. You were like a wild beast, Malthor said, and he hoped you had not harmed the Lady Varra, as he could see from Egil's wounds that there had been trouble.

"The Lord Egil turned quite purple. I thought he was going to fall in a fit."

"Yes," said Stark. "That was the wrong thing to say." The ludicrous side of it struck him, and he was suddenly roaring with laughter. "Malthor should have kept his mouth shut!"

"Egil called his guard and ordered them to take Malthor. And when he realized what had happened, Malthor turned on me, trying to say that it was all my fault, that I let you escape."

Stark stopped laughing.

Her voice went on slowly, "Egil seemed quite mad with fury. I have heard that the Lhari are all mad, and I think it is so. At any rate, he ordered me taken too, for he wanted to stamp Malthor's seed into the mud forever. So we are here."

There was a long silence. Stark could think of no word of comfort, and as for hope, he had better wait until he was sure he could at least raise his head. Egil might have damaged him permanently, out of spite. In fact, he was surprised he wasn't dead.

He glanced again at the collar on Zareth's neck. Slave. Slave to the Lhari, in the city of the Lost Ones.

What the devil did they do with slaves, at the bottom of the sea?

The heavy gases conducted sound remarkably well, except for an odd property of diffusion which made it seem that a voice came from everywhere at once. Now, all at once, Stark became aware of a dull clamor of voices drifting toward him.

He tried to see, and Zareth turned his head carefully so that he might.

The Lost Ones were returning from whatever work it was they did.

*

Out of the dim red murk beyond the open door they swam, into the long, long vastness of the hall that was filled with the same red murk, moving slowly, their white bodies trailing wakes of sullen flame. The host of the damned drifting through a strange red-litten hell, weary and without hope.

One by one they sank onto pallets laid in rows on the black stone floor, and lay there, utterly exhausted, their pale hair lifting and floating with the slow eddies of the sea. And each one wore a collar.

One man did not lie down. He came toward Stark, a tall

pt. ends next p.

barbarian who drew himself with great strokes of his arms so that he was wrapped in wheeling sparks. Stark knew his face.

"Helvi," he said, and smiled in welcome.

"Brother!"

Helvi crouched down—a great handsome boy he had been the time Stark saw him, but he was a man now, with all the laughter turned to grim deep lines around his mouth and the bones of his face standing out like granite ridges.

"Brother," he said again, looking at Stark through a glitter of unashamed tears. "Fool." And he cursed Stark savagely because he had come to Shuruun to look for an idiot who had gone the same way, and was already as good as dead.

"Would you have followed me?" asked Stark.

"But I am only an ignorant child of the swamps," said Helvi. "You come from space, you know the other worlds, you can read and write—you should have better sense!"

Stark grinned. "And I'm still an ignorant child of the rocks. So we're two fools together. Where is Tobal?"

Tobal was Helvi's brother, who had broken tabu and looked for refuge in Shuruun. Apparently he had found peace at last, for Helvi shook his head.

"A man cannot live too long under the sea. It is not enough merely to breathe and eat. Tobal over-ran his time, and I am close to the end of mine." He held up his hand and then swept it down sharply, watching the broken fires dance along his arms.

"The mind breaks before the body," said Helvi casually, as though it were a matter of no importance.

Zareth spoke. "Helvi has guarded you each period while the others slept."

"And not I alone," said Helvi. "The little one stood with me."

"Guarded me!" said Stark. "Why?"

For answer, Helvi gestured toward a pallet not far away. Malthor lay there, his eyes half open and full of malice, the fresh scar livid on his cheek.

"He feels," said Helvi, "that you should not have fought upon his ship."

Stark felt an inward chill of horror. To lie here helpless, watching Malthor come toward him with open fingers reaching for his helpless throat . . .

He made a passionate effort to move, and gave up, gasping. Helvi grinned.

"Now is the time I should wrestle you, Stark, for I never could throw you before." He gave Stark's head a shake, very gentle for all its apparent roughness. "You'll be throwing me again. Sleep now, and don't worry."

He settled himself to watch, and presently in spite of himself Stark slept, with Zareth curled at his feet like a little dog.

There was no time down there in the heart of the Red Sea. No daylight, no dawn, no space of darkness. No winds blew, no rain nor storm broke the endless silence. Only the lazy currents whispered by on their way to nowhere, and the red sparks danced, and the great hall waited, remembering the past.

Stark waited, too. How long he never knew, but he was used to waiting. He had learned his patience on the knees of the great mountains whose heads lift proudly into open space to look at the Sun, and he had absorbed their own contempt for time.

Little by little, life returned to his body. A mongrel guard came now and again to examine him, pricking Stark's flesh with his knife to test the reaction, so that Stark should not malinger.[1]

He reckoned without Stark's control. The Earthman bore his prodding without so much as a twitch until his limbs were completely his own again. Then he sprang up and pitched the man half the length of the hall, turning over and over, yelling with startled anger.

At the next period of labor, Stark was driven with the rest out into the City of the Lost Ones.

[1] To feign or exaggerate illness.

Part 7

Stark had been in places before that oppressed him with a sense of their strangeness or their wickedness—Sinharat, the lovely ruin of coral and gold lost in the Martian wastes; Jekkara, Valkis—the Low-Canal towns that smell of blood and wine; the cliff-caves of Arianrhod on the edge of Darkside, the buried tomb-cities of Callisto. But this—this was nightmare to haunt a man's dreams.

He stared about him as he went in the long line of slaves, and felt such a cold shuddering contraction of his belly as he had never known before.

Wide avenues paved with polished blocks of stone, perfect as ebon mirrors. Buildings, tall and stately, pure and plain, with a calm strength that could outlast the ages. Black, all black, with no fripperies[1] of paint or carving to soften them, only here and there a window like a drowned jewel glinting through the red.

Vines like drifts of snow cascading down the stones. Gardens with close-clipped turf and flowers lifting bright on their green stalks, their petals open to a daylight that was gone, their head bending as though to some forgotten breeze. All neat, all tended,

[1] Pretentious or unnecessary.

the branches pruned, the fresh soil turned this morning—by whose hand?

Stark remembered the great forest dreaming at the bottom of the gulf, and shivered. He did not like to think how long ago these flowers must have opened their young bloom to the last light they were ever going to see. For they were dead—dead as the forest, dead as the city. Forever bright—and dead.

Stark thought that it must always have been a silent city. It was impossible to imagine noisy throngs flocking to a market square down those immense avenues. The black walls were not made to echo song or laughter. Even the children must have moved quietly along the garden paths, small wise creatures born to an ancient dignity.

He was beginning to understand now the meaning of that weird forest. The Gulf of Shuruun had not always been a gulf. It had been a valley, rich, fertile, with this great city in its arms, and here and there on the upper slopes the retreat of some noble or philosopher—of which the castle of the Lhari was a survivor.

A wall or rock had held back the Red Sea from this valley. And then, somehow, the wall had cracked, and the sullen crimson tide had flowed slowly, slowly into the fertile bottoms, rising higher, lapping the towers and the tree-tops in swirling flame, drowning the land forever. Stark wondered if the people had known the disaster was coming, if they had gone forth to tend their gardens for the last time so that they might remain perfect in the embalming gases of the sea.

*

The columns of slaves, herded by overseers armed with small black weapons similar to the one Egil had used, came out into a broad square whose farther edges were veiled in the red murk. And Stark looked on ruin.

A great building had fallen in the center of the square. The

pt. ends p. 214

gods only knew what force had burst its walls and tossed the giant blocks like pebbles into a heap. But there it was, the one untidy thing in the city, a mountain of debris.

Nothing else was damaged. It seemed that this had been the place of temples, and they stood unharmed, ranked around the sides of the square, the dim fires rippling through their open porticoes.[2] Deep in their inner shadows Stark thought he could make out images, gigantic things brooding in the spark-shot gloom.

He had no chance to study them. The overseers cursed them on, and now he saw what use the slaves were put to. They were clearing away the wreckage of the fallen building.

Helvi whispered, "For sixteen years men have slaved and died down here, and the work is not half done. And why do the Lhari want it done at all? I'll tell you why. Because they are mad, mad as swamp-dragons gone *musth* in the spring!"

It seemed madness indeed, to labor at this pile of rocks in a dead city at the bottom of the sea. It was madness. And yet the Lhari, though they might be insane, were not fools. There was a reason for it, and Stark was sure it was a good reason—good for the Lhari, at any rate.

An overseer came up to Stark, thrusting him roughly toward a sledge already partly loaded with broken rocks. Stark hesitated, his eyes turning ugly, and Helvi said,

"Come on, you fool! Do you want to be down flat on your back again?"

Stark glanced at the little weapon, blunt and ready, and turned reluctantly to obey. And there began his servitude.

It was a weird sort of life he led. For a while he tried to reckon time by the periods of work and sleep, but he lost count, and it did not greatly matter anyway.

He labored with the others, hauling the huge blocks away, clearing out the cellars that were partly bared, shoring up weak

[2] Porches; covered entrances to buildings or structures.

walls underground. The slaves clung to their old habit of thought, calling the work-periods "days" and the sleep-periods "nights".

Each "day" Egil, or his brother Cond, came to see what had been done, and went away black-browed and disappointed, ordering the work speeded up.

Treon was there also much of the time. He would come slowly in his awkward crabwise[3] way and perch like a pale gargoyle on the stones, never speaking, watching with his sad beautiful eyes. He woke a vague foreboding in Stark. There was something awesome in Treon's silent patience, as though he waited the coming of some black doom, long delayed but inevitable. Stark would remember the prophecy, and shiver.

It was obvious to Stark after a while that the Lhari were clearing the building to get at the cellars underneath. The great dark caverns already bared had yielded nothing, but the brothers still hoped. Over and over Cond and Egil sounded the walls and the floors, prying here and there, and chafing at the delay in opening up the underground labyrinth. What they hoped to find, no one knew.

Varra came, too. Alone, and often, she would drift down through the dim mist-fires and watch, smiling a secret smile, her hair like blown silver where the currents played with it. She had nothing but curt words for Egil, but she kept her eyes on the great dark Earthman, and there was a look in them that stirred his blood. Egil was not blind, and it stirred his too, but in a different way.

*

Zareth saw that look. She kept as close to Stark as possible, asking no favors, but following him around with a sort of quiet devotion, seeming contented only when she was near him. One "night" in the slave barracks she crouched beside his pallet, her

[3] Sideways.

hand on his bare knee. She did not speak, and her face was hidden by the floating masses of her hair.

Stark turned her head so that he could see her, pushing the pale cloud gently away.

"What troubles you, little sister?"

Her eyes were wide and shadowed with some vague fear. But she only said, "It's not my place to speak."

"Why not?"

"Because . . . " Her mouth trembled, and then suddenly she said, "Oh, it's foolish, I know. But the woman of the Lhari . . . "

"What about her?"

"She watches you. Always she watches you! And the Lord Egil is angry. There is something in her mind, and it will bring you only evil. I know it!"

"It seems to me," said Stark wryly, "that the Lhari have already done as much evil as possible to all of us."

"No," answered Zareth, with an odd wisdom. "Our hearts are still clean."

Stark smiled. He leaned over and kissed her. "I'll be careful, little sister."

Quite suddenly she flung her arms around his neck and clung to him tightly, and Stark's face sobered. He patted her, rather awkwardly, and then she had gone, to curl up on her own pallet with her head buried in her arms.

Stark lay down. His heart was sad, and there was a stinging moisture in his eyes.

The red eternities dragged on. Stark learned what Helvi had meant when he said that the mind broke before the body. The sea-bottom was no place for creatures of the upper air. He learned also the meaning of the metal collars, and the manner of Tobal's death.

Helvi explained.

"There are boundaries laid down. Within them we may range, if we have the strength and the desire after work. Beyond them we may not go. And there is no chance of escape by breaking through the barrier. How this is done I do not understand, but it is so, and the collars are the key to it.

"When a slave approaches the barrier the collar brightens as though with fire, and the slave falls. I have tried this myself, and I know. Half-paralyzed, you may still crawl back to safety. But if you are mad, as Tobal was, and charge the barrier strongly . . . "

He made a cutting motion with his hands.

Stark nodded. He did not attempt to explain electricity or electronic vibrations to Helvi, but it seemed plain enough that the force with which the Lhari kept their slaves in check was something of the sort. The collars acted as conductors, perhaps for the same type of beam that was generated in the hand-weapons. When the metal broke the invisible boundary line it triggered off a force-beam from the central power station, in the manner of the obedient electric eye that opens doors and rings alarm bells. First a warning—then death.

*

The boundaries were wide enough, extending around the city and enclosing a good bit of forest beyond it. There was no possibility of a slave hiding among the trees, because the collar could be traced by the same type of beam, turned to low power, and the punishment meted out to a retaken man was such that few were foolish enough to try that game.

The surface, of course, was utterly forbidden. The one unguarded spot was the island where the central power station was, and here the slaves were allowed to come sometimes at night. The Lhari had discovered that they lived longer and worked better if they had an occasional breath of air and a look at the sky.

Many times Stark made that pilgrimage with the others. Up from the red depths they would come, through the reeling bands of fire where the currents ran, through the clouds of crimson sparks and the sullen patches of stillness that were like pools of

pt. ends next p.

blood, a company of white ghosts shrouded in flame, rising from their tomb for a little taste of the world they had lost.

It didn't matter that they were so weary they had barely the strength to get back to the barracks and sleep. They found the strength. To walk again on the open ground, to be rid of the eternal crimson dusk and the oppressive weight on the chest—to look up into the hot blue night of Venus and smell the fragrance of the *liha*-trees borne on the land wind . . . They found the strength.

They sang here, sitting on the island rocks and staring through the mists toward the shore they would never see again. It was their chanting that Stark had heard when he came down the gulf with Malthor, that wordless cry of grief and loss. Now he was here himself, holding Zareth close to comfort her and joining his own deep voice into that primitive reproach to the gods.

While he sat, howling like the savage he was, he studied the power plant, a squat blockhouse of a place. On the nights the slaves came guards were stationed outside to warn them away. The blockhouse was doubly guarded with the shock-beam. To attempt to take it by force would only mean death for all concerned.

Stark gave that idea up for the time being. There was never a second when escape was not in his thoughts, but he was too old in the game to break his neck against a stone wall. Like Malthor, he would wait.

Zareth and Helvi both changed after Stark's coming. Though they never talked of breaking free, both of them lost their air of hopelessness. Stark made neither plans nor promises. But Helvi knew him from of old, and the girl had her own subtle understanding, and they held up their heads again.

Then, one "day" as the work was ending, Varra came smiling out of the red murk and beckoned to him, and Stark's heart gave a great leap. Without a backward look he left Helvi and Zareth, and went with her, down the wide still avenue that led outward to the forest.

Part 8

They left the stately buildings and the wide spaces behind them, and went in among the trees. Stark hated the forest. The city was bad enough, but it was dead, honestly dead, except for those neat nightmare gardens. There was something terrifying about these great trees, full-leafed and green, rioting with flowering vines and all the rich undergrowth of the jungle, standing like massed corpses made lovely by mortuary art. They swayed and rustled as the coiling fires swept them, branches bending to that silent horrible parody of wind. Stark always felt trapped there, and stifled by the stiff leaves and the vines.

But he went, and Varra slipped like a silver bird between the great trunks, apparently happy.

"I have come here often, ever since I was old enough. It's wonderful. Here I can stoop and fly like one of my own hawks." She laughed and plucked a golden flower to set in her hair, and then darted away again, her white legs flashing.

Stark followed. He could see what she meant. Here in this strange sea one's motion was as much flying as swimming, since the pressure equalized the weight of the body. There was a queer sort of thrill in plunging headlong from the tree-tops, to arrow down through a tangle of vines and branches and then sweep upward again.

She was playing with him, and he knew it. The challenge got his blood up. He could have caught her easily but he did not, only now and again he circled her to show his strength. They sped on and on, trailing wakes of flame, a black hawk chasing a silver dove through the forests of a dream.

But the dove had been fledged in an eagle's nest. Stark wearied of the game at last. He caught her and they clung together, drifting still among the trees with the momentum of that wonderful weightless flight.

Her kiss at first was lazy, teasing, and curious. Then it changed. All Stark's smoldering anger leaped into a different kind of flame. His handling of her was rough and cruel, and she laughed, a little fierce voiceless laugh, and gave it back to him, and remembered how he had thought her mouth was like a bitter fruit that would give a man pain when he kissed it.

She broke away at last and came to rest on a broad branch, leaning back against the trunk and laughing, her eyes brilliant and cruel as Stark's own. And Stark sat down at her feet.

"What do you want?" he demanded. "What do you want with me?"

She smiled. There was nothing sidelong or shy about her. She was bold as a new blade.

"I'll tell you, wild man."

He started. "Where did you pick up that name?"

"I have been asking the Earthman Larrabee about you. It suits you well." She leaned forward. "This is what I want of you. Slay me Egil and his brother Cond. Also Bor, who will grow up worse than either—although that I can do myself, if you're adverse to killing children, though Bor is more monster than child. Grandmother can't live forever, and with my cousins out of the way she's no threat. Treon doesn't count."

"And if I do—what then?"

"Freedom. And me. You'll rule Shuruun at my side."

Stark's eyes were mocking. "For how long, Varra?"

"Who knows? And what does it matter? The years take care of themselves." She shrugged. "The Lhari blood has run out, and it's time there was a fresh strain. Our children will rule after us, and they'll be men."

Stark laughed. He roared with it.

"It's not enough that I'm a slave to the Lhari. Now I must be executioner and herd bull as well!" He looked at her keenly. "Why me, Varra? Why pick on me?"

"Because, as I have said, you are the first man I have seen since my father died. Also, there is something about you . . . "

She pushed herself upward to hover lazily, her lips just brushing his.

"Do you think it would be so bad a thing to live with me, wild man?"

She was lovely and maddening, a silver witch shining among the dim fires of the sea, full of wickedness and laughter. Stark reached out and drew her to him.

"Not bad," he murmured. "Dangerous."

He kissed her, and she whispered, "I think you're not afraid of danger."

"On the contrary, I'm a cautious man." He held her off, where he could look straight into her eyes. "I owe Egil something on my own, but I will not murder. The fight must be fair, and Cond will have to take care of himself."

"Fair! Was Egil fair with you—or me?"

He shrugged. "My way, or not at all."

*

She thought it over a while, then nodded. "All right. As for Cond, you will give him a blood debt, and pride will make him fight. The Lhari are all proud," she added bitterly. "That's our curse. But it's bred in the bone, as you'll find out."

pt. ends p. 220

"One more thing. Zareth and Helvi are to go free, and there must be an end to this slavery."

She stared at him. "You drive a hard bargain, wild man!"

"Yes or no?"

"Yes *and* no. Zareth and Helvi you may have, if you insist, though the gods know what you see in that pallid child. As to the other . . . " She smiled very mockingly. "I'm no fool, Stark. You're evading me, and two can play that game."

He laughed. "Fair enough. And now tell me this, witch with the silver curls—how am I to get at Egil that I may kill him?"

"I'll arrange that."

She said it with such vicious assurance that he was pretty sure she would arrange it. He was silent for a moment, and then he asked,

"Varra—what are the Lhari searching for at the bottom of the sea?"

She answered slowly, "I told you that we are a proud clan. We were driven out of the High Plateaus centuries ago because of our pride. Now it's all we have left, but it's a driving thing."

She paused, and then went on. "I think we had known about the city for a long time, but it had never meant anything until my father became fascinated by it. He would stay down here days at a time, exploring, and it was he who found the weapons and the machine of power which is on the island. Then he found the chart and the metal book, hidden away in a secret place. The book was written in pictographs—as though it was meant to be deciphered—and the chart showed the square with the ruined building and the temples, with a separate diagram of catacombs underneath the ground.

"The book told of a secret—a thing of wonder and of fear. And my father believed that the building had been wrecked to close the entrance to the catacombs where the secret was kept. He determined to find it."

Sixteen years of other men's lives. Stark shivered. "What was the secret, Varra?"

"The manner of controlling life. How it was done I do not know, but with it one might build a race of giants, of monsters, or of gods. You can see what that would mean to us, a proud and dying clan."

"Yes," Stark answered slowly. "I can see."

The magnitude of the idea shook him. The builders of the city must have been wise indeed in their scientific research to evolve such a terrible power. To mold the living cells of the body to one's will—to create, not life itself but its form and fashion . . .

A race of giants, or of gods. The Lhari would like that. To transform their own degenerate flesh into something beyond the race of men, to develop their followers into a corps of fighting men that no one could stand against, to see that their children were given an unholy advantage over all the children of men . . . Stark was appalled at the realization of the evil they could do if they ever found that secret.

Varra said, "There was a warning in the book. The meaning of it was not quite clear, but it seemed that the ancient ones felt that they had sinned against the gods and been punished, perhaps by some plague. They were a strange race, and not human. At any rate, they destroyed the great building there as a barrier against anyone who should come after them, and then let the Red Sea in to cover their city forever. They must have been superstitious children, for all their knowledge."

"Then you all ignored the warning, and never worried that a whole city had died to prove it."

She shrugged. "Oh, Treon has been muttering prophecies about it for years. Nobody listens to him. As for myself, I don't care whether we find the secret or not. My belief is it was destroyed along with the building, and besides, I have no faith in such things."

"Besides," mocked Stark shrewdly, "you wouldn't care to see Egil and Cond striding across the heavens of Venus, and you're doubtful just what your own place would be in the new pantheon."

She showed her teeth at him. "You're too wise for your own good. And now goodbye." She gave him a quick, hard kiss and

pt. ends next p.

was gone, flashing upward, high above the tree-tops where he dared not follow.

Stark made his way slowly back to the city, upset and very thoughtful.

As he came back into the great square, heading toward the barracks, he stopped, every nerve taut.

Somewhere, in one of the shadowy temples, the clapper of a votive bell was swinging, sending its deep pulsing note across the silence. Slowly, slowly, like the beating of a dying heart it came, and mingled with it was the faint sound of Zareth's voice, calling his name.

Part 9

He crossed the square, moving very carefully through the red murk, and presently he saw her.

It was not hard to find her. There was one temple larger than all the rest. Stark judged that it must once have faced the entrance of the fallen building, as though the great figure within was set to watch over the scientists and the philosophers who came there to dream their vast and sometimes terrible dreams.

The philosophers were gone, and the scientists had destroyed themselves. But the image still watched over the drowned city, its hand raised both in warning and in benediction.

Now, across its reptilian knees, Zareth lay. The temple was open on all sides, and Stark could see her clearly, a little white scrap of humanity against the black unhuman figure.

Malthor stood beside her. It was he who had been tolling the votive bell. He had stopped now, and Zareth's words came clearly to Stark.

"Go away, go away! They're waiting for you. Don't come in here!"

"I'm waiting for you, Stark," Malthor called out, smiling. "Are you afraid to come?" And he took Zareth by the hair and struck her, slowly and deliberately, twice across the face.

All expression left Stark's face, leaving it perfectly blank except for his eyes, which took on a sudden lambent gleam. He began to move toward the temple, not hurrying even then, but moving in such a way that it seemed an army could not have stopped him.

Zareth broke free from her father. Perhaps she was intended to break free.

"Egil!" she screamed. "It's a trap . . . "

Again Malthor caught her and this time he struck her harder, so that she crumpled down again across the image that watched with its jeweled, gentle eyes and saw nothing.

"She's afraid for you," said Malthor. "She knows I mean to kill you if I can. Well, perhaps Egil is here also. Perhaps he is not. But certainly Zareth is here. I have beaten her well, and I shall beat her again, as long as she lives to be beaten, for her treachery to me. And if you want to save her from that, you outland dog, you'll have to kill me. Are you afraid?"

Stark was afraid. Malthor and Zareth were alone in the temple. The pillared colonnades[1] were empty except for the dim fires of the sea. Yet Stark was afraid, for an instinct older than speech warned him to be.

It did not matter. Zareth's white skin was mottled with dark bruises, and Malthor was smiling at him, and it did not matter.

Under the shadow of the roof and down the colonnade he went, swiftly now, leaving a streak of fire behind him. Malthor looked into his eyes, and his smile trembled and was gone.

He crouched. And at the last moment, when the dark body plunged down at him as a shark plunges, he drew a hidden knife from his girdle and struck.

Stark had not counted on that. The slaves were searched for possible weapons every day, and even a sliver of stone was forbidden. Somebody must have given it to him, someone . . .

---

[1] A series of arches supported by evenly-spaced columns.

The thought flashed through his mind while he was in the very act of trying to avoid that death blow. *Too late, too late, because his own momentum carried him onto the point . . .*

Reflexes quicker than any man's, the hair-trigger reactions of a wild thing. Muscles straining, the center of balance shifted with an awful wrenching effort, hands grasping at the fire-shot redness as though to force it to defy its own laws. The blade ripped a long shallow gash across his breast. But it did not go home. By a fraction of an inch, it did not go home.

While Stark was still off balance, Malthor sprang.

*

They grappled. The knife blade glittered redly, a hungry tongue eager to taste Stark's life. The two men rolled over and over, drifting and tumbling erratically, churning the sea to a froth of sparks, and still the image watched, its calm reptilian features unchangingly benign and wise. Threads of a darker red laced heavily across the dancing fires.

Stark got Malthor's arm under his own and held it there with both hands. His back was to the man now. Malthor kicked and clawed with his feet against the backs of Stark's thighs, and his left arm came up and tried to clamp around Stark's throat. Stark buried his chin so that it could not, and then Malthor's hand began to tear at Stark's face, searching for his eyes.

Stark voiced a deep bestial sound in his throat. He moved his head suddenly, catching Malthor's hand between his jaws. He did not let go. Presently his teeth were locked against the thumb-joint, and Malthor was screaming, but Stark could give all his attention to what he was doing with the arm that held the knife. His eyes had changed. They were all beast now, the eyes of a killer blazing cold and beautiful in his dark face.

There was a dull crack, and the arm ceased to strain or fight. It bent back upon itself, and the knife fell, drifting quietly down.

pt. ends p. 227

Malthor was beyond screaming now. He made one effort to get away as Stark released him, but it was a futile gesture, and he made no sound as Stark broke his neck.

He thrust the body from him. It drifted away, moving lazily with the suck of the currents through the colonnade, now and again touching a black pillar as though in casual wonder, wandering out at last into the square. Malthor was in no hurry. He had all eternity before him.

Stark moved carefully away from the girl, who was trying feebly now to sit up on the knees of the image. He called out, to some unseen presence hidden in the shadows under the roof,

"Malthor screamed your name, Egil. Why didn't you come?"

There was a flicker of movement in the intense darkness of the ledge at the top of the pillars.

"Why should I?" asked the Lord Egil of the Lhari. "I offered him his freedom if he could kill you, but it seems he could not—even though I gave him a knife, and drugs to keep your friend Helvi out of the way."

He came out where Stark could see him, very handsome in a tunic of yellow silk, the blunt black weapon in his hands.

"The important thing was to bait a trap. You would not face me because of this—" He raised the weapon. "I might have killed you as you worked, of course, but my family would have had hard things to say about that. You're a phenomenally good slave."

"They'd have said hard words like 'coward', Egil," Stark said softly. "And Varra would have set her bird at you in earnest."

Egil nodded. His lip curved cruelly. "Exactly. That amused you, didn't it? And now my little cousin is training another falcon to swoop at me. She hooded you today, didn't she, Outlander?"

He laughed. "Ah well. I didn't kill you openly because there's a better way. Do you think I want it gossiped all over the Red Sea that my cousin jilted me for a foreign slave? Do you think I wish it known that I hated you, and why? No. I would have killed Malthor anyway, if you hadn't done it, because he knew. And when I have killed you and the girl I shall take your bodies to the barrier and leave them there together, and it will be obvious to everyone, even Varra, that you were killed trying to escape."

The weapon's muzzle pointed straight at Stark, and Egil's finger quivered on the trigger stud. Full power, this time. Instead of paralysis, death. Stark measured the distance between himself and Egil. He would be dead before he struck, but the impetus of his leap might carry him on, and give Zareth a chance to escape. The muscles of his thighs stirred and tensed.

A voice said, "And it will be obvious how and why *I* died, Egil? For if you kill them, you must kill me too."

*

Where Treon had come from, or when, Stark did not know. But he was there by the image, and his voice was full of a strong music, and his eyes shone with a fey light.

Egil had started, and now he swore in fury. "You idiot! You twisted freak! How did you come here?"

"How does the wind come, and the rain? I am not as other men." He laughed, a somber sound with no mirth in it. "I am here, Egil, and that's all that matters. And you will not slay this stranger who is more beast than man, and more man than any of us. The gods have a use for him."

He had moved as he spoke, until now he stood between Stark and Egil.

"Get out of the way," said Egil.

Treon shook his head.

"Very well," said Egil. "If you wish to die, you may."

The fey gleam brightened in Treon's eyes. "This is a day of death," he said softly, "but not of his, or mine."

Egil said a short, ugly word, and raised the weapon up.

Things happened very quickly after that. Stark sprang, arching up and over Treon's head, cleaving the red gasses like a burning

pt. ends next p.

arrow. Egil started back, and shifted his aim upward, and his finger snapped down on the trigger stud.

Something white came between Stark and Egil, and took the force of the bolt.

Something white. A girl's body, crowned with streaming hair, and a collar of metal glowing bright around the slender neck.

Zareth.

They had forgotten her, the beaten child crouched on the knees of the image. Stark had moved to keep her out of danger, and she was no threat to the mighty Egil, and Treon's thoughts were known only to himself and the winds that taught him. Unnoticed, she had crept to a place where one last plunge would place her between Stark and death.

The rush of Stark's going took him on over her, except that her hair brushed softly against his skin. Then he was on top of Egil, and it had all been done so swiftly that the Lord of the Lhari had not had time to loose another bolt.

Stark tore the weapon from Egil's hand. He was cold, icy cold, and there was a strange blindness on him, so that he could see nothing clearly but Egil's face. And it was Stark who screamed this time, a dreadful sound like the cry of a great cat gone beyond reason or fear.

Treon stood watching. He watched the blood stream darkly into the sea, and he listened to the silence come, and he saw the thing that had been his cousin drift away on the slow tide, and it was as though he had seen it all before and was not surprised.

Stark went to Zareth's body. The girl was still breathing, very faintly, and her eyes turned to Stark, and she smiled.

Stark was blind now with tears. All his rage had run out of him with Egil's blood, leaving nothing but an aching pity and a sadness, and a wondering awe. He took Zareth very tenderly into his arms and held her, dumbly, watching the tears fall on her upturned face. And presently he knew that she was dead.

Sometime later Treon came to him and said softly, "To this end she was born, and she knew it, and was happy. Even now she smiles. And she should, for she had a better death than most of us." He laid his hand on Stark's shoulder. "Come, I'll show you where to put her. She will be safe there, and tomorrow you can bury her where she would wish to be."

Stark rose and followed him, bearing Zareth in his arms.

Treon went to the pedestal on which the image sat. He pressed in a certain way upon a series of hidden springs, and a section of the paving slid noiselessly back, revealing stone steps leading down.

Part 10

Treon led the way down, into darkness that was lightened only by the dim fires they themselves woke in passing. No currents ran here. The red gas lay dull and stagnant, closed within the walls of a square passage built of the same black stone.

"These are the crypts," he said. "The labyrinth that is shown on the chart my father found." And he told about the chart, as Varra had.

He led the way surely, his misshapen body moving without hesitation past the mouths of branching corridors and the doors of chambers whose interiors were lost in shadow.

"The history of the city is here. All the books and the learning, that they had not the heart to destroy. There are no weapons. They were not a warlike people, and I think that the force we of the Lhari have used differently was defensive only, protection against the beasts and the raiding primitives of the swamps."

With a great effort, Stark wrenched his thoughts away from the light burden he carried.

"I thought," he said dully, "that the crypts were under the wrecked building."

"So we all thought. We were intended to think so. That is why the building was wrecked. And for sixteen years we of the Lhari have killed men and women with dragging the stones of it away. But the temple was shown also in the chart. We thought it was there merely as a landmark, an identification for the great building. But I began to wonder . . . "

"How long have you known?"

"Not long. Perhaps two rains. It took many seasons to find the secret of this passage. I came here at night, when the others slept."

"And you didn't tell?"

"No!" said Treon. "You are thinking that if I had told, there would have been an end to the slavery and the death. But what then? My family, turned loose with the power to destroy a world, as this city was destroyed? No! It was better for the slaves to die."

He motioned Stark aside, then, between doors of gold that stood ajar, into a vault so great that there was no guessing its size in the red and shrouding gloom.

"This was the burial place of their kings," said Treon softly. "Leave the little one here."

Stark looked around him, still too numb to feel awe, but impressed even so.

They were set in straight lines, the beds of black marble—lines so long that there was no end to them except the limit of vision. And on them slept the old kings, their bodies, marvelously embalmed, covered with silken palls, their hands crossed upon their breasts, their wise unhuman faces stamped with the mark of peace.

Very gently, Stark laid Zareth down on a marble couch, and covered her also with silk, and closed her eyes and folded her hands. And it seemed to him that her face, too, had that look of peace.

He went out with Treon, thinking that none of them had earned a better place in the hall of kings than Zareth.

"Treon," he said.

"Yes?"

pt. ends p. 234

"That prophecy you spoke when I came to the castle—I will bear it out."

Treon nodded. "That is the way of prophecies."

He did not return toward the temple, but led the way deeper into the heart of the catacombs. A great excitement burned within him, a bright and terrible thing that communicated itself to Stark. Treon had suddenly taken on the stature of a figure of destiny, and the Earthman had the feeling that he was in the grip of some current that would plunge on irresistibly until everything in its path was swept away. Stark's flesh quivered.

*

They reached the end of the corridor at last. And there, in the red gloom, a shape sat waiting before a black, barred door. A shape grotesque and incredibly misshapen, so horribly malformed that by it Treon's crippled body appeared almost beautiful. Yet its face was as the faces of the images and the old kings, and its sunken eyes had once held wisdom, and one of its seven-fingered hands were still slim and sensitive.

Stark recoiled. The thing made him physically sick, and he would have turned away, but Treon urged him on.

"Go closer. It is dead, embalmed, but it has a message for you. It has waited all this time to give that message."

Reluctantly, Stark went forward.

Quite suddenly, it seemed that the thing spoke.

Behold me. Look upon me, and take counsel before you grasp that power which lies beyond the door!

Stark leaped back, crying out, and Treon smiled.

"It was so with me. But I have listened to it many times since then. It speaks not with a voice, but within the mind, and only when one has passed a certain spot."

Stark's reasoning mind pondered over that. A thought-record, obviously, triggered off by an electronic beam. The ancients had taken good care that their warning would be heard and understood by anyone who should solve the riddle of the catacombs. Thought-images, speaking directly to the brain, know no barrier of time or language.

He stepped forward again, and once more the telepathic voice spoke to him.

"We tampered with the secrets of the gods. We intended no evil. It was only that we love perfection, and wished to shape all living things as flawless as our buildings and our gardens. We did not know that it was against the Law . . .

"I was one of those who found the way to change the living cell. We used the unseen force that comes from the Land of the Gods beyond the sky, and we so harnessed it that we could build from the living flesh as the potter builds from the clay. We healed the halt[1] and the maimed, and made those stand tall and straight who came crooked from the egg, and for a time we were as brothers to the gods themselves. I myself, even I, knew the glory of perfection. And then came the reckoning.

"The cell, once made to change, would not stop changing. The growth was slow, and for a while we did not notice it, but when we did it was too late. We were becoming a city of monsters. And the force we had used was worse than useless, for the more we tried to mold the monstrous flesh to its normal shape, the more the stimulated cells grew and grew, until the bodies we labored over were like things of wet mud that flow and change even as you look at them.

"One by one the people of the city destroyed themselves. And those of us who were left realized the judgment of the gods, and our duty. We made all things ready, and let the Red Sea hide us forever from our own kind, and those who should come after.

"Yet we did not destroy our knowledge. Perhaps it was our pride only that forbade us, but we could not bring ourselves to do it. Perhaps other gods, other races wiser than we, can take away the

[1] The physically disabled.

pt. ends p. 234

evil and keep only the good. For it is good for all creatures to be, if not perfect, at least strong and sound.

"But heed this warning, whoever you may be that listen. If your gods are jealous, if your people have not the wisdom or the knowledge to succeed where we failed in controlling this force, then touch it not! Or you, and all your people, will become as I."

*

The voice stopped. Stark moved back again, and said to Treon incredulously, "And your family would ignore that warning?"

Treon laughed. "They are fools. They are cruel and greedy and very proud. They would say that this was a lie to frighten away intruders, or that human flesh would not be subject to the laws that govern the flesh of reptiles. They would say anything, because they have dreamed this dream too long to be denied."

Stark shuddered and looked at the black door. "The thing ought to be destroyed."

"Yes," said Treon softly.

His eyes were shining, looking into some private dream of his own. He started forward, and when Stark would have gone with him he thrust him back, saying, "No. You have no part in this." He shook his head.

"I have waited," he whispered, almost to himself. "The winds bade me wait, until the day was ripe to fall from the tree of death. I have waited, and at dawn I knew, for the wind said, *Now is the gathering of the fruit at hand*."

He looked suddenly at Stark, and his eyes had in them a clear sanity, for all their feyness.

"You heard, Stark. 'We made those stand tall and straight who came crooked from the egg.' I will have my hour. I will stand as a man for the little time that is left."

He turned, and Stark made no move to follow. He watched Treon's twisted body recede, white against the red dusk, until it passed the monstrous watcher and came to the black door. The long thin arms reached up and pushed the bar away.

The door swung slowly back. Through the opening Stark glimpsed a chamber that held a structure of crystal rods and discs mounted on a frame of metal, the whole thing glowing and glittering with a restless bluish light that dimmed and brightened as though it echoed some vast pulse-beat. There was other apparatus, intricate banks of tubes and condensers, but this was the heart of it, and the heart was still alive.

Treon passed within and closed the door behind him.

Stark drew back some distance from the door and its guardian, crouched down, and set his back against the wall. He thought about the apparatus. Cosmic rays, perhaps—the unseen force that came from beyond the sky. Even yet, all their potentialities were not known. But a few luckless spacemen had found that under certain conditions they could do amazing things to human tissue.

It was a line of thought Stark did not like at all. He tried to keep his mind away from Treon entirely. He tried not to think at all. It was dark there in the corridor, and very still, and the shapeless horror sat quiet in the doorway and waited with him. Stark began to shiver, a shallow animal-twitching of the flesh.

He waited. After a while he thought Treon must be dead, but he did not move. He did not wish to go into that room to see.

He waited.

Suddenly he leaped up, cold sweat bursting out all over him. A crash had echoed down the corridor, a clashing of shattered crystal and a high singing note that trailed off into nothing.

The door opened.

A man came out. A man tall and straight and beautiful as an angel, a strong-limbed man with Treon's face, Treon's tragic eyes. And behind him the chamber was dark. The pulsing heart of power had stopped.

The door was shut and barred again. Treon's voice was saying, "There are records left, and much of the apparatus, so that the secret is not lost entirely. Only it is out of reach."

pt. ends next p.

He came to Stark and held out his hand. "Let us fight together, as men. And do not fear. I shall die, long before this body changes." He smiled, the remembered smile that was full of pity for all living things. "I know, for the winds have told me."

Stark took his hand and held it.

"Good," said Treon. "And now lead on, stranger with the fierce eyes. For the prophecy is yours, and the day is yours, and I who have crept about like a snail all my life know little of battles. Lead, and I will follow."

Stark fingered the collar around his neck. "Can you rid me of this?"

Treon nodded. "There are tools and acid in one of the chambers."

He found them, and worked swiftly, and while he worked Stark thought, smiling—and there was no pity in that smile at all.

They came back at last into the temple, and Treon closed the entrance to the catacombs. It was still night, for the square was empty of slaves. Stark found Egil's weapon where it had fallen, on the ledge where Egil died.

"We must hurry," said Stark. "Come on."

Part 11

The island was shrouded heavily in mist and the blue darkness of the night. Stark and Treon crept silently among the rocks until they could see the glimmer of torchlight through the window-slits of the power station.

There were seven guards, five inside the blockhouse, two outside to patrol.

When they were close enough, Stark slipped away, going like a shadow, and never a pebble turned under his bare foot. Presently he found a spot to his liking and crouched down. A sentry went by not three feet away, yawning and looking hopefully at the sky for the first signs of dawn.

Treon's voice rang out, the sweet unmistakable voice. "Ho, there, guards!"

The sentry stopped and whirled around. Off around the curve of the stone wall someone began to run, his sandals thud-thudding on the soft ground, and the second guard came up.

"Who speaks?" one demanded. "The Lord Treon?"

They peered into the darkness, and Treon answered, "Yes." He had come forward far enough so that they could make out the pale blur of his face, keeping his body out of sight among the rocks and the shrubs that sprang up between them.

"Make haste," he ordered. "Bid them open the door, there." He spoke in breathless jerks, as though spent. "A tragedy—a disaster! Bid them open!"

One of the men leaped to obey, hammering on the massive door that was kept barred from the inside. The other stood goggle-eyed, watching. Then the door opened, spilling a flood of yellow torchlight into the red fog.

"What is it?" cried the men inside. "What has happened?"

"Come out!" gasped Treon. "My cousin is dead, the Lord Egil is dead, murdered by a slave."

He let that sink in. Three or more men came outside into the circle of light, and their faces were frightened, as though somehow they feared they might be held responsible for this thing.

"You know him," said Treon. "The great black-haired one from Earth. He has slain the Lord Egil and got away into the forest, and we need all extra guards to go after him, since many must be left to guard the other slaves, who are mutinous. You, and you—" He picked out the four biggest ones. "Go at once and join the search. I will stay here with the others."

It nearly worked. The four took a hesitant step or two, and then one paused and said doubtfully,

"But, my lord, it is forbidden that we leave our posts, for any reason. Any reason at all, my lord! The Lord Cond would slay us if we left this place."

"And you fear the Lord Cond more than you do me," said Treon philosophically. "Ah, well. I understand."

He stepped out, full into the light.

A gasp went up, and then a startled yell. The three men from inside had come out armed only with swords, but the two sentries had their shock-weapons. One of them shrieked,

"It is a demon, who speaks with Treon's voice!"

And the two black weapons started up.

Behind them, Stark fired two silent bolts in quick succession, and the men fell, safely out of the way for hours. Then he leaped for the door.

He collided with two men who were doing the same thing. The third had turned to hold Treon off with his sword until they were safely inside.

Seeing that Treon, who was unarmed, was in danger of being spitted on the man's point, Stark fired between the two lunging bodies as he fell, and brought the guard down. Then he was involved in a thrashing tangle of arms and legs, and a lucky blow jarred the shock-weapon out of his hand.

Treon added himself to the fray. Pleasuring in his new strength, he caught one man by the neck and pulled him off. The guards were big men, and powerful, and they fought desperately. Stark was bruised and bleeding from a cut mouth before he could get in a finishing blow.

Someone rushed past him into the doorway. Treon yelled. Out of the tail of his eyes Stark saw the Lhari sitting dazed on the ground. The door was closing.

Stark hunched up his shoulders and sprang.

*

He hit the heavy panel with a jar that nearly knocked him breathless. It slammed open, and there was a cry of pain and the sound of someone falling. Stark burst through, to find the last of the guards rolling every which way over the floor. But one rolled over onto his feet again, drawing his sword as he rose. He had not had time before.

Stark continued his rush without stopping. He plunged headlong into the man before the point was clear of the scabbard, bore him over and down, and finished the man off with savage efficiency.

He leaped to his feet, breathing hard, spitting blood out of his mouth, and looked around the control room. But the others had fled, obviously to raise the warning.

The mechanism was simple. It was contained in a large black metal oblong about the size and shape of a coffin, equipped with grids and lenses and dials. It hummed softly to itself, but what its source of power was Stark did not know. Perhaps those same cosmic rays, harnessed to a different use.

He closed what seemed to be a master switch, and the humming stopped, and the flickering light died out of the lenses. He picked up the slain guard's sword and carefully wrecked everything that was breakable. Then he went outside again.

Treon was standing up, shaking his head. He smiled ruefully.

"It seems that strength alone is not enough," he said. "One must have skill as well."

"The barriers are down," said Stark. "The way is clear."

Treon nodded, and went with him back into the sea. This time both carried shock-weapons taken from the guards—six in all, with Egil's. Total armament for war.

As they forged swiftly through the red depths, Stark asked, "What of the people of Shuruun? How will they fight?"

Treon answered, "Those of Malthor's breed will stand for the Lhari. They must, for all their hope is there. The others will wait, until they see which side is safest. They would rise against the Lhari if they dared, for we have brought them only fear in their lifetimes. But they will wait, and see."

Stark nodded. He did not speak again.

They passed over the brooding city, and Stark thought of Egil and of Malthor who were part of that silence now, drifting slowly through the empty streets where the little currents took them, wrapped in their shrouds of dim fire.

He thought of Zareth sleeping in the hall of kings, and his eyes held a cold, cruel light.

They swooped down over the slave barracks. Treon remained on watch outside. Stark went in, taking with him the extra weapons.

The slaves still slept. Some of them dreamed, and moaned in their dreaming, and others might have been dead, with their hollow faces white as skulls.

Slaves. One hundred and four, counting the women.

Stark shouted out to them, and they woke, starting up on their pallets, their eyes full of terror. Then they saw who it was that called them, standing collarless and armed, and there was a great surging and a clamor that stilled as Stark shouted again, demanding silence. This time Helvi's voice echoed his. The tall barbarian had wakened from his drugged sleep.

Stark told them, very briefly, all that happened.

"You are freed from the collar," he said. "This day you can survive or die as men, and not slaves." He paused, then asked, "Who will go with me into Shuruun?"

They answered with one voice, the voice of the Lost Ones, who saw the red pall of death begin to lift from over them. The Lost Ones, who had found hope again.

Stark laughed. He was happy. He gave the extra weapons to Helvi and three others that he chose, and Helvi looked into his eyes and laughed too.

Treon spoke from the open door. "They are coming!"

*

Stark gave Helvi quick instructions and darted out, taking with him one of the other men. With Treon, they hid among the shrubbery of the garden that was outside the hall, patterned and beautiful, swaying its lifeless brilliance in the lazy drifts of fire.

The guards came. Twenty of them, tall armed men, to turn out the slaves for another period of labor, dragging the useless stones.

And the hidden weapons spoke with their silent tongues.

Eight of the guards fell inside the hall. Nine of them went down outside. Ten of the slaves died with blazing collars before the remaining three were overcome.

pt. ends next p.

Now there were twenty swords among ninety-four slaves, counting the women.

They left the city and rose up over the dreaming forest, a flight of white ghosts with flames in their hair, coming back from the red dusk and the silence to find the light again.

Light, and vengeance.

The first pale glimmer of dawn was sifting through the clouds as they came up among the rocks below the castle of the Lhari. Stark left them and went like a shadow up the tumbled cliffs to where he had hidden his gun on the night he had first come to Shuruun. Nothing stirred. The fog lifted up from the sea like a vapor of blood, and the face of Venus was still dark. Only the high clouds were touched with pearl.

Stark returned to the others. He gave one of his shock-weapons to a swamplander with a cold madness in his eyes. Then he spoke a few final words to Helvi and went back with Treon under the surface of the sea.

Treon led the way. He went along the face of the submerged cliff, and presently he touched Stark's arm and pointed to where a round mouth opened in the rock.

"It was made long ago," said Treon, "so that the Lhari and their slavers might come and go and not be seen. Come—and be very quiet."

They swam into the tunnel mouth, and down the dark way that lay beyond, until the lift of the floor brought them out of the sea. Then they felt their way silently along, stopping now and again to listen.

Surprise was their only hope. Treon had said that with the two of them they might succeed. More men would surely be discovered, and meet a swift end at the hands of the guards.

Stark hoped Treon was right.

They came to a blank wall of dressed stone. Treon leaned his weight against one side, and a great block swung slowly around on a central pivot. Guttering torchlight came through the crack. By it Stark could see that the room beyond was empty.

They stepped through, and as they did so a servant in bright silks came yawning into the room with a fresh torch to replace the one that was dying.

He stopped in mid-step, his eyes widening. He dropped the torch. His mouth opened to shape a scream, but no sound came, and Stark remembered that these servants were tongueless—to prevent them from telling what they saw or heard in the castle, Treon said.

The man spun about and fled, down a long dim-lit hall. Stark ran him down without effort. He struck once with the barrel of his gun, and the man fell and was still.

Treon came up. His face had a look almost of exaltation, a queer shining of the eyes that made Stark shiver. He led on, through a series of empty rooms, all somber black, and they met no one else for a while.

He stopped at last before a small door of burnished gold. He looked at Stark once, and nodded, and thrust the panels open and stepped through.

Part 12

They stood inside the vast echoing hall that stretched away into darkness until it seemed there was no end to it. The cluster of silver lamps burned as before, and within their circle of radiance the Lhari started up from their places and stared at the strangers who had come in through their private door.

Cond, and Arel with her hands idle in her lap. Bor, pummelling the little dragon to make it hiss and snap, laughing at its impotence. Varra, stroking the winged creature on her wrist, testing with her white finger the sharpness of its beak. And the old woman, with a scrap of fat meat halfway to her mouth.

They had stopped, frozen, in the midst of these actions. And Treon walked slowly into the light.

"Do you know me?" he said.

A strange shivering ran through them. Now, as before, the old woman spoke first, her eyes glittering with a look as rapacious as her appetite.

"You are Treon," she said, and her whole vast body shook.

The name went crying and whispering off around the dark walls, *Treon! Treon! Treon!* Cond leaped forward, touching his cousin's straight strong body with hands that trembled.

"You have found it," he said. "The secret."

"Yes." Treon lifted his silver head and laughed, a beautiful ringing bell-note that sang from the echoing corners. "I found it, and it's gone, smashed, beyond your reach forever. Egil is dead, and the day of the Lhari is done."

There was a long, long silence, and then the old woman whispered, "*You lie!*"

Treon turned to Stark.

"Ask him, the stranger who came bearing doom upon his forehead. Ask him if I lie."

Cond's face became something less than human. He made a queer crazed sound and flung himself at Treon's throat.

Bor screamed suddenly. He alone was not much concerned with the finding or the losing of the secret, and he alone seemed to realize the significance of Stark's presence. He screamed, looking at the big dark man, and went rushing off down the hall, crying for the guard as he went, and the echoes roared and racketed. He fought open the great doors and ran out, and as he did so the sound of fighting came through from the compound.

The slaves, with their swords and clubs, with their stones and shards of rock, had come over the wall from the cliffs.

Stark had moved forward, but Treon did not need his help. He had got his hands around Cond's throat, and he was smiling. Stark did not disturb him.

The old woman was talking, cursing, commanding, choking on her own apoplectic[1] breath. Arel began to laugh. She did not move, and her hands remained limp and open in her lap. She laughed and laughed, and Varra looked at Stark and hated him.

"You're a fool, wild man," she said. "You would not take what I offered you, so you shall have nothing—only death."

She slipped the hood from her creature and set it straight at Stark. Then she drew a knife from her girdle and plunged it into Treon's side.

---

[1] Extremely angry or furious.

pt. ends p. 248

*

Treon reeled back. His grip loosened and Cond tore away, half throttled, raging, his mouth flecked with foam. He drew his short sword and staggered in upon Treon.

Furious wings beat and thundered around Stark's head, and talons were clawing for his eyes. He reached up with his left hand and caught the brute by one leg and held it. Not long, but long enough to get one clear shot at Cond that dropped him in his tracks. Then he snapped the falcon's neck.

He flung the creature at Varra's feet, and picked up the gun again. The guards were rushing into the hall now at the lower end, and he began to fire at them.

Treon was sitting on the floor. Blood was coming in a steady trickle from his side, but he had the shock-weapon in his hands, and he was still smiling.

There was a great boiling roar of noise from outside. Men were fighting there, killing, dying, screaming their triumph or their pain. The echoes raged within the hall, and the noise of Stark's gun was like a hissing thunder. The guards, armed only with swords, went down like ripe wheat before the sickle, but there were many of them, too many for Stark and Treon to hold for long.

The old woman shrieked and shrieked, and was suddenly still.

Helvi burst in through the press, with a knot of collared slaves. The fight dissolved into a whirling chaos. Stark threw his gun away. He was afraid now of hitting his own men. He caught up a sword from a fallen guard and began to hew his way to the barbarian.

Suddenly Treon cried his name. He leaped aside, away from the man he was fighting, and saw Varra fall with the dagger still in her hand. She had come up behind him to stab, and Treon had seen and pressed the trigger stud just in time.

For the first time, there were tears in Treon's eyes.

A sort of sickness came over Stark. There was something horrible in this spectacle of a family destroying itself. He was too much the savage to be sentimental over Varra, but all the same he could not bear to look at Treon for a while.

Presently he found himself back to back with Helvi, and as they swung their swords—the shock-weapons had been discarded for the same reason as Stark's gun—Helvi panted,

"It has been a good fight, my brother! We cannot win, but we can have a good death, which is better than slavery!"

It looked as though Helvi was right. The slaves, unfortunately, weakened by their long confinement, worn out by overwork, were being beaten back. The tide turned, and Stark was swept with it out into the compound, fighting stubbornly.

The great gate stood open. Beyond it stood the people of Shuruun, watching, hanging back—as Treon had said, they would wait and see.

In the forefront, leaning on his stick, stood Larrabee the Earthman.

Stark cut his way free of the press. He leaped up onto the wall and stood there, breathing hard, sweating, bloody, with a dripping sword in his hand. He waved it, shouting down to the men of Shuruun.

"What are you waiting for, you scuts,[2] you women? The Lhari are dead, the Lost Ones are freed—must we of Earth do all your work for you?"

And he looked straight at Larrabee.

Larrabee stared back, his dark suffering eyes full of a bitter mirth. "Oh, well," he said in English. "Why not?"

He threw back his head and laughed, and the bitterness was gone. He voiced a high, shrill rebel yell and lifted his stick like a cudgel,[3] limping toward the gate, and the men of Shuruun gave tongue and followed him.

After that, it was soon over.

[2] Foolish or contemptible persons.

[3] A short heavy club.

pt. ends p. 248

*

They found Bor's body in the stable pens, where he had fled to hide when the fighting started. The dragons, maddened by the smell of the blood, had slain him very quickly.

Helvi had come through alive, and Larrabee, who had kept himself carefully out of harm's way after he had started the men of Shuruun on their attack. Nearly half the slaves were dead, and the rest wounded. Of those who had served the Lhari, few were left.

Stark went back into the great hall. He walked slowly, for he was very weary, and where he set his foot there was a bloody print, and his arms were red to the elbows, and his breast was splashed with the redness. Treon watched him come, and smiled, nodding.

"It is as I said. And I have outlived them all."

Arel had stopped laughing at last. She had made no move to run away, and the tide of battle had rolled over her and drowned her unaware. The old woman lay still, a mountain of inert flesh upon her bed. Her hand still clutched a ripe fruit, clutched convulsively in the moment of death, the red juice dripping through her fingers.

"Now I am going, too," said Treon, "and I am well content. With me goes the last of our rotten blood, and Venus will be the cleaner for it. Bury my body deep, stranger with the fierce eyes. I would not have it looked on after this."

He sighed and fell forward.

Bor's little dragon crept whimpering out from its hiding place under the old woman's bed and scurried away down the hall, trailing its dragging rope.

*

Stark leaned on the taffrail,[4] watching the dark mass of Shuruun recede into the red mists.

The decks were crowded with the outland slaves, going home. The Lhari were gone, the Lost Ones freed forever, and Shuruun was now only another port on the Red Sea. Its people would still be wolf's-heads and pirates, but that was natural and as it should be. The black evil was gone.

Stark was glad to see the last of it. He would be glad also to see the last of the Red Sea.

The off-shore wind set the ship briskly down the gulf. Stark thought of Larrabee, left behind with his dreams of winter snows and city streets and women with dainty feet. It seemed that he had lived too long in Shuruun, and had lost the courage to leave it.

"Poor Larrabee," he said to Helvi, who was standing near him. "He'll die in the mud, still cursing it."

Someone laughed behind him. He heard a limping step on the deck and turned to see Larrabee coming toward him.

"Changed my mind at the last minute," Larrabee said. "I've been below, lest I should see my muddy brats and be tempted to change it again." He leaned beside Stark, shaking his head. "Ah, well, they'll do nicely without me. I'm an old man, and I've a right to choose my own place to die in. I'm going back to Earth, with you."

Stark glanced at him. "I'm not going to Earth."

Larrabee sighed. "No. No, I suppose you're not. After all, you're no Earthman, really, except for an accident of blood. Where are you going?"

"I don't know. Away from Venus, but I don't know yet where."

Larrabee's dark eyes surveyed him shrewdly. "'A restless, cold-eyed tiger of a man', that's what Varra said. He's lost something, she said. He'll look for it all his life, and never find it."

---

[4] The rail around a ship's stern or rear.

pt. ends next p.

After that there was silence. The red fog wrapped them, and the wind rose and sent them scudding[5] before it.

Then, faint and far off, there came a moaning wail, a sound like broken chanting that turned Stark's flesh cold.

All on board heard it. They listened, utterly silent, their eyes wide, and somewhere a woman began to weep.

Stark shook himself. "It's only the wind," he said roughly, "in the rocks by the strait."

The sound rose and fell, weary, infinitely mournful, and the part of Stark that was N'Chaka said that he lied. It was not the wind that keened so sadly through the mists. It was the voices of the Lost Ones who were forever lost—Zareth, sleeping in the hall of kings, and all the others who would never leave the dreaming city and the forest, never find the light again.

Stark shivered, and turned away, watching the leaping fires of the strait sweep toward them.

---

[5] Moving fast in a straight line.

HONORARY HEATHEN

"Oh N'Chaka, oh Man-without-a-tribe, I Call You!"

Printed in Great Britain
by Amazon

6fef5361-8ef1-4346-9eca-e89e8da30fd8R01